Over the years I'd been part ▊▊▊▊▊▊▊
that had played out here in my ▊▊▊▊
of my neighbors already looked at me with a jaundiced
eye. To my knowledge, I was the only resident who'd
ever actually shot anyone on the premises.

WHO IN HELL IS WANDA FUCA?

"ONE OF THE BEST DETECTIVE POTBOILERS
IN SOME TIME . . .
Waterman is a great character . . .
WHO IN HELL IS WANDA FUCA? guarantees at least
one big surprise every couple of chapters,
not to mention a shocker of an ending."
Diversion

"SOLID . . . MEMORABLE . . .
A TWIST ON THE PRIVATE EYE CONVENTION"
Alfred Hitchcock Mystery Magazine

"COMPELLING AND WELL-WRITTEN . . .
Ford blends the faintly bitter humor
of the hardboiled genre with the
grit and social decay of the '90s."
South Bend Tribune

"A CLEVER, FUNNY MYSTERY . . .
EVERYONE WILL LIKE LEO WATERMAN"
Booklist

"A WELCOME ADDITION
TO THE LITERARY WORLD . . .
Ford is a witty and spunky writer
who not only knows his terrain but how to
bring it vividly to the printed page."
West Coast Review of Books

WHO IN HELL IS WANDA FUCA?

A LEO WATERMAN MYSTERY

G. M. FORD

AVON
TWILIGHT

All the characters and events portrayed in this work are fictitious.

AVON BOOKS, INC.
1350 Avenue of the Americas
New York, New York 10019

Copyright © 1995 by G. M. Ford
Published by arrangement with Walker and Company
Visit our website at www.AvonBooks.com/Twilight
Library of Congress Catalog Card Number: 94-37349
ISBN: 0-380-72761-7

First Avon Books Printing: October 1996

AVON TWILIGHT TRADEMARK REG. U.S. PAT. OFF. AND IN OTHER COUNTRIES,
MARCA REGISTRADA, HECHO EN U.S.A.

Printed in the U.S.A.

WCD 10 9 8 7 6 5 4

WHO IN HELL IS WANDA FUCA?

1

"LEAVE ME ALONE, will you?" he pleaded. "Please, just leave me alone." I inched closer along the windowsill, hoping he wouldn't notice. He noticed. "Stay where you are. You come any closer, I'm gonna jump, you hear me?"

"I hear you," I said. "My feet hurt. I was just sitting down."

Thomas Greer was standing on an eighteen-inch concrete ledge, fourteen stories above Third Avenue, his arms extended, palms flat against the surface, fingers searching for any purchase among the breaks and cracks, his back trying to press its way through the blond brick facing of the building. All he needed to do was cross his feet.

He didn't want to talk anymore. On the other hand, he didn't look to me like he wanted to take a dive either, but I couldn't be sure. I kept my distance and waited for the professionals to arrive. They were taking their time. We live in a society where pizza will get to you quicker than the police.

The hotel manager stood half in, half out of the doorway, watching the scene in the window and keeping an eye on the hall leading to the elevators, his head swiveling out of control as if he were watching a tennis match in fast-forward. In spite of the weather, he had sweat all the way through his gray silk suit in several places. I turned my attention back to the jumper. I leaned out a little and spoke to him soothingly.

"Come on, Greer, you don't want to do this . . ." Before it was out of my mouth, I knew I'd made a mistake. He instantly picked up on it.

"How do you know my name?" he asked without ever moving his eyes from the street below. "How do you know my name?"

"Just a lucky guess," I said. It was weak.

"You found us, didn't you? You're the one. She hired you, didn't she?"

"Come on in here, Mr. Greer. You don't want to do this. There's nothing to be gained from this." He wasn't listening.

"That bitch. That fucking bitch. She hired you, didn't she?" He looked at me for the first time. My assessment of the chances of him jumping instantly changed. I knew that look. Something in him had shaken loose. There was only the here and now. I kept talking.

"Whatever problems you think you've got," I said, "this isn't going to help. This is only going to make things worse. You don't want your son to remember you this way, do you? This is no way for a boy to remember his dad. Come on in here." I held out my hand. He sidestepped two feet farther away, stopped, and sidestepped back, reaching for my hand. His eyes showed a distinct lack of future.

I pulled my hand back inside and braced myself against the sill with both hands.

"Come on," he screamed. "Come with me." He bent and extended his hand toward me. "Come on, earn your blood money."

I shook my head. He stood back up and pressed himself to the building.

"Come on back inside, Mr. Greer. You're not doing anybody any good out there. Look, I'm sure things look pretty bad to you right now. I'm sure—"

My babbling was interrupted by the arrival of the Seattle Police Department. A uniformed officer swept the manager out into the hall and cleared the way for two detectives and a woman.

The larger of the two detectives I'd seen somewhere before. Big features, too much loose, florid skin, a pair of wide, distended nostrils that seemed to be constantly testing the air. This was not a face to forget. Everything about him was thick and wrinkled, as if he'd been thrown in a corner and allowed to dry. He was fifty or so with brush-cut hair and a quarter-inch gap between his front teeth. His deep-set eyes showed minimal interest as they swept the room. Trask. Bill Trask, maybe. I tried to dredge up where we'd met, but at the moment I was too scattered to recall.

His partner and the woman were strangers. She wasn't a cop. They stayed just inside the doorway and beckoned me over. I spoke to Thomas Greer.

"I'll be right back, Mr. Greer. Just hang in there. Okay? Just hang in there. I'll be right back."

"Go on, get outta here, you bloodsucker," he spat at me.

I slid slowly from the sill and walked over to the cops. The woman was removing her full-length blue wool coat. She folded the coat neatly and laid it on the nearest unmade bed. About thirty-five, a natural redhead, small features dwarfed by oversize glasses, wearing a bright blue two-piece suit, she looked like a grammar school teacher. Except for the eyes. An array of fine lines radiated from the corners of her eyes and worked their way through the freckles toward her high cheekbones.

The big detective got things rolling. Apparently, his memory was better than mine.

"One of your creditors finally had enough, Waterman?" Failing to get so much as a grimace, he moved on to the introductions.

"Leo Waterman." He turned to me. "It is Leo, isn't it?" I said it was. "This is Saasha Kennedy. She's a volunteer with Community Services."

It didn't take an expert to read his tone of voice. Like most cops, he hated social workers.

"Ms. Kennedy, this is Leo Waterman. As I remember, he passes himself off as a private investigator."

"What," she asked me, "have we got here?"

"I think he's serious," I replied.

"They're all serious, Mr. Waterman. You have to be serious to get out on a ledge like that. Are you just a bystander, Mr. Waterman, or are you part of the problem?" she asked.

The big cop couldn't resist. "P.I.'s are never just bystanders. They're always part of the problem."

"I'll handle this, Sergeant Trask," she snapped. "Why don't you and your partner keep the hall clear and check on the team on the roof."

As the detectives reluctantly shuffled off, she turned her attention back to me. "What have we got here?" she repeated.

"Custody battle."

"I take it he's the loser."

"He seems to think so."

"Tell me about it."

"His name's Thomas Greer. He picked up his son Jason ten days ago in Spokane for his weekend visitation and neglected to bring the boy back. The mother hired me to find them. She wasn't getting a whole lot of help from the local authorities. I traced them to the hotel here last night. This morning, on their way out to breakfast, I managed to get them separated. The boy's with hotel security. Mr. Greer here"— I gestured toward the window—"was quicker than he looked.

He got back into the room and got the door locked before I could get a hold on him. The rest, as they say, is history."

"Where's the boy now?"

"He's downstairs with Jack Moody in the security office."

"Does your client know you've found the boy?"

"I called her last night. She's probably in town by now."

"We'd better get her down here."

"I don't think so," I said.

"Why not?"

"Mr. Greer seems to blame all of this on his ex-wife. Having met this particular woman, I think he may have a point. If the object of the exercise is to get him down off that ledge, she's not going to be much of a help."

"Let me be the judge of that, Mr. Waterman."

"No," I said. Her eyes opened wide. I got the impression that it had been some time since anyone had dared utter that awful syllable in her august presence.

"No? Did you say no? Perhaps you don't understand the situation here, Mr. Waterman——"

"I understand the situation just fine, Ms. Kennedy. I've spent the last twenty-five minutes talking to the guy. I'll tell you what we've got here. We've got a guy here who makes good money but lives in this ratty little apartment in Ballard because the poor bastard wanted to do the right thing and because his ex-wife had a better lawyer. We've got a guy here whose ex-wife, without so much as a by-your-leave, picks up and drags his son clear over to the other side of the state. We've got a guy here who, every time he tries to call his son on the phone, gets to talk to some new boyfriend. A new one every time. His life's in the dumper. He feels like he needs to do something. This is it. The right audience is all he needs for his big recital. She's it. Trust me."

"You have a degree in psychology, Mr. Waterman?" She didn't wait for an answer. "I didn't think so. I have a master's in clinical psychology, and——"

"I'm sure your credentials are quite impressive, Ms. Kennedy, but I do have a degree in irresponsibility with a minor in feeling sorry for myself. You give this guy the right audience and he's going to take the Nestea plunge, believe me."

"We'll see," she said and headed over toward the window.

She sat on the windowsill, leaned out, and said something to Greer. I couldn't catch the words. She leaned out farther, exposing a length of freckled thigh, still talking. A commotion in the hall diverted my attention from the window.

Two more uniforms and a pair of paramedics slid silently into the room. Without ever taking her attention from the ledge, Saasha Kennedy held up a hand for silence. Everyone stood still. I could vaguely hear Greer now.

"I want to see her. Get her down here"—something I couldn't catch—"She's the one."

After a series of reassuring hand gestures, Kennedy disengaged herself from her perch and backed into the center of the room. She turned to me.

"You have a number for the wife?"

"She's staying with her brother in Magnolia, but I don't think—"

"Don't think, Mr. Waterman, just get me the number."

I pulled my notebook from my jacket pocket. I was about to read her the number when she snatched the whole notebook and handed it to the nearest uniform.

"Find an empty room; call her and get her down here," she said. He scurried off. She turned to the remaining patrolman.

"Mr. Waterman will be waiting in the hall." He started to take my elbow, but I pulled free and turned to face him. He was young, blond, thick in the neck. Probably only had to shave every other day. He reached for me. I stiff-armed him back three steps. His hand crept toward the service revolver at his side and hovered there. A voice from the doorway interrupted the standoff.

"Easy, Eagan." It was Trask. "You have any idea how many forms you're going to have to fill out if you pull that thing?" Eagan blinked. He relaxed his hand and took a step my way, but the big detective stopped him midstride.

"I said easy." Trask sauntered over close to the young cop. "First of all, there's the forms for drawing your weapon. Endless, son, I assure you. Endless. Waterman here's"—he jabbed a thumb in my direction—"definitely not worth the trouble." He turned to me.

"Get your ass out in the hall." Reluctantly, I complied. I put my feet in the hall but left the rest of me in the doorway.

When his little joke failed to lighten Eagan up, Trask stepped in still closer and got serious. "Besides that, use a little judgment, kid. We've got enough problems here already. Don't you think? This guy look to you like he's going quietly, huh? Look at him." Eagan eyed me up and down. He shook his head.

"All the way in the hall, Waterman." Trask made a grand gesture down the hall toward the elevators. I took my time, keeping my eyes on Eagan. Trask followed me two steps down the hall.

"Unlike you, Waterman, he's just a kid. Also unlike you, he doesn't know any better. At least he's got an excuse."

"He stays as jumpy as he is now," I said, "he's never going to get a chance to get educated." Trask shrugged.

The hall was filling up. The other uniform pinballed his way through the throng and skidded to a halt in front of the door.

Trask stepped aside and let him into the room. I stepped around him so I could see back into the room.

The uniform stood just inside the door and whispered to Eagan, who kept glancing ominously my way, then quickly trotted over toward the window.

"She's downstairs with the boy," the kid blurted. "She saw it on TV."

Saasha Kennedy never got a chance to register her shock and disapproval. Greer heard it all.

I could hear Thomas Greer from the hall.

"I want to see her," he screamed. "Get her up here. Where is she! Goddammit, is she here? I want to see her."

Kennedy left her perch on the window and hurried back to the center of the room, pushing the two uniforms before her.

"Great. Just great." She turned on Trask. "Get these two morons out of here. *Now.*" Trask quickly herded the two patrolmen past me into the hall. She shook her head in disbelief. I wandered back in.

"Sure am glad I waited for the professionals," I said.

"Fuck you, Waterman."

"You learn that in grad school?" I asked.

She ignored me and went after Trask again.

"Get the woman up here. We don't have any choice now. He's very unstable." Before he could leave, she stopped him. "How's the team on the roof? Are they almost ready?"

Trask shook his head. "There's a cornice around the top of the building. By the time they rappel down here, they figure they'll be six feet out from the wall. I don't think we're going to get much help from above, but they're standing by."

"Get the woman." Trask hurried off. Ms. Kennedy headed back for Thomas Greer and the window.

Trask's partner appeared at my elbow. A little guy with an overbite. His laminated ID card read "Henderson, Earl D."

"What do you think?" he asked, peering over my shoulder.

"I think the way this is being handled, somebody better call sanitation. Where the hell is the regular negotiation unit anyway?"

"They're all down in Rainier Valley. We've had a hostage

situation going on down there all night long." He leaned in. "I've never seen her before. I think this is her first one."

"I think so too," I said. She kept whispering out onto the ledge. I strained to hear, but could only catch bits and pieces. Henderson broke my concentration.

"You think he's going to jump, huh?"

"It's a distinct possibility," I said.

We stood silently and watched Saasha Kennedy talk soothingly to Greer. I still couldn't hear her end, but I sure could hear Greer's. It never varied. No matter what Kennedy said to him, he screamed for the woman.

He got his wish. Trask stepped away from the elevator door and let my client precede him down the crowded hallway.

She was a short, sturdily built little woman carrying a poodlelike mass of dark, curly hair that bounced as she walked. Pretty in a grossly over-made-up sort of way. One more layer of foundation on her face and she'd be Madam Tussaud material. Eyebrows plucked into pencil-thin question marks. Lipstick too red for a woman her age. Halloween on Hollywood Boulevard.

She was wearing a red one-piece jumpsuit, the full-length gold zipper alarmingly low, the elastic cinching her wasp waist further accentuating her remarkably prominent prow, which she pushed aggressively before her like twin battering rams.

"Where is he?" she demanded of no one in particular. I stepped into the doorway and blocked her path.

"How's the boy?" I asked. The question momentarily slowed her.

She blinked and focused in on me.

"He's fine," she said. "Where's Tom?"

"He's inside. But listen, before you go in there——"

I never got a chance to finish. Eagan shouldered his way

through me, dragging Mrs. Greer along. She clung to his arm as if it were a life preserver.

I started into the room. Trask dug a hand into my shoulder.

"Butt out, Waterman."

"This is going to get ugly, Trask. I can feel it. I'm telling you."

"Even better reason to stay butted out," he said. Henderson grunted in agreement.

Saasha Kennedy had disengaged herself once again and was whispering into Monica Greer's ear. Thomas Greer was screaming something unintelligible. Monica Greer listened distractedly. She had other things on her mind.

Even as Kennedy spoke, Mrs. Greer's attention was riveted on the brawny Officer Eagan, whose elbow she was now rhythmically polishing with her breasts. The hunter had become the hunted. Eagan was beginning to sweat. He repeatedly glanced over his shoulder. Another few minutes and Monica Greer was going to be locked onto his kneecap like a terrier.

Kennedy was oblivious. She droned on. When she finished, she looked to the other woman for agreement. Feedback was not forthcoming. Monica's total attention was focused on making a meticulous estimate of young Officer Eagan's inseam.

Undaunted, Saasha Kennedy pried Monica Greer from her quarry and led her slowly toward the window. From the hall, I could hear Eagan's sigh of relief. Kennedy leaned out and spoke briefly. Greer said something. Kennedy spoke again. More yelling. With Kennedy's attention focused on the ledge, Monica Greer turned back toward Eagan, clasped her hands below waist level, and used her upper arms to squeeze her breasts nearly up and out of the jumpsuit. Eagan resumed sweating.

"Looks like she's got two baldheaded midgets under that jumpsuit," Trask whispered from behind me.

"Not at all beyond the realm of possibility," I said through my teeth.

Eagan tugged at his collar, looking for backup.

Kennedy stepped back and beckoned Monica Greer forward. Monica wasn't looking. Kennedy had to walk over and take her by the shoulder.

Slowly, one foot carefully in front of the other, Monica Greer allowed her stiletto heels to propel her across the carpet. Her obviously unencumbered derriere rolled and thrashed inside the jumpsuit. She snuck a coy glance over her shoulder to make sure she was having the desired effect, pushed Kennedy aside with a sweep of her arm, and leaned out the window.

"Go ahead, you fuck. Jump!" she screamed. "You haven't got the balls. You've never had any balls. Go ahead jump, you wimp. I've got you insured to the teeth. You—"

There was more, but I didn't hear it. Trask, Henderson, and I were too busy barreling into the room to catch the rest of the tirade. Saasha Kennedy made an attempt to pull Mrs. Greer from the window but was elbowed backward over an end table. She went ass over teakettle. Her dress up around her head, her heavily freckled legs sticking up like a pair of rabbit ears, she wedged into the corner.

In one smooth motion, Henderson clamped his hand over Monica Greer's mouth and lifted her completely off the ground. She struggled and kicked her legs madly. Trask and I ducked as one deadly spiked shoe slipped from her foot and sailed spearlike into the bathroom on the far side of the suite. Henderson quickly began to carry Monica toward the hall. She bit him. He yanked his hand away.

"Jump, you son of a bitch!" she bellowed before Henderson could replace his hand. He yarded her into the hall and kicked the door shut.

Trask took the window.

"Take it easy, Mr. Greer," he said soothingly.

Saasha Kennedy had regained her feet and was smoothing her dress around her. "My God," she muttered. "Oh my God, I never—"

"Look on the bright side," I said. "At least you were wearing clean underwear. Your mother would be so proud."

She began to stammer something in reply but was interrupted by Thomas Greer.

"Where is she? I want her to see this. Where is she?" He wasn't screaming anymore. His voice was tight and flat. Trask kept talking.

"There's no need for this, Tom," he said. "You don't mind if I call you Tom, do you?" There was no reply from the ledge. Trask leaned in.

"I'm losing him," he breathed. "He's gonna do it."

Saasha Kennedy was rooted in place, her hands over her mouth, her eyes huge behind the oversize glasses. No help there.

I slipped between Trask and the sill and looked out. Thomas Greer was focused on the sidewalk below, rocking slightly on the balls of his feet, building up a rhythm.

"You're not gonna let her win again, are you?" I asked Greer. I wasn't expecting a reply and didn't get one. I stayed at it. "You dive off this building and that bitch wins again. You know that, don't you? She wins. You gonna let her manipulate you one last time? You like being manipulated? You gonna leave your son alone with that tramp?" Trask grabbed me by the belt.

Thomas Greer turned his attention to me. Trask let go.

"I'll show her."

"You're not gonna show her shit, man. She wants you to jump, for Chrissake. All you're going to do is make her day, you dumb fuck. A week from now Jason will be in some strange daycare center, and Monica will be in the Bahamas shacked up with an Australian rugby team or something. All you're gonna do is finance the trip."

I don't know whether it was the mention of his son's name or the image of the rugby team, but either way it got his attention. He stared at me, bobbed his head up and down, and started to cry. He removed one hand from the bricks and used it to wipe his eyes.

"Where's Jason?" he asked between gulps.

"He's safe here in the hotel. He's not with your wife," I added. "Come on in here."

Greer hesitated, wiped his eyes again, and began to slowly slide toward me a horizontal foot at a time. He almost made it.

Six feet from safety, he wobbled once, swam with his arms, recovered, and welded himself to the bricks, too terrified to move. I turned to Trask.

"Get the roof team," I said. Trask headed for the hall.

"Just take it easy, Mr. Greer. Help's on the way." I thought I detected a slight nod of the head. Saasha Kennedy was at my elbow. She started to speak, changed her mind, and stepped back again. I kept talking, saying anything, just talking. Greer was shaking violently, his fingers scratching at the bricks as if he were picking at scabs.

The team rappelled down in unison. First just two pairs of booted feet, then two uniformed officers in full climbing gear. One black, one white. Bright orange climbing harnesses segmenting their arms and legs. They were six feet out from the ledge, trying to get up enough momentum to swing over to the building. They weren't having much luck. I turned to Eagan, who was still standing in the center of the room.

"Get the far window. Help him in. I'll get this one." He hustled.

The officer was trying to swing over. I timed his swing, stretched out of the window, and got two fingers hooked in his harness. As he swung back toward perpendicular, the force pulled me up horizontal to the floor, balancing on the windowsill, my feet off the ground. I tottered, rocking on my belt buckle.

"Easy now," the cop in the harness whispered.

I should have listened. Instead, I tried to brace myself on the bricks below the window. Bad move. The movement of my arm put me further out of balance, and an inch at a time, I began to slide face-first out the window.

Trask saved the day by grabbing my belt, rearing back, and jerking me to the floor. Unconsciously, I held on to the harness. My weight dragged the officer to the side of the building. He got settled on the ledge, pried my fingers loose, and turned to me.

"You okay?" he asked calmly. I had the shakes so bad it looked like I was nodding. He turned his attention to Greer. I checked Eagan. Kennedy was lending a hand over at the other window. Everything seemed to be in order. I stayed on the floor. Trask's knees appeared in front of me. He held out a hand. I declined the invitation. Trask did the commentary.

"They've got a harness on him. They're hooking him up."

I rolled to my knees and peeked up over the sill. Greer was now connected to the roof. I slowly levered myself up onto my feet, legs heavy, tingling like I'd run a marathon. I had to lock my knees to keep them under control. I leaned back against the wall.

The room was full of people. A complete medical team had assembled, collapsible gurney and all, without me noticing. The hotel manager was back. Four more cops had arrived.

Everybody was accounted for except Henderson and Monica Greer.

"You don't look so good, Waterman," said Detective Trask, a smirk bending his lips.

"Most observant. Must be how come you made plainclothes," I said.

Before he could get cute again, I asked, "Anybody checked on Henderson and the woman?"

Trask turned to Eagan's partner. "Olson, go find Henderson and lend him a hand."

"Or a condom," suggested Eagan from across the room.

The tension shattered. We were still laughing when they stuffed Thomas Greer back in the window and rolled him out strapped to the gurney.

"You're a shit magnet, Waterman," said Trask, "a true shit magnet."

I suddenly remembered where Trask and I had met. We'd had much this same discussion at the time. Saasha Kennedy appeared on my left, rubbing her temple, her glasses in her hand.

"Mr. Waterman. I don't know what to say. I mean . . . I've never . . ."

"Don't worry about it," I said.

She wouldn't let it go. "I mean . . . I'm so sorry . . . I . . ."

"It was my first jumper too."

"I was sure the wife—"

I tried again. "You had no way of knowing."

"I mean . . . I should have . . . I wouldn't want you to think . . ."

"The only thing I'm thinking about, Ms. Kennedy, is having a drink." I bumped myself off the wall and started for the door. She was still mumbling when I rounded the corner and headed for the back stairs.

2

THE EMBERS WAS dark. Interstellar-space dark. Black-hole dark. Patsy liked it that way. I'd asked him about it once, several years back when I was spending most of my days and nights working on a stool implant. I'd always figured that the lighting was merely another example of Patsy's bizarre sense of humor.

We'd watched an executive drunk wobble from his stool at the other end of the bar and head for relief in the men's room. Four lurches from the dim glow of the light over the register, the poor bastard realized he was flying blind. He'd stopped, hiked up his drooping trousers, put his hands up in front of his body, and begun to shuffle slowly across the room, working his hands like a mime in a box. Patsy had chuckled into the back of his hand.

"You think it's funny, don't you?" I'd said. He smiled.

"It is funny," he said. "But that's not why I keep it so dark. Drunks drink to forget, Leo," he sighed. "It's easier to forget in the dark. They don't have to wipe anything out. All they've got to do is make up new material."

"Very thoughtful of you, Patsy."

"One does what one can, Leo."

I'd bolted from the hotel certain I needed a drink. By the time I made it all the way across town to the Embers, I was positive I'd better not start. I was still waffling between the poles when I stepped inside. I'd learned from experience not to make any sudden moves, just to step inside, close the door, and wait for my eyes to adjust.

Slowly, like a fade-in, my pupils expanded to the point where I could make out the two couples engaged in quiet conversation at one of the booths facing the bar. Another ten seconds and I was able to make out the three solitary drinkers holding down bar stools. I headed for the far end of the bar.

I plopped myself down on the single stool facing the door. Patsy finished up his conversation with the guy on my right and shuffled over. He read my face like a book.

"Leo," he said with a phony Mr. Ed smile, "haven't seen you in a while. Just when I thought you'd fixed that drinking problem of yours."

"I don't have a drinking problem," I said. "I have a stopping problem."

Patsy'd heard them all. Within the limits of commerce, he'd always made it a point to keep me as sober as possible. When sobriety wasn't possible, he'd always shoveled me into a cab and seen to it that I got home.

"What'll it be today?"

"Better make it an iced tea, Patsy."

With an almost invisible nod of approval, Patsy receded into the gloom, only to appear a minute later with my drink. Before we had a chance to exchange further pleasantries, the guy on the stool at my right piped up.

"I'm tellin' you, mister, I'll cut you a hell of a deal."

"I'm sure you would, my good man," Patsy replied, "but, as I was saying, I don't need a new car."

Before the guy could go back into his spiel, Patsy inclined his head at me.

"Now Leo here is a guy who could use a new car." He turned to face me. "Friends don't let friends drive Fiats," he said with a real smile this time.

The guy didn't seem to know when he was being kidded. On autopilot, he stayed with the sales pitch. We tried to ignore him.

"Rough day?" Patsy asked.

"As a cob," I said, sipping my tea. The salesman wasn't finished.

"Sixty months, five-point-one financing—"

"Stay sober," Patsy whispered.

"—a five-year lease with a minimal payoff—"

"I will," I said without much conviction.

"Leo"—Patsy leaned in close—"you got anything going with Tim Flood? I mean, I don't want to pry or anything, but—"

Before he could explain, the salesman clambered from his stool and weaved over. He put a brotherly arm around my shoulder. Patsy, knowing how little I liked to be touched, began sweeping the immediate area with his eyes, looking for expensive, breakable items.

A dark circle of perspiration stained the underside of the suit jacket where it made contact with my shoulder. The alcohol was beginning to separate his skin from his bones. His face looked partially melted, as the whole puffy mass of veined skin worked its way south. A couple more years and he'd be a walking neck. He slobbered in my ear.

"I can put you in a Probe."

"A what?"

"A Probe. A Ford Probe." He bobbed his head up and down.

"Who in hell would name a car that?" I asked. "Kinda makes it sound like the seats would be uncomfortable, don't you think?" He stared at me blankly. "Thanks, but I'm holding out for the Chevy Catheter."

He must have had some experience with hospitals. Unconsciously, he dropped his arm from my shoulder and reached protectively for his groin.

"Hey, I was just tryin' to be helpful, man. No need to talk like that."

"We appreciate it, buddy, we really do," I said. "It's just that neither of us is in the market for a car right at the moment."

Before he could respond, Patsy jumped in.

"Why don't you let the house buy you a drink, my friend?"

The guy waved him off. "Gotta get back to work. Got a couple coming in to pick up a new Explorer." He headed for the door, stopped briefly, turned. "I'll be back after my shift."

"See you then," said Patsy. We watched as he lurched over, yanked open the door, and stood for a moment transfixed by the light.

"See, Patsy, now you've got something to look forward to."

"I'll quiver with anticipation until his return."

The door hissed shut. Everyone inside was blind again. I turned back to Patsy. "You were saying?"

"Oh, yeah, I was asking whether you had anything going with Tim Flood." He mopped the section of bar where the guy had been sitting and changed the ashtray.

"Why do you ask?"

"Well, I was wondering . . ." Patsy was seldom at a loss for words.

"Is this just part of some massive list of philosophical problems that you've been pondering, or was there some special reason for your interest?"

He finished up and leaned in close again. "Frankie Ortega's been in a couple of times this week asking around for you. Real laid-back-like."

"Interesting," I said. "Laid-back? You mean like he wasn't working?"

"Yeah," said Patsy. "Had a drink each time. Real relaxed."

Frankie Ortega worked for Tim Flood. Tim liked to call Frankie his arranger. The Nelson Riddle of violence. If you got behind in your payments to Tim, Frankie arranged for your appliances to disappear. If you still didn't get your vig paid on time, Frankie arranged some sort of colorful maiming. A broken arm, something like that. Nothing too serious. Nothing fatal. The dead can't pay.

"Nope," I said. "Tim and I haven't exchanged words since the old man's funeral. Hell, I figured he was dead by now."

"How old you figure he is?" Patsy asked. I thought about it.

"Well, if my old man was still alive, he'd be eighty-one. They were just about the same age. Tim's maybe a couple of years older, so he's gotta be in his mid-eighties. Somewhere in there."

Tim Flood and my father had started out together working for Dave Beck and the Teamsters. At the time, they'd been known as labor organizers.

Revisionist history now labeled them as thugs. Neither of them minded the shift. My father had parlayed his local notoriety into eleven terms on the Seattle city council. He'd run for mayor four times and had been narrowly defeated each time. While it was fun to have Wild Bill Waterman sitting on the council, making absurd proposals, keeping the bureaucrats on their toes, the good people of Seattle had instinctively known that Wild Bill was not the kind of guy you'd want running the whole show.

Tim Flood had gone in another direction. He'd used his Teamster connections to become the Northwest's biggest and most successful fence. My first apartment had been furnished with a wide array of items that, according to Frankie Ortega, had "fallen offa truck."

Tim, like any good conglomerate, had branched out. If Seattle had anything that could be labeled as organized crime, Tim was it. Mostly it was loan-sharking, bookmaking, punch cards, and the old-time trades. He stayed away from drugs and women. By the time my father died, about ten years ago, Tim was mostly legitimate. Mostly. Old habits die hard.

I hadn't heard from him since the day of my father's funeral. With Frankie Ortega carefully holding a huge black umbrella over him, Tim had waited for the bereavement line to end before approaching me. As I watched the last of the throng tiptoe off through the steady drizzle that had turned the graveyard into a bog, I felt someone beside me.

"He was a hell of a good man, Leo," Tim had said. I agreed. "If it hadn't been for me, he'd have been mayor." I nodded again.

My father's political opponents had never failed to exploit his well-known association with the shadowy Tim Flood. The old man never denied it. He always responded to the effect that those were different, desperate times for organized labor, calling for different, desperate measures. Besides, as he pointed out, nobody had ever convicted Tim Flood of a damn thing. This was America, wasn't it? A man was still innocent until proven guilty, wasn't he? It was just the sort of speech my father favored.

In reality, Tim Flood hadn't cost my father a thing. The old man ran strictly for the fun it. It gave him a chance to exercise his sense of humor. He showed up for the first great mayoral debate dressed as Mahatma Gandhi, leading a goat. He campaigned from atop a spewing beer wagon, wearing a red tuxedo. When questioned about the ongoing issue of daylight savings time, he took a firm stand in favor of waltz time. "Three-four for evermore," was his slogan.

I couldn't come up with a single good reason why Tim Flood should be looking for me. Patsy waited.

"So, you say Frankie didn't seem to be working?" I asked him.

"Well, we both know he don't break wind unless Tim tells him, but if you ask me, it was informal." I was about to inquire how he'd reached that conclusion, but he anticipated me. "Frankie don't drink when he's on the job. He's all business. Besides that, he told me to tell you it was personal, not professional. Whatever the hell that means. I figured you'd know."

"Not a clue," I said. "I even have trouble with the notion that either of those guys has anything you could call a personal life."

"Yeah, me too," said Patsy. "You haven't gotten any messages from them or anything?"

I shook my head. "I can't see either of them leaving their names and numbers at the beep, can you?"

"Mules will sing opera first."

Another pilgrim wandered in from the light and took over the stool to my right. Patsy took care of him and came back.

"What should I tell Frankie when he comes back?" he asked.

"What makes you think he's coming back?"

"He's been in every day this week. He'll be back."

The matron at the other end of the bar banged her glass three times in what I supposed to be a prearranged signal for another double.

"Tell him you told me," I said to his back.

"You going to get in touch?" He was still walking.

"Just tell him you told me. That gets you out of it."

"I'll tell him," he said, refilling the old lady. I chugged the rest of my tea. Patsy wandered back. I reached in my pocket. He stopped me.

"Tea's free."

"But vodka's—"

"Nothing rhymes with vodka," he said with a wink.

3

I MADE IT home sober. I stopped at four more bars but managed to stick to soft drinks. I told myself that it was the atmosphere, the camaraderie, the easy laughter and built-in excuses that I craved, not the buzz. I tell myself a lot of things. My last stop before turning up the hill to my place was the Zoo.

It was an old-time saloon in the truest sense of the word. An ornately carved stand-up bar, complete with brass footrail, ran the full length of the room. I'd always favored stand-up bars. They kept a guy honest. It was too easy for a guy to drink himself senseless while perched on a padded stool.

Standing up was another matter. A guy had to maintain some semblance of sanity or risk falling among the phlegm, the cigarette butts, and the peanut shells littering the filthy planked floor. Around here, it was known as huggin' the rail. Too much huggin' the rail would get a guy eighty-sixed.

Much like the Alaskan caribou, drunks follow a strict migrational pattern. The process usually begins in some neighborhood fern bar hard by the office, where the stressed-out go for just a few after work.

The Zoo is at the other end of the spectrum. The Zoo is the last stop a Seattle drunk makes before tottering down to Pioneer Square and taking up permanent residence in the streets. When it got so bad a guy got eighty-sixed from the Zoo, from then on he did his drinking alfresco.

The left-hand wall comprised a series of brown leatherette booths. The management kept the regulars standing. The booths were for walk-ins. The booths were empty. The bar was full. Two steps inside the place, I was greeted like a returning war hero.

"Leo, Leo, where've you been?" It was Buddy Knox. A short, dumpy little guy, Buddy looked a bit like Fred Mertz. Buddy had, years before, been an editor at the *Times*. A taste for single-malt Scotch had careened Buddy through three short-lived marriages and a series of increasingly less responsible editing positions into his present status as resident arts and literature critic of the Zoo. Hereabouts, Buddy was the final authority.

"How you been, Buddy?"

"Hanging in there, Leo. We haven't seen much of you lately."

"By design, Buddy."

"Staying sober, huh?"

"I'm working at it. You're looking good. Looks like you've gained a little weight, right?' I said, poking him gently in the waist.

"Maybe a few pounds," he admitted, checking himself out. "But remember, Leo"—patting his formidable girth—"a waist is a terrible thing to mind."

He pivoted back toward the bar. "Hey Terry, how about a Coke down here?" He turned back to me. "Coke okay?"

"Coke's fine," I said. Buddy set about creating a reunion.

"Harold, Ralph, George, look who's here," he shouted down the bar. "It's Leo." One after the other, like the June Taylor Dancers, they each leaned back and squinted up front to see what the commotion was. One by one, they detached themselves from the bar and wandered up. Handshakes all around. The bartender shuffled over like he was walking on broken glass and set my Coke on the bar. I ordered a round for the boys. The gesture was greeted with unanimous acclaim.

Harold Green, Ralph Batista, and George Paris had, like Buddy, once been local people of some note. The four of them shared the enormous front room of a rooming house up the hill on Franklin. Last time I'd had business cards printed, I'd briefly considered changing the logo to read Waterman and Associates. I did, after all, use these guys quite a bit. Maybe they deserved billing. Sanity prevailed. I stuck with Waterman Investigations. God forbid anybody wanted to meet the associates.

Harold had sold men's shoes at the Bon. He used to be taller. The years had carved even more meat from his already gaunt frame, further emphasizing his baseball-size Adam's apple and prominent ears.

Ralph, who'd picked up and kept whatever weight Harold had lost, used to be some sort of port official. The extra folds of skin on his face, combined with a startling lack of functioning brain cells, gave him the benign countenance of the Mona Lisa. Inner peace by default.

George had been one of the first high-level bankers to get the axe in the great merger mania but was hanging in there pretty good. His finely chiseled features and slicked-back mane of white hair made him look like a boxing announcer. If you didn't look into his eyes or down at his shoes, you could mistake George for a functioning member of society.

Other than a sadness for the past and a taste for the grape, there seemed to be two factors keeping these guys together. One was their financial status. Each had managed to hang in there long enough to have garnered a meager monthly stipend from his respective employer. Not a full pension, not enough to make it alone, but enough, when you added in the money I paid them, to collectively keep them in liquor and out of the rain.

The other factor was their wardrobes. None of them had yet reached the Dumpster stage. Each was attired in the last remnants of his executive wardrobe. Finely tailored coats and slacks, stained and worn to a shine, hung mismatched on their bloated, sagging bodies, a credit to their tailors and a link to their pasts.

We drank to the good old days. I sported them to another round. We drank to my father. One by one, as it became obvious that a third round was not forthcoming, Harold, Ralph, and George said their good-byes and drifted back to their deeded spots along the bar, leaving Buddy and me alone. Buddy stepped in close. He smelled like an attic.

"You got anything going that we can help you with, Leo?"

I often used Buddy and his friends as field operatives. The destitute and the homeless had become so prevalent and so bothersome in Seattle that they were able to operate under a cloak of cultural invisibility. They were there, but nobody saw them. They could hang around places for days at a time without being noticed. It was as if they had their own little socioeconomic force field. Even better, they took great pride in their work and didn't require much in the way of fringe benefits. When they worked for me, they stayed relatively sober. When I paid them, they got drunk. It worked.

"Things are a little slow right now, Buddy. Mostly paper trails, but if I get anything, I'll let you know."

Buddy eyed me closely. His eyes were filigreed with red. I watched as he went through one of those instantaneous mood swings that only drunks and menstruating women can manage.

"You wouldn't be getting self-righteously sober on us now, would you, Leo? Maybe too good to be working with a bunch of old drunks like us anymore?"

"No way, Buddy. I'm just a mostly sober drunk, that's all."

Buddy relaxed. "Good," he said, downing a Scotch followed by a beer chaser. " 'Cause I got a little information I'd like to pass your way." He patted his chest as the liquor made its way down. His eyes watered.

"Smoooooth," he wheezed. I waited. "That's why I thought you might have something interesting going on."

"Why's that?"

"Guess who's been around looking for you?" he asked smugly.

"Frankie Ortega," I said.

"Goddammit, Leo."

"Just a wild guess."

Buddy was pissed. I'd ruined his surprise. He ordered another boilermaker. I paid for it. He went through the same routine as he gulped it down. This time, his nose started to run. He wiped it on his sleeve.

"He found you, huh?"

"Nope," I said. Buddy leaned close again.

"You're not into Tim for money, are you? I mean, Jesus Christ, Leo—"

"Don't worry, Buddy. I'm not into Tim for money."

"Good." He breathed out heavily, and the air reeked of mothballs. "We're gonna have to move. Did I tell you that?"

"No. How come?"

"Mrs. Paultz is retiring. Wants to move down to Arizona to be closer to her kids. She's selling the house. They'll tear the old place down for sure."

"Sorry to hear that."

"I don't know what the hell we're gonna do, Leo. There's not many old places—" He was about to lapse into maudlin. I didn't have it in me.

"Gotta go, Buddy. You take care now, okay?"

"Come on, Leo, stick around. Things are just starting. Nearly Normal Norman will be in in a bit. The whole gang'll be here. Come on," he whined.

I swilled my Coke, fished out the cherry, ate it, and threw the stem back in the glass. "Gotta go, Buddy."

"You'll be back." He'd changed again. His pouched face was suddenly hard. He was beginning to slur.

"I don't think so, Buddy." He smiled and moved his head up and down. His eyes failed to keep pace with the movement.

"I don't mean today. I just mean you'll be back." He pointed down at his feet. "One of these nights when I've slid down—when I'm huggin' the rail with my pants full of shit— I'll look over to the side and you'll be there. Don't doubt it. You'll be there, Leo." He turned back to the bar. I headed out.

Probably because I was so busy ruminating on the likelihood of Buddy's prophecy coming true, I got sloppy. I have my own little security system for my combination office-apartment. Years before, in a drunken rage, I'd tried to kick the door in one night when I'd lost my keys. The door held fast, but somewhere in the locking mechanism something had snapped. Since that night, whenever the door is locked from the outside, the handle tilts violently to the right. Locked from the inside, it stays straight up.

I was three steps inside my apartment before I snapped to the fact that I wasn't alone. Great cumulus clouds of cigarette smoke swam in the sunlight that angled in through the front windows. Frankie Ortega was leaning all the way back in my white leather recliner, working on his second beer.

Frankie was a little guy. No more than five-six or so. I'd always thought he looked like Cab Calloway. Thick, black processed hair combed straight back. A bold, wide mouth accented by a pencil-thin mustache clinging precisely to the outline of his upper lip. He was sporting a fawn-colored suit, a bright yellow tie, and two-tone loafers, brown and white.

"Relax, Leo," he said. I relaxed. I was unarmed. In spite of the fact that he must be pushing sixty by now, Frankie Ortega was not somebody I had any desire to take on. Whatever he may have lacked in size, he more than made up for in speed and ruthlessness. For the past thirty-five years he had handled Tim Flood's problems without so much as wrinkling his suits.

"Make yourself at home, Frankie." When in doubt, try irony.

"Thanks, Leo. I knew you wouldn't mind." He smiled and pushed the handle forward, bringing himself to an upright, seated position. He stood and smoothed out his slacks. "Nice quiet place you've got here."

"You looking to sublease, Frankie?"

"Still the comedian, eh, Leo. You really ought to get over that, you know. I told you before, there's no long-term future in it."

"Other than career counseling, did you have some other purpose for stopping by to see me today, Frankie?"

"You know I been looking for you." It was a statement.

"I might have heard a rumor to that effect," I said.

"You know if I'm looking for a guy, I'm gonna find him, right?"

I didn't feel any great need to answer. His ego didn't need the boost.

He walked over and stood too close to me. He kept his hands in his pockets, letting his cologne grab me instead.

"Tim needs to see you," he said evenly.

"So where is he?" I said, looking around the apartment. "I'm in the book. W for Waterman or I for Investigations." He shook his head sadly and started for the door.

"Tim don't get around so good anymore, Leo," he said as he passed.

"I'm kind of busy right now, Frankie. Tell Tim—"

"Dinner at seven at the house. We'll be expecting you."

He opened the door and stepped silently into the hallway. Before closing the door, he looked me up and down. "You probably ought to clean up a bit, Leo. That suit's a mess," he said shaking his head again. He was gone. Only the smoke remained. I opened the windows.

IN SOME PERVERSE way, it was probably fitting that Tim Flood had ended up on Capitol Hill. For nearly a century the Victorian mansions of the Hill had gazed disapprovingly out over Lake Union like crotchety maiden aunts. The wealth of the Klondike, the spoils of the sea, and the offspring of the founders had competed cheek by jowl in a thirty-year frenzy of bourgeois building, each hoping to appear more firmly settled and less nouveau riche than his neighbors.

This same neighborhood had, for many years, been a major bone of contention between my parents. My mother had wanted to get in on the building program. She'd envisioned an Edwardian mansion at the very zenith of the hill as the type of home that befitted both my father's political status and her own social-climbing fixation. The old man had disagreed.

He saw himself as a man of the people and had steadfastly refused to budge from the ancestral digs on lower Queen Anne. As, one by one, my mother's friends had abandoned the old neighborhood in favor of the Hill, she had become increasingly strident in her demands. The old man was a rock. He wasn't going anywhere. They'd carried the argument to their graves. Probably beyond.

I slid the Fiat to the curb atop the thick layer of sodden maple leaves that blanketed Tenth Avenue, two blocks south of Tim Flood's house. As I locked the car, I tried to remember the last time I'd been up here. A couple of years at least. I turned my collar against the wet breeze and looked around.

At first glance the street appeared timeless. The maples and elms formed towering Gothic arches above the street. The immense old houses seemed to have been hewn directly from the landscape. A Northwest Norman Rockwell. A frozen fantasy of the American dream.

The illusion was transitory. Even from here, nearly the epicenter of the neighborhood, the steady gnawing away of the Hill's exclusivity was plain.

Broadway, the heartland of the leather geek, was pissing on the back steps. Pill Hill, with its ever-expanding megamedical facilities, crept steadily in from the south. To the west, trendy new condos rapidly devoured the modest homes that used to litter the side of the hill. It wouldn't be long.

I slipped my hands into the pockets of my overcoat and meandered slowly up the street, wondering how much a month it cost to heat one of these monsters. A sure sign that I didn't belong here.

I still hadn't settled on a figure when I reached the gate. The house, like most of its neighbors, was better than twenty rooms. Three stories of tapered columns, gabled windows, and gingerbread flourishes covered in brown shingles. A three-foot brick wall, into which an ornately wrought gate had been set, separated the sidewalk from the small front yard. I opened the gate and walked up the broad front steps to the double doors. I never got a chance to knock.

A young guy of about thirty opened the right-hand door as I reached for the brass knocker. Samoan maybe, five-eleven but a solid two-twenty or so, with a neck wider than his head. He looked funny in a suit. Suits weren't made for that kind of bulk. Even the custom tailoring couldn't fully disguise the bulge under his left arm. He stared dispassionately at me as if I were something blown onto the porch by the breeze. He made no move to invite me in. He stood with one hand on the door and the other on the frame like Samson chained to the temple.

"Leo Waterman to see Tim Flood," I said.

He moved his thick, spiked hair an inch or so, opened the door wider, and stepped aside. He had a twin. Same spiked hair, same impassive face, same bulging suit, leaning back against the inside wall, hidden by the frosted glass of the doors. I stepped in and gazed from one to the other. Number one closed the door. Number two closed ranks.

They waddled before me down the marble-covered hall that bisected the residence. Their gait was remarkably splay-footed. It appeared that at any moment each twin was likely to split down the middle and march away from his other half straight into one of the mahogany-wainscoted walls.

We marched all the way to the end of the hallway and on through the double French doors at the end of the passage. We were in a small foyer between the main house and the giant solarium at the back. They stepped back and ushered me into the stifling sunroom. It was at least eighty-five degrees inside, as humid as New Orleans in August. The doors closed behind me.

A dazzling array of tropical plants and shrubs, some pushing the thirty-foot glass roof, dripped in the moist air. A greenhouse with furniture.

"Leo." A hoarse voice beckoned from the far end of the room.

I wandered over. Tim Flood, or what was left of him, was nearly lost amid the cushions of the ancient wicker settee that fanned out behind his head like a halo.

"Sit," he said, motioning toward a green wicker chair that had been drawn up by his side. Sweat was beginning to form on my scalp, deodorant failure was imminent, but Tim Flood, beneath the bright afghan, was wearing a sweater. I sat.

He looked pretty good. Smaller than I remembered, beginning the same descent back inside himself that I'd watched my father take, but holding up pretty well. His hawk-like nose had become more prominent with advancing age and his bony liver-spotted hands rested limply on the padded arms of the lounger like bird's feet, but the eyes were as hard as they'd always been.

"Thanks for coming, Leo." His voice was husky enough to pull a dogsled. "What can we get you to drink?"

"Bourbon rocks."

The words were hardly out of my mouth before Frankie Ortega appeared, drink in hand. Back over his shoulder, through the massive ferns, I could see a portable bar along the north wall.

Frankie had taken his own advice. He'd changed into a blue three-piece suit highlighted by a blue-and-green-striped tie riding above a tight collar pin. He hadn't broken a sweat. Tim spoke.

"If you don't mind, Leo, we'll eat in here." Runnels of sweat trickled down my back, soaking the elastic of my shorts. Serving food in this room probably saved the cook a great deal of time. By the time he got the stuff carted over to Tim, it was probably poached. I took a pull of my drink, trying to will myself to stop sweating. No go.

Tim turned his attention to me. "Been a long time, Leo." When I didn't respond, he went on. "Your father's funeral was the last time, wasn't it?" I agreed. "We come a long way together, me and him. From Hooverville to the halls of power, he liked to say." I had heard all the stories before, but was determined to be polite. I didn't want to end up fertilizing one of the palms.

Tim seemed to find new strength as he selectively rooted through the past. Now, more than fifty years later, even the rain-soaked nights spent in a reeking board shack on the tide flats seemed to hold a certain romantic appeal for him. He seemed to pine for the long nights spent huddled around a bark-fired cookstove, the inevitable smoke filling the upper half of the shack, the sopping bedrolls and mattresses serving as the only furniture.

He recited the oft-told tale of how he and my father had first made their mark as part of Hooverville's vigilante Sanitation Committee. To Tim, the building of the privies and catwalks seemed to be the perfect dinner conversation. He reached full animation as he recounted how, on a particularly foul night in December—1933, he thought it was—a dissolute stonecutter named Herman somethingorother had slipped on one of the greasy catwalks, tumbled headfirst into a privy, and unceremoniously drowned amid the collected effluent in the hand-dug pit below. Yessir, bring on the food.

"Well, Tim," I interjected the first time he came up for air, "you've gone to a bunch of trouble to get me here. Frankie's been spending more time in my favorite hangouts than I have. As much as I enjoy talking about old times, I don't figure that's what you got me down here for. What can I do for you?"

His face crinkled into a smile. At least I hoped it was a smile.

"You always were a cheeky kid, Leo. Always."

"It's genetic."

He nodded approvingly. "You're probably right," he agreed. He got serious. "It played better on your old man than it does on you though, Leo. Something about him put people at ease, the same way you put people on edge." I waited.

He rearranged himself, sitting up straighter, leaning on the arm closest to me.

"I got troubles, Leo. Troubles I can't handle in the usual way, if you know what I mean." I waited for him to elaborate. He fixed me with a stare. His black eyes were covered with a thin, blue, rubbery film.

"None of this leaves this room. You understand me?"

I understood. "Don't worry about it, Tim. For you or for anybody else, I sell discretion. It's all I've got to sell."

He smiled again. "I'm not worried, Leo. Besides that, it's the better part of valor, right?" He laughed. I had to agree.

"Not that you've been short on valor, Leo. You do nice work. You're quite a local celebrity, you are. I been following you in the papers. I even saw you on the TV during that court battle over them frozen babies."

"Embryos. Frozen embryos."

"You did good there, Leo. What was it the papers called it?"

"The Leggo My Eggo Trial." Frankie chuckled.

Although that particular episode was never going to appear on my résumé, I let them have their fun. Compliments from Tim Flood made me nervous. My angst was interrupted by the arrival of dinner. The bruise brothers materialized with a lap tray for Tim and a stand-up tray for me.

We ate in silence. Tim's tray looked more like an artist's palette. Dabs of variously colored pastes were arranged about the plate. He worked methodically from one to another. Mine was a steak, a baked potato, and an assortment of parboiled vegetables, probably from a nearby restaurant. By the time I'd finished, I was in a full runner's sweat. Tim's tray had disappeared. He was leaning back, apparently napping.

Frankie removed my tray. "You want coffee?" he asked.

"No thanks, I try to move in one direction at a time."

I watched as he left the room. When I looked back at Tim Flood, he was sitting with his legs over the side of the lounger, his hands on his knees, leaning in close to me.

"It's my granddaughter, Leo," he whispered. "Gene's girl."

"What about her?" I asked. His daughter Gene, I remembered. We'd been stuck at a lot of public functions together. It had been important to our respective fathers that we get along. We'd been unable to oblige. I hadn't seen her in over twenty years.

"She's a wild one, Leo. In all my years, I've never met anybody like this kid. She's into some deep shit. I can feel it."

"What's she into, Tim?"

"That's what I want you to find out, shamus."

I was wary now. Tim could fix just about anything. If he needed me, it must be a humdinger. Tim was shaking his head, reading my mind.

"There's only Frankie and the brothers now. She knows them all, Leo. Up until a few months ago, she lived here in the house with me. She was here almost a year. No, it's gotta be somebody from the outside." He thought for a moment. "Besides that, she's family, Leo. You know what I mean? I don't want to be mixing her up in any of this. It's gotta be from the outside."

"Maybe you better tell me about it." I don't know why I said it. It was stupid. I regretted it the minute it passed my lips. Probably the bourbon. I'd been planning to refuse gracefully. Now it was going to be tough. If I let him tell me the story, there'd be no backing out. I tried to head him off. Better now than later. He started to speak. I stopped him.

"Just so we understand each other, Tim. I haven't agreed to anything yet. If you want to tell me this, tell me. I'll respect your confidence. But I haven't agreed to anything. Understood?"

"Understood," he said quietly.

He searched my face. I felt like he was going through my pockets. I remembered the stories my old man used to tell me about Tim's style. How he used to advise people not to borrow money from him. How he used to make sure they were every bit as desperate for cash as they thought they were before lending them any money. How he'd advise them that unless they were absolutely certain they could at least make the vig payments every week, this was going to be the worst mistake they'd ever made. No threats. Nothing specific anyway. He let the customer's imagination do the rest.

"Caroline Nobel—that's my granddaughter—she come back here to live with me a little over a year ago. She and Gene just couldn't stand each other no more."

He waved himself off. "Wait, you need some background here so's you'll understand. Gene, she's . . . well she's . . . Hell, she's working on either her fourth or fifth husband now, I've lost track. Some fag of an Englishman. Claims to have a title. Spends most of her time commuting between Europe and Palm Springs. Fancies herself a real jet-setter. Never wanted the kid. She's been farming the kid out to private school since Caroline was six."

He wiped the corners of his mouth with his thumb and forefinger.

"This mess is probably my fault for giving Caroline that damn trust fund, but you know, I figured she didn't have nothin' you could call parents, so I figured she might as well have some money. So what does she do? She gives the fucking money to these Save the Earth assholes."

He shook his head sadly.

"It probably would have been better if I'd let her find her own way, like your old man did, but you know, Leo, we all want it to be better for our kids than it was for us."

I gave him the reinforcement he was looking for. He continued.

"Anyway, about a year ago, she calls me one night. She's been kicked out of her fancy private school. Asks if she can come and live with me, go to high school here. I almost shit. I mean, I don't need no high school kid running around, you know what I mean, I was still heavily into things then, not like now. But she's family, so what can I say? I tell her if it's all right with Gene, I guess it's all right with me. I'm figuring Gene will put the kibosh on it, but Gene she don't give a damn. She wants to get rid of the kid as bad as the kid wants to go, so what am I gonna do? I tell her, okay, come on." He leaned back to his former reclining position as if gathering himself.

"I figured it was time to scale back anyway. Hell, I was damn near eighty. So I let most everybody go. All that's left is Ricky and Nicky."

"And Frankie," I amended.

"Frankie's like family. He don't count as help." He sat up again. "She did okay for a while. Got pretty good grades. Hell, I even went to one of those parent-teacher conferences once." I looked at him quizzically. "Frankie waited in the hall," he said immediately. The image held a certain manic appeal.

"Then, about four months ago, it all changed. She started getting political. Started hanging out with scumbags. Rallies, demonstrations. Got herself arrested a few times. Seemed like she had a new cause every week." He spread his gnarled hands. "No problem, you know, I figure it's all part of growing up. Your old man and I spent a few nights inside together." He smiled as remembered. "The last time she got busted was for throwing blood on some old lady wearing a fur coat down at Westlake. Animal rights, some shit like that." He was having trouble finding an end to the story. I tried to give him a hand.

"So, what's she into now?" I asked.

"God only knows."

"What makes you think she needs any help?"

"I was getting to that," he snapped. He was tiring. "So after I bail her out the last time, she announces that she's moving out. She's had enough of my meddling." Tim shook his head. "Like getting her ass out of jail is meddling, right? But, I can't say nothing. She's damn near twenty years old, if she wants to move out that's her business. Like I said, she gives all her money to the group. I figure I'll hear from her when she needs money, you know? Two months go by. Nothing."

He slashed the air with the bony edge of his hand. "So I send Frankie out to see what's up. We don't have a hell of a lot going on anymore. I figured he'd enjoy the exercise. Nothing." He slashed the air again. "Even Frankie can't seem to find her." I started to speak. Only the dead could hide from Frankie Ortega. He stopped me.

"About a week later Frankie gets a sniff from one of his sources that Caroline's hanging around with this Save the Earth group down by the square. He tools around a bit to see what's going on, but on the second day she makes him. She calls here in the middle of the night and tells me to keep out of her business. Tells me it's people like me who've ruined the planet and hangs up." He was out of gas. He motioned to the far side of the room. Frankie emerged from the mist and sidled over. "Tell him, Frankie," he croaked. Frankie patted his shoulder and turned to me.

"I don't know what she's into, Leo, but it's not good. She lives like she's on the run." Frankie would know.

"You sure she's not?" I asked.

"Positive," Tim wheezed. "I checked. Nobody official wants her for nothing." Tim rested between outbursts, breathing deeply and pulling the covers close about him.

Frankie jumped in. "This group she's with, now that's another matter. They're suspects in a whole lot of shit. You remember that Japanese fishing trawler that got rammed a couple of months ago?" He didn't wait for a response. "The heat is looking at them for that. Also all that damage a couple months back over at the research labs at the university."

Two months ago someone had ransacked the research labs at the U, freed all the animals, and set the place on fire. The fire had spread to an adjoining campus building, causing damage in the millions. Every legitimate animal rights and environmental organization had decried the action as that of the terminally misguided. A couple had even posted rewards for the capture of the perpetrators. If Caroline Nobel was part of this mess, things were ugly. Taking a case for Tim Flood was one thing, failing at it was another.

Turning to Frankie Ortega, I asked, "What makes you say she acts like she's on the run?" Maybe if I could put their collective mind at ease, I could get out of this. No go. Tim had been waiting for this part.

"These screwballs have a whole building way down on First. I had Frankie take me down there. It's like Prohibition all over again. They got these assholes in green berets hanging out on the sidewalk handing out leaflets. Nobody, but nobody, gets into the building. They live in there, for Chrissake. They eat there. When they want to leave, they back these vans up to the side door, everybody files out into the vans. They got other vans makin' sure they ain't being followed. They're just a bunch of kids. They think they're the fuckin' CIA or something. I never seen anything like it. They shouldn't be playin' at shit like that. They're a bunch of amateurs. They haven't got a clue. They're gonna get hurt." I'd never seen Tim Flood quite this riled.

"I still don't see why you need me."

"Frankie I need around, Leo. Nicky and Ricky, well— they have their talents but it's not for finding out stuff, if you know what I mean.

"I want to know about this Save the Earth group. I want to know what they're into. I want to make sure she's not getting in too far, where even I can't get her out of it."

"I don't know, Tim. I—"

"Expenses, your daily rate, and a ten-grand bonus."

Tim knew the way to my heart. No "for old times' sake." No playing on his relationship with my father. Just filthy lucre.

"What's your daily rate, Leo?"

"Four hundred and expenses," I shot back.

"Bullshit," he said with a smile. "You get three. I checked."

Before I could protest he stopped me. "I'll go the four hundred."

He leaned back once again and closed his eyes. "You need anything, you call Frankie," he sighed. He was snoring softly before I could work up a clever refusal.

Frankie Ortega walked me all the way to my car. I was freezing, shivering almost uncontrollably inside my topcoat. Frankie didn't notice. He was deep in thought. As I unlocked the car door, he put his hand on my arm. "Take care of this for him, huh, Leo? She's family. He's an old man."

I said I'd try. He handed me an envelope. I opened the door.

Frankie held the door as I got in. "Watch out for this kid, Leo. She's scary." Now he had my attention.

Anything that would scare Frankie Ortega automatically put the fear of God in me. I started sweating again.

"Why's that, Frankie?"

"Something's loose in that kid," he said.

"Oh," I deadpanned.

"Tim, he wouldn't say so. He's too proud, her being family and all, but this one's definitely trouble, Leo. Nineteen, going on fifty. A wild child. Never seen anything quite like it, Leo.

This one's a cross between little Miss Muffet and Debbie Does Dallas. One minute she's stomping her feet, acting like a baby; next minute she's offering to sit on your face."

He stopped and cast his eyes furtively up and down the street, as if the old man's tentacles reached everywhere. Satisfied, he continued.

"We couldn't keep regular help. You remember Tim never much liked women around since the wife died. We always had male help. You remember from when your dad used to bring you here." I remembered. "I had to let them all go. If she couldn't get what she wanted out of them one way, she'd get it another. We had guys threatening to shoot one another over her, for Chrissake. She'd fuck a snake if somebody'd hold the head still."

"How'd you make out, Frankie?" I asked. He wasn't amused.

"Don't fuck around," he said gravely. "Before this is over, you may need some help with this one, Leo. You need anything, you call. I'll send you the twins, okay?" I said it was okay. I lied. Frankie was still musing about the dangerous Caroline Nobel. Almost sounded like professional jealousy.

"She's a pretty package, all right. No doubt about it. There's a picture in the envelope. You'll see." He still held the door. "You been around, Leo. You know the score. You spend any time with her, you'll see what I mean. She plays men like some broads play the piano."

He leaned down and got close to my face. "You know, Leo, years ago I learned to look in people's eyes. I needed to know right away whether they was reaching for their wallet or they was reaching for a gun. This one, I don't see nothin'. Before you leap—take a good look in her eyes. It'll shrivel your dick up like a roll of dimes." He slammed the door.

5

"ANY OF YOU still have a driver's license?" I asked.

The question brought on another round of head shaking, foot shuffling, and staring at my living room floor. Buddy, as was his custom, took the lead.

"You might as well ask a fish if he still has his bicycle," Buddy muttered under his breath.

"Okay. Okay," I said. "For the time being, we'll take the bus."

While Buddy was generally in charge of the bitching for this group, this particular suggestion even brought complaints from Harold, Ralph, and George. "How in hell can we be real operatives from the bus?" said George, jamming his hands into the pockets of his buttonless tweed overcoat.

"Yeah, Leo, it just ain't right," whined Harold.

"What if we have to follow somebody or something?" asked Ralph.

"If you have to follow anyone, which I doubt," I added, "take a cab. It's expenses. I'll give it back to you later."

"Won't work," said Buddy.

"Why not?"

"Most of the cabbies won't pick us up."

Buddy had a point. I'd forgotten that once a guy was officially enshrined in the local Degenerate Hall of Fame, public transport was no longer a viable option. About the third time a guy puked, pissed, or passed out in a cab or a bus, the drivers spread the word.

"Wave money at 'em," I suggested.

"Won't work," Buddy said again, shaking his head. "They'll just think it's old Ralph here waving his balls at 'em again."

I'd heard about that particularly sordid little episode.

"They're both green," offered George.

"Yeah, and if you fold the bills enough times, they're about the same size," Harold added. They yukked it up.

This led to a prolonged round of accusations centering on the legendary personal hygiene deficiencies of each. I let them have their fun. They were right. I needed to come up with a car that we could all fit in. Renting one was out of the question. Anything new and shiny would get these guys arrested for car theft within four blocks. I decided to handle the problem once I'd gotten them all staked out.

"Okay, you guys have got a point. I'll get you a vehicle this afternoon. Today, though, just this once, we're going to have to take the bus downtown."

They grumbled but went along with the program.

The bus driver was no rookie. I hid the crusty quartet in a dark doorway nearby. As the doors hissed open, I inserted myself between them and waved the crew forward. The driver tried to cut me in half with the doors. It took my promise that, if necessary, I'd use my leather jacket to clean up any little surprises the boys might leave, to get us all on board. He opened his little side window and drove with his nose in the breeze like a spaniel.

As soon as I'd pulled the pictures from the envelope Frankie Ortega had given me, I'd recognized the building. If I remembered correctly, it used to be an old shoe factory. The building squatted midway down a long row of degenerate architecture along the west side of the Kingdome, hard by the side of the viaduct, occupying nearly the same ground as Tim Flood's beloved Hooverville had so many years before. What goes around, comes around.

This very building had been part of a discussion that Patsy and I had last summer. We'd been taking our seventh-inning stretch on the ramp adjacent to the three-hundred level of the Kingdome. Patsy was sucking down Kools and bemoaning the fact that smoking was no longer permitted in the Dome.

To the south the gutted hulk of a building, painted bright blue as if to draw attention to itself, stood gap-toothed among the surrounding rubble. On the two lower floors, each and every window had been systematically stoned out by local rock throwers. Some merely had been holed; others were gone entirely. I commented to Patsy that they weren't making rock throwers like they used to. In our day, we'd have gotten the top floor too. He'd agreed.

"It's these goddamn Little League programs with all their pussy rules about how many innings the kids can throw and all that shit. The kids never develop any arm strength. They're all like that Blackmore kid in there tonight." The M's were losing big. Patsy had lost his sense of humor.

"That son of a bitch doesn't throw hard enough to raise lumps on anybody. M's ought to have a ticket promotion," he sneered. "Buy one, get one free. Buy two, you can pitch."

Last year's hideous blue had been painted over with a uniform coat of beige. The windows had been replaced. I made a note to call a friend of mine in Planning. It might be interesting to see how Save the Earth had come into posses-sion of such a property.

The boys and I marched like Caesar and his lesions from the bus stop down to the far side of the south Kingdome parking lot. The building was a good quarter mile away across the lots. Close enough to reconnoiter, but far enough for us to be invisible.

"All right," I started. "I want one of you hanging around at each corner of the building. I want—"

The bitching started immediately. They all wanted the viaduct side.

"I got friends over there by pillar six," Ralph claimed.

"Me too," chimed George.

Buddy took over. "Screw you guys. You just want to be able to stay out of the rain, that's all. Harold and George, you guys are the oldest, you get the viaduct side. Try to stay dry. Ralph and I will work from the street." He looked to me.

"Great," I said. "Take these." I handed each a small spiral notebook and a couple of pencils. Their grimy hands clutched the booty like it was the Holy Grail. It wasn't much, but it was brand-new.

"I want license numbers for every vehicle of any sort that either enters or leaves." They scribbled away. "I want descriptions, ages, and anything else you can come up with on any foot traffic." More scribbling. "If anybody leaves on foot, I want one of you to see where he goes. But"—I waved a finger in front of their faces—"I want at least one of you to stay out front and out back at all times. At no time is either the front or the back to be completely unattended. Got it?" Ralph raised his hand.

"Could you go over that again, Leo?"

"Which part?" I tried to hide my exasperation.

"All of it," he said sheepishly. I looked over the top of his hand to see what notes he'd been taking. Stick figures. Either Ralph was taking notes in Egyptian hieroglyphics, or he was experiencing a serious shortage of brain cells. I was beginning to worry.

Buddy jumped in again. "I'll fill him in, Leo." He patted Ralph's arm.

"Okay," I said. "Everybody pay attention." They stopped scribbling.

"Here's the important part." I brought out four copies of Caroline's photo that I'd made that morning.

As Frankie Ortega had promised, she was indeed one slick package. Blond, blue-eyed, high cheekbones, solid chiseled features. Definite cover girl potential. The picture only showed her from the neck up, wearing a square-necked peasant blouse, but, presuming she was still in possession of all of her appendages, the rest of her held great promise. I gave each guy a copy.

They made noises like a pack of feeding hyenas, elbowing one another and trying lamely to look down the front of the blouse.

"This is who we're looking for." They weren't paying attention. Ralph was sniffing the picture. "Hey," I shouted. They snapped to. Contrite.

"This," I said, shaking the picture, "is what we're here about. This young lady is the one exception to the two-guys-have-to-stay-here-at-all-times rule. If any of you see her leaving, follow her Use as many guys as it takes but keep track of her. Do whatever it takes. Understood?"

"What if she leaves by car?"

"Follow on foot as far as you can. As bad as traffic is, you can probably stay ahead of them. Try for a taxi. I'll work on getting you guys a car for this afternoon. In the meantime, fake it. Okay?"

It was okay. "You've each got the twenty-five I gave you this morning. If you spend any of it in the line of duty, I'll replace it. Get receipts. You hear me? This isn't the honor system. If you want to be reimbursed, get a receipt." En masse scribbling. "I'm going to dig up a car for you now. I don't know how long it'll take. I might be back to pick you guys up this afternoon or I might not. If I miss any of you between now and then, be at my place again at eight A.M. sharp tomorrow." They nodded in unison. I headed off in search of a cab.

The job had seemed like a natural. I had an extra hundred a day coming in from Tim Flood. Buddy and the boys could blend into the surroundings like so much refuse. It seemed like a hell of a lot better idea than staking the place out myself. Three or four days and we ought to have a pretty good picture of the activities originating at the building.

In the meantime, I knew a place I could probably come up with a car and some information on Save the Earth all at the same time.

I had the cabbie drop me in front of the University Bookstore. The Ave was humming. An elderly black man played solo sax in the doorway to the bookstore. A bebop version of "For All We Know" buzz-sawed its way along the street. Across the street in front of Tower Records, a dobro player had attracted a small crowd.

The sidewalks were jammed with the usual eclectic sampling of life's rich pageant that clung to the belly of any major university. Students, would-be students, used-to-be students, hawkers, hustlers, hangers-on, punkers, and a whole new generation of bums all flowed and eddied about, forming a meandering stream of partially washed plurality.

I shouldered my way through the melee and headed downhill toward the Cucumber Castle. In its present manifestation, it was a combination head shop, clothing store, and CD exchange. Arnie Robbins had a knack for keeping up with the times.

Thirty years ago, in the back row of the balcony of the Varsity Theatre, Arnie'd slipped me my first joint. We'd found Charlton Heston's antics in *The Ten Commandments* so inexplicably funny that we'd eventually been escorted out. While for most of us the tribal fantasy of the sixties had been merely a brief respite along life's highway, a welcome excuse to avoid the imagined terrors of responsibility for just one more endless summer, for Arnie it had become a permanent way of life.

Arnie was on his usual stool behind the counter. A tie-dyed Dorian Gray, seemingly impervious to the ravages of time, he looked exactly like he had back in the early seventies. His frizzy red hair and walrus mustache showed no signs of gray. Unlike the rest of us, he seemed to lose a few pounds every year. As one by one we'd trudged off toward serious jobs and serious responsibilities, I'd initially been saddened by what I'd perceived to be Arnie's arrested development. The last few times I'd seen him, however, I'd experienced something a great deal more akin to envy.

The store was full. He glanced up briefly as I walked in, handed the blue ceramic bong he'd been holding over to a leather-clad kid with an orange mohawk, and walked down to the display of vintage horror comics at the far end of the counter. I followed.

We engaged in the old hippie thumbs-only handshake and checked one another out.

"Looking good, Leo," he said with a smile.

"You too, Arnie. I mean, Jesus Christ, you look great."

"Clean living," he said gravely. "I went full fruitarian five years ago, changed my whole life, Leo. You wouldn't believe—"

Mercifully, two clean-cut coeds had decided on a pair of wild tie-dyed T-shirts. Arnie hustled down to take their money. I looked around the shop.

Tie-dye was back with a vengeance. I was still shaking my head at the vagaries of devolution when Arnie came back.

"It's the Age of Aquarius all over again, Leo." God forbid, I thought.

"Listen, Arnie, have you still got that collection of semi-running beaters out back of your house?"

"I'm preserving the earth's resources, Leo. Do you have any idea what our addiction to the automobile is costing this planet? Do you—"

"Any of them big and still in running condition?"

"Well"—stroking his mustache—"there's that Buick station wagon we used to tool around in. A real gas hog though."

"It still runs?"

"You bet." He headed off to wait on a customer. He was back.

"You'd have to take the battery out of the red Chevy with the camper on it. Other than that I think it's just fine. Ran okay the last time I fired it up. Burns a little oil. You want to borrow it?"

I said I did. "Tags current?" I asked.

"Not since sixty-three," he laughed. "Take the plates off the Opel station wagon; they're good for another couple of months."

The crowd was thinning out. Mostly just wasting time. I jumped on the lull to pick up a little information.

"Arnie, tell me what you know about an environmental group called Save the Earth." The question pulled him up short.

"Bad news, brother, bad news," he intoned gravely. "Making all the legitimate movements look bad. People like that make me wish I was a CPA, man." I somehow doubted it. He elaborated. "They don't understand that violence begets violence. They're a bunch of vigilantes. Bought this big old armored cargo ship. Been tearing up fishing nets. Rammed what they thought was a Japanese fishing trawler out in the Straits, turned out to be outgoing, full of machine parts. Shit like that." He trotted over and sold the kid the blue bong.

We were alone in the store now. For the first time I noticed that the Blues Project was coming through the ceiling-mounted speakers. Paul Butterfield was wailing his heart out. It still sounded good. Another hour of this and I was going to spend the next three days calling everybody man or sister or some such shit. As the door closed silently behind the kid, Arnie spoke down the length of the store.

"They see most of the old-time movements as part of the problem. Greenpeace, the Sierra Club, even Earth First! These kids hate all of them, think they're a bunch of wussies. Don't attend any of the symposiums or anything. I'm telling you brother, they're going to set the movement back thirty years is what they're going to do."

"What else?" I asked when he stopped.

"That's all I know, Leo. You want more, I know a guy, a writer, who can maybe help you. He's more tied into that area than I am." I said I did.

Arnie reached beneath the counter and came out with an ornately tooled leather address book. He copied down a name and number on a blue Post-it and stuck it on my shirt front. I peeled it off and slipped it in my pocket.

"Is the gate locked?" I asked.

"Nope. You can just waltz in."

"No dogs or anything like that?"

"Just Nadine," he said with a chuckle. "She's my current squeeze. She's probably not up yet though. Just tell her I said it was okay."

We repeated the secret handshake, promised to get together more often, which we both knew to be a lie, and parted company.

I walked the fifteen blocks through the U ghetto to Arnie's place. As promised, the gate was open. Ten or twelve dilapidated cars filled the backyard. The famous "No Hope Without Dope" VW van rested like a piece of sculpture on cement blocks. A family of pigeons was living inside. They made no move to escape as I peered through the dusty windows.

The Buick was backed up against the fence at the far end of the yard. A true land yacht. A car for the long-gone nuclear family, its once woody sides faded white. It had originally been either blue or gray—the level of oxidation made it hard to tell. I took a tour. The tires were mismatched but looked serviceable. I opened the passenger door. The interior was filled with more spare parts. An axle lay across the front seat. Fifteen or twenty old rims, some with tires, some without, filled the rest of the car, floorboard to ceiling. I went back around the front to the driver's side, leaned in, and popped the hood release, leaving that door open too. The rusted parts smelled decadent and organic, like a roadkill drying in the sun.

The engine was cleaner than the rest of the car. My hopes buoyed, I walked over to the little shack tacked on the back of the house and found Arnie's toolbox right where he'd always kept it.

I scrounged the plates from the Opel and the battery from the Chevy. I had the newer battery bolted into the Buick and was wedged in between the fence and the back bumper cold-chiseling the last license-plate bolt off when I heard the screen door squeak.

"That you honey?" Female voice, thick southern drawl. "That you bangin' around out there?" I gave the rusted bolt three more strokes. The plate fell into my lap. I butt-bumped my way out from behind the Buick and stood to dust myself. She was standing on the back steps of the little house wrapped in a blue bath towel.

I guessed she was slightly less than half Arnie's age. Twenty or so. Fresh from the shower, her black hair glistened. I set the ball-peen hammer and the chisel on the fender and started over. If all women looked like this one, makeup and fashion sales would go in the dumper. She didn't need any help. Even at a distance, my envy returned.

"Arnie's loaning me the Buick," I said, still walking.

"What's yo name, darlin'?"

"Leo." This was not last-name material.

"Not yo sign, yo name, honey."

"That *is* my name."

"Well then, Leo the lion, what's yo sign?"

"If I go to my cap, it's a hit and run." She didn't have a clue.

"You're funny, just like Arnie. You a friend of his?"

"We go way back," I said, stopping just in front of the battered steps. "What about you?" I asked.

"Oh, ahm just stayin' here for a bit," she said, slowly peeling the blue towel from around her body and rubbing it around in her hair. She seemed totally at ease standing out on the back steps in the nude. She was perfect. Small pert breasts stood at attention above her flat stomach, a small trail of dark fuzz led invitingly down into her thick black bush. Not a stretch mark. Not a blemish. Not a single vein in sight. Not a chance in hell.

She finished working on her hair, draped the towel around her neck, and, still holding the ends, smiled at me through her hair.

"You just gonna stand there gawkin' or you want to come inside?" I presumed she meant the house.

"I'd better get the Buick going," I said weakly.

"Whatsamatter, you a queer or somethin', honey? Or maybe you're just shy." I was beginning to wonder myself. She moved down a step. I retreated. I kept my mouth shut. My silence was making her nervous.

She retrieved the towel and wound it quickly back around her body.

"Just a guy that knows his limitations," I said, trying to put her at ease.

She shrugged. "And here I had a notion you'd be kinda

grateful like old whatshisname that lives here. You been listenin' to too much of that safe-sex talk, Leo, become a prisoner of the media."

"In my day, safe sex meant a padded headboard."

She shook her pretty head, turned on her heel, and headed back into the house, slamming the door behind her. My envy returned.

My fingers didn't want to work as I bolted the new plates on. Probably insufficient blood supply. It took a while, but I got it done. I was better at the heavy work. I cleaned out the interior in record time, piling the parts neatly by the side of the fence.

The moment of truth was at hand. The keys were in the ignition. I brushed the driver's seat, sat, and turned the key. The big V-8 rolled over slowly. I got out and checked the oil. A quart down, no problem.

I tried again. The Buick shook and rocked as the engine caught, sputtered, and finally died once again. On the fifth try it ran. For the first thirty seconds the dry valves sounded as if they were about to come right out of the block, but gradually, as the oil pump managed to move the sludgelike oil through the system, things quieted down. I gunned it, looking in the mirror.

It looked like I was crop dusting. Thick blue smoke billowed into the air. The smoke got blacker as I put the pedal to the metal. I let up. The big boat idled nicely, if you didn't count the noxious blue smoke. I got out and closed the hood. I replaced Arnie's tools in the little shed, opened the gate, and drove through. As I reclosed the gate, my peripheral vision said she was standing above me in the window. I looked the other way. The exhaust from the Buick had left a two-foot black circle on the cedar fence.

All in all, the Buick drove pretty well, a bit spongy in the turns perhaps, and the squealing of the brakes would probably open garage doors within a three-mile radius, but overall, not too bad. I stopped at a BP station on Eastlake with a do-it-yourself car wash. I hosed her down inside and out, filled her up, and added a quart of oil. I checked the stick. Burned a little oil, Arnie'd said. I'd burned half a quart since I'd left his yard. I went back inside and bought a case of oil and a blue plastic funnel and tooled downtown to check on the crew.

6

BY THURSDAY MORNING we'd worked up a preliminary picture of how Save the Earth spent its day and were formulating a plan for getting a line on the elusive Caroline Nobel.

The boys had been thrilled by the Buick. A Bentley couldn't have pleased them more. They'd spent a full twenty minutes kicking the tires, slapping the roof, and reminiscing about the days when Detroit made real cars like this one. I led them on a run-through of checking the oil and extracted a promise that they'd check it twice a day. I'd burned another half quart getting downtown. They'd christened it "The Drunk Tank." Buddy, by default, had been appointed designated driver.

Last I'd seen them, Monday afternoon, Buddy, his eyes barely above the wheel, was tooling up Occidental with George riding shotgun. Harold and Ralph had appropriated the rear seat and rode facing backward like a pair of those spring-loaded hula dolls. They disappeared in a carbon monoxide fog as Buddy eased her away from the light. Tailgaters beware.

"They're just fancy panhandlers, Leo. That's all," said Buddy. Buddy was holding down my recliner, contentedly flossing with a matchbook cover. The rest of the crew were lined up on the couch. To George's never-ending chagrin, Buddy fancied himself management. Harold and Ralph always sided with whoever was winning at the moment.

"Those vans take them around to whatever events are going on in town. They stand out front and panhandle with those little cans they carry." He consulted his notes. "So far, we been to a couple of ball games, the Opera. They make regular rounds over at the locks and down on the waterfront."

"How do they do?" I asked.

"No more than twenty a day each," said George, who was deemed to be the resident expert on panhandling. "They're too pushy."

"How many of them?"

"Twelve out at a time. Two vans." Buddy again.

"How many people live in the building?"

"We figure twenty total. Give or take a few." Harold.

"It's hard to tell, there's a lot of traffic in and out." George.

"These kids all look alike to me." Ralph.

"What they all look is *dumb*." Buddy.

"Specially the hairdo on the kid who seems to be in charge." Ralph laughed. "Leo, you ought to see—" We were getting way off track. I pulled them back.

"Tell me about Caroline." This produced the usual round of snorting, elbowing, and rude remarks. Buddy broke it up.

"She don't panhandle, Leo. She's got something else going on."

"Tell me about it." Buddy checked his notes again.

"She keeps meeting this guy down by Pier Fifty-seven. Around two in the afternoon. They both drive up, find a parking space, and just sit there for a while, looking all around."

"In the same car?" I asked.

"Nope." Harold.

"In the cars they come in. She drives this little blue Toyota. He drives this big old Ford pickup. Big tires. Real muddy."

"And they just sit there in their cars?"

"For a while," said Buddy.

"Then what?"

"Well, on Monday he got out and walked over and got in her car. On Wednesday she got out and went over and sat in his car."

"For how long?"

George fanned his notes. "Half hour or so on Monday. Forty minutes on Wednesday."

"Boyfriend?" I asked.

"No way," said Buddy quickly.

"Could be," offered George. Harold and Ralph shrugged and waited.

"Looked like they were arguing to me," insisted Buddy.

"They was sittin' right on top of one another, for Chrissake," said George. Harold and Ralph nodded in agreement.

"He's an Eskimo," said Harold.

"Mexican," mumbled Ralph.

George held out for some sort of Indian. East, West, American, he wasn't sure.

"What then?"

"They get back in their own cars and take off." Buddy.

"Where to?" I asked.

"She goes right back to headquarters." Buddy again.

"What about him?"

They all looked at Buddy. There was a problem.

"You tell him, George," said Buddy. When in doubt, delegate.

"You were driving, you tell him."

Buddy fidgeted around in the recliner, took a deep

breath, and started. "Well. Leo, on Wednesday George and I were ready. Ralph stayed back at headquarters. Harold found this great old Safeway cart and was pushing it around down there where they park."

"Got right up next to their car," bragged Harold.

"George and I were ready to follow him—"

"Found four bucks worth of cans too." Harold again.

Buddy shot him a murderous glance. "Anyway, Leo. To make a long story short. He lost us." Buddy hung his head.

"Guy drives like Barney Oldfield," said George, staring at his mismatched wing tips.

"Any idea which way he was headed?"

"Up University. That's as far as we got."

"Toward the freeway?" Buddy and George nodded.

"Okay," I said. "Good work. Here's what we're going to do."

"You're not pissed?" asked Buddy.

"We're not fired?" George showed great relief.

"Hell, no," I said. "You guys did just fine." Buddy staged a recovery.

"If George here wasn't so goddamn slow, we'd a kept him in sight, Leo. I know we would have. He"—pointing at George—"wouldn't ride in the backseat."

"I get carsick riding backward," whined George.

"You're the one insisted on sitting back there," Buddy snorted.

"The passenger seat's sopping wet," George shot back.

"Who are you shittin', George? How could you tell? You're generally a bit damp down there anyway." Buddy looked around the group for agreement. I put a stop to it.

"Is there a pay phone handy down there?" These were the guys to know. Checking coin slots was part of the daily routine.

"Three," said Ralph immediately. "One all the way over by the Curiosity Shop. One inside the Antique Mart and one by the Hot Dog Stand."

"Okay," I said. "Here's what we're going to do." They got out their notepads. "You guys are going to do the same thing you did the last time they met, with one exception. This time I want Ralph over at one of the pay phones."

"Which one?" asked Ralph, pencil poised.

"It doesn't matter, Ralph," I snapped. "You decide."

Chastened, Ralph went back to drawing in his pad. "Harold, you get your cart and wander about. Buddy, you and George be ready in the car same as before, but this time"—I paused for effect—"the minute they're both there, you guys have Ralph give me a call. I'll be waiting at home. If the pattern holds, I ought to have plenty of time to get down there. I'll follow him."

"What do we do, then?" asked Buddy.

"You guys pile in the wagon and follow her. If she goes back to the building, stake it out and keep taking license numbers." I remembered. "Where's the license numbers you guys have gotten so far?"

Buddy rummaged around in the pocket of his parka and handed me the list.

"What if she don't go back to headquarters?" he asked.

"Then try to follow her." I waited for it to sink in. "Any questions?"

Ralph started to raise his hand, but an elbow from Buddy made him reconsider. "We're ready," Buddy said.

"All right then, fellas. Back to work."

They rose as a unit and headed out the door. From the doorway, I reminded them. "Take the stairs." They waved agreement. I closed the door. Having the crew around was hard enough on my neighbors. Over the years I'd been part of a couple of ugly scenes that had played out here in the building. Most of my neighbors already looked at me with a jaundiced eye. To my knowledge, I was the only resident who'd ever actually shot anybody on the premises. I was afraid that getting caught in an elevator with this group might push one of the neighbors over the edge. I watched until the boys opened the fire door and started down.

I was behind in my paperwork. I owed a couple of expense reports on a skip-tracing job I was working on and a final report and billing on a prenuptial investigation I'd just completed. And this was just the old business.

Last evening, I'd retrieved a list of nine new possibles off my answering machine, weeded it down to the six most promising, and made a note to follow up sometime today. Sometime was now.

I started with Jed James. Jed was a local attorney whose investigative work I handled when the time and finances permitted. He did mostly pro bono work, but usually scammed up a way to get me paid full rate for my work.

Jed was the scourge of the local law enforcement community. His ten years spent as the ACLU's chief litigator back in New York had given him both a taste for the underdog and a grating, abrasive manner seldom seen this far west. Jed was interested in rights. It didn't matter whose rights, just rights. No cause was too unpopular. No infringement too slight. To my knowledge, if you counted appeals, he was undefeated.

Judges, when faced with the prospect of presiding over one of Jed's cases, had been known to hastily disqualify themselves on obscure technical grounds in favor of a couple of weeks of tranquil trout fishing in the eastern part of the state.

The district attorney's office, after years of having its best and brightest ground into fodder, had wisely taken to utilizing Jed's peculiar talents to cull their own ranks of deadwood. Many a marginal prosecutor, ineffective but immovable because of the arcane civil service statutes, had been jettisoned either into private practice or into a completely new career path after being buried in court by Jed James.

Most of the experienced local attorneys, rather than trotting their thousand-dollar suits into open court only to be hammered mercilessly by this obnoxious little guy spouting lyrical phrases with the Brooklyn accent, usually settled out of court. Contrary to rumor, there are some things that attorneys won't do for money. Not coincidentally, Jed was also my attorney.

"James, Junkin, Rose, and Smith." A cheery little voice.

"Jed James, please."

"Can I tell Mr. James who's calling, please?"

"Leo Waterman."

"Leo, it's Cynthia. How are you doing?"

"Cynthia, I thought you'd retired to full-time child rearing."

"I have. But Suzanne had a baby last Thursday. I'm filling in for a few weeks till she gets back on her feet."

"What did she have?" I asked.

"A boy, and catch this, eleven pounds three ounces."

I winced. "Sounds painful."

"No kidding."

"She home yet?" I asked.

"Oh, sure. They let her out Monday."

"Let me have her address. I'll send her something." She read me an address up in Snohomish County.

"Let me get Jed for you. He's been trying to get me to call you every fifteen minutes. You know how he gets." I knew. Type A all the way. "I, on the other hand, know you'll check in when you get damn good and ready."

"One of the perks of the self-employed."

"I'll get him for you." I waited on the line as the Embalmed Strings sawed their way through a particularly turgid instrumental rendition of "Moon River." The line clicked.

"Leo, you slime, I've been looking for you."

"You'll have to take a number, like a bakery."

"I knew fame would spoil you, Leo. I knew it."

"The only thing that's going to spoil me, Jed, is that music you play over the phone system. Is that the best you can do? I mean, 'Moon River,' give me a break." I made gagging noises.

"It's soothing, Leo," he chuckled. "We do criminal defense work, remember. I don't think 'Stairway to Heaven' is what most of the people calling here are looking for."

"Point well taken, Jed. What can I do for you?"

"I've got a kid accused of a drive-by shooting over in Medina. He—"

"A drive-by shooting in Medina? Come on, Jed. You sure it wasn't more like a drive-by snubbing? That would be more like Medina."

Medina is the Beverly Hills of the Greater Seattle area. Spacious homes bordering Lake Washington, Japanese gardeners tending acres of mature landscaping, estates set back a quarter mile from the road. The only way you could stage a drive-by in that neighborhood would be with a Mercedes-seeking cruise missile.

"I swear to God, Leo."

"I can't handle it this time, Jed."

"Sure you can. He's black, so naturally he's guilty."

"I'm swamped."

"Find a way. I need you."

"No can do. Send one of those eager young associates of yours."

" 'Fraid not, friend. I already sent one of the neophytes on a foray to ferret out the friends."

"How do you do that?"

"What?"

"Make up whole sentences using the same letter."

"It's a gift. How about it?"

"I'm working for Tim Flood." This slowed even Jed down.

"You have a living will?"

"I'm just helping him with a problem."

"Most of Tim's problems wind up wearing the concrete kimono."

"He's retired. This is personal."

"Your ass."

"I'll check in when I'm finished."

"No, my man, you'll probably check out before you're finished. Ta ta." He was gone. Before I could dial again, the phone rang. I answered it.

"Waterman Investigations."

"Hello." I waited. "Can I help you?"

"Is this Leo?"

"Yes, it is."

"Leo Waterman?"

"Is this Ralph?" Just a wild guess.

"Leo, it's Ralph." I was trying to stay calm, but this conversation needed a boost. Five more minutes and we'd be at Ralph's last name.

"Are they meeting again?"

"Yep. They're sittin' in her car. We're all here like you said."

"Stay where you are. I'll be right down."

"Should I tell Buddy you're comin'?"

"Just stay where you are. I'm on the way." I hung up.

I'd already packed a cooler full of food and Pepsi and a day pack full of clothes. Preparation is the essence of stakeouts. I'd spent some of the most miserable days of my life staked out unprepared. I'm a slow learner, but eventually it gets through. I hustled over to the hall closet, threw a flashlight in the side pocket of the pack, grabbed my sleeping bag just in case, and put on my coat. With my nine-millimeter in one pocket and the little thirty-two auto in the other, the coat was as heavy as chain mail and every bit as comforting.

I slung the strap of the little cooler over my shoulder, reached through, and picked up the pack. The sleeping bag went under my free arm. It was clumsy, but I managed to get out the door and down to the car.

7

IT WASN'T HARD to find the boys. Harold's shopping cart leaned heavily against the front bumper of the Buick, blocking half of one of the already narrow lanes of traffic beneath the overhead highway. I pulled up behind the cart and left the Fiat running. I moved the cart over to the side. There was a party going on in the Buick. I rapped hard on the window. The window slid down.

"You guys paying attention, or what?"

Buddy cleaned the windshield with his sleeve and peered up the street in terror. "Still there, Leo. You see that primered red Ford?"

"The one with the big tires?" I asked.

"They're still in there," he said smugly. He smelled of cheap whiskey.

"I thought we'd agreed to stay sober on the job," I said loud enough for all of them to hear. They went silent. Buddy took the lead.

"We've only got a pint, Leo. That's mouthwash for the four of us. Just a bracer," he said with a watery wink.

I appreciated that Buddy hadn't tried to bullshit me, but the bracer part made me nervous. These guys had names for every conceivable drinking situation. They liked to have a little eye-opener to get themselves going in the morning, a midmorning bracer before attempting anything serious, a few modest cocktails at lunch, followed by the obligatory afternoon pick-me-up, which segued neatly right into happy hour and ended with a little one just to help them sleep. For purely medicinal purposes, of course. What the hell had I expected, anyway?

"Okay," I said reasonably. "I'm going to ignore this little breach of manners this time." They visibly relaxed. I checked the street. The Ford four-by-four was still nosed in, sixty yards up the street. I leaned down to the window.

"So you guys follow her, right?"

"To the ends of the earth," said Buddy.

"All the way to Bellingham, if we have to," added Ralph.

Buddy, bless his heart, tried to run interference.

"From the mighty Columbia to the Straits of Juan de Fuca, Leo."

"Who in hell is Wanda Fuca?" asked Ralph.

We never did get it settled. Caroline Nobel, wearing a yellow down vest over a camouflage jacket, strode briskly across the street toward her car. The pickup backed out in a rush. I sprinted back to the Fiat.

The big Ford made the first available right and started up toward the square. I had to run the light to keep up. The boys were right. As a driver, this guy took no prisoners. Passenger cars, their roofs barely above the truck's tire level, seemed disinclined to compete for space.

He intimidated his way through the midafternoon madness at breakneck pace, turned left on First Avenue, and headed uptown. By the time I rounded the corner, he was three blocks up, whistling along in the right-hand lane while

the bulk of the traffic inexplicably crawled along on the left.
I started to follow along in the right lane but was stopped by
a tandem Metro bus, which pulled to the curb, blocking both
my path and my view.

By the time the bus disgorged its passengers and got back
underway, I was sure I'd lost him. I nearly sideswiped a new
green Wagoneer as I rocketed around the bus and tried to
make up ground. I got lucky.

Six blocks up the hill, the Ford looked like it was long
gone until, just before University, a UPS van veered suddenly
into its path. I could see the nose of the truck dive as he stood
on the brakes. Even from this distance I could see some of
the collected mud that layered the sides of the truck break
loose and turn to dust on the street.

The UPS driver was already out of the truck and on his
way inside one of the buildings. They may run the tightest
ship in the shipping business, but they're a pain in the ass
in traffic. As far as UPS drivers are concerned, the world is
their parking lot.

I'd made up nearly four blocks by the time the pickup
had managed to force its way out into the left lane. I had no
trouble making the light as he turned right up University. He
was heading for the freeway.

I stayed a respectful quarter mile back as we worked our
way up I-5. He wove in and out of traffic, missing no opportunity to make additional time, zigzagging through the building stream of afternoon commuters. I had no choice but to do
likewise. When I was younger, I used to drive like this all the
time. Today I expected to be pulled over, pummeled, and
summarily arrested at any moment. I felt old and stodgy.

For the next fifteen miles only the constant thickening of the
traffic allowed me to keep him in sight. As we roared through
the confluence of I-5 and I-405, something was ejected from the
truck window. It bounced several times and came to a stop on

the shoulder. The Rainier can was still spinning as I shot past.

As the traffic thinned out on the north side of Everett, the driver put the hammer down. He was cruising at a smooth eighty. Bits of debris parachuted from the bed of the truck. The Fiat was flat out and losing ground. Another can was thrown from the truck. I was standing on the accelerator. The little car didn't have any more to give. Five more minutes and I was going to be history. I backed off. No point in eating an engine in a lost cause.

As I crested the top of a small rise, I saw the Ford, now a half mile ahead, veer sharply to the right and head down the Marysville exit ramp. There was still hope. I got back on the gas.

It was better than that. The ramp was full. The light was red. The truck was no more than a hundred yards ahead when I ran the yellow and made the turn toward downtown Marysville. For the first time, I could make out the red-and-blue flannel shirt of the driver through the dusty back window.

We wound our way back out the east side of town, first through lower-income residential neighborhoods, then through a seedy commercial zone, and finally, nearly at the edge of civilization itself, through an unpopulated area of defunct sawmills and construction companies.

Without so much as tapping the brakes, the driver made a ninety-degree turn into the gravel parking lot, spewing dust and stones as the truck fought for traction. I continued up past the next building and turned right.

The narrow driveway led back past the building. I pulled to a stop. I was in the back parking lot of Johnson Logging Supply. Several concrete dividers separated this little lot from the big one next door. I had a perfect view of the parking lot and the front door. The Ford was empty.

The Last Stand was a large bunkerlike bar surrounded by

five acres of empty gravel parking lot. Two tiny windows marred the otherwise smooth block front of the building. They probably just needed a place to put the flashing beer signs.

The oversize lot was full of pickups and aging American sedans, parked here and there in no discernible pattern, some north and south, some east and west, some at odd angles like they'd died on the spot. Free-form parking. An affront to civilized society.

The flannel shirt was standing to the left of the front door making conversation with a couple of other Indians. He was no more than twenty, slim but well put together. From what I could see, he was a good-looking kid. A wide, smooth expanse of face accented by oversize dark eyes. His black hair was cut longer than was presently fashionable downtown but was nowhere in the ballpark of the flowing manes of the two guys he was talking to.

They could have been father and son. One was about the kid's age, his long hair held down by a black-and-white baseball cap. The Raiders maybe. His back was partially turned, but even from this distance I could see the acne scars that dominated his ruined face. The other guy was about sixty and moved with the lean stiffness of a cowboy. Three feet of graying hair sprouted from under his battered cowboy hat. He kept his arms tightly folded over his chest.

It wasn't hard to read the body language. The kid I'd been following was animated enough. He used his arms like an orchestra leader, punctuating his points with a series of sweeps and jabs. The other two might as well have been cast in bronze. They listened impassively, the older one occasionally turning away to sweep the dirt with a boot tip, glancing my way once or twice. They were otherwise unmoved and unmoving. While I was too far away to catch the words, they sure as hell weren't catching up on old times. The kid was in their faces about something serious, but they weren't going for it.

A one-ton flatbed roared into the lot and slid to a stop directly between my position and the front door. Through the dust, I could see six or eight more Indians, a couple of them women, climb down from the bed and start inside. The truck zoomed off, showering dirt and gravel as it made a wide loop around the lot, bounced back into the street, turned left, and headed back the way it had come. The local Metro shuttle.

The two other guys had used the diversion to make their escape. By the time the dust settled enough for me to see again, the pair were backing slowly toward the nearest jumble of parked cars, agreeing as they retreated.

They got into a peeling puke-green Nova. The older guy was driving. He must have missed the local driver's ed class. He pulled slowly from the lot, casting a tentative wave at the Ford driver as he went by. The kid shook his head sadly and went inside.

As the last of the dust settled to the ground, I considered my next move. It seemed a good bet that the Last Stand was not the watering hole of choice of the local yuppie set. I was betting on a full-scale, balls-to-the-wall, shit-kicker Saturday-night Indian bar. I stayed put.

I rummaged around in the cooler, came up with a turkey sandwich and a Pepsi. I punched the button for KPLU and was rewarded with an old Ike Quebec tune. One of those excuse-me-while-I-slip-into-something-more-comfortable saxophone riffs that speaks of jagged skylines, wet streets, and slippery lingerie. I sat back, munching slowly, and waited it out.

For the first few hours arrivals far outnumbered departures. By ten-thirty the trend had reversed itself, and the lot began to clear. When the midnight NPR news interrupted my reverie, the big Ford pickup was but one of a dozen or so cars left in the lot. The Last Stand was getting down to the hard core. People with no better place to be. I was getting itchy.

I got out and stretched for the umpteenth time. I wandered

over to the chain-link fence at the back of Johnson's little lot and pissed on the fence.

Loud talk and laughter rolled across the lot as two more cars filled up and headed elsewhere. The Ford stayed put.

I considered going inside but discarded the idea again. My initial impression had proved correct. The clientele had been exclusively Native American. I wondered whether my assumption that I would not be welcome was the product of prejudice or just common sense. Either way I'd stick out like a sore thumb, and the kid was almost certain to get a look at me. I stayed put.

It was one-twelve by the dashboard clock when the kid came out, walking a crooked path, and ambled over to his truck. He was carrying one for the road in his left hand. The Ford turned over, sputtered, and died. In the surrounding stillness, I could hear him pumping the gas pedal. The truck roared to life on the fourth try. I backed the Fiat into the fence, shot up the narrow drive, and was waiting at the street when the Ford came into view. The kid wasn't taking any chances. He drove like he was looking for an address. Staying well within the posted limits, using his signals. I followed at a respectful distance as we wound our way back along the path we'd traveled earlier.

We cut under the freeway, past the Tulalip Cultural Center, and out toward the reservation. Traffic was light. I slowed and left more distance between us. He tooled along at forty for another five miles. Traffic was now nonexistent. We were the only two people out here. As the Ford disappeared around a sweeping left turn, I cut my lights and sped up. I stayed just far enough back to be invisible, hoping there were no cops around.

Another mile and the brake lights on the pickup flashed briefly and then came on full-bore. I slowed. He turned left into a dirt driveway. I pulled the Fiat to the right-hand shoulder, got out, and sprinted across the road. I had no way of knowing how far back the driveway ran or if there was a turnaround. The only safe course was to follow on foot.

As I started down the lane, I could see the pickup roll to a stop about a quarter mile down. I relaxed. The Ford's dome light came on briefly. I stepped into the thick bushes that lined the roadway. The kid got out, walked around the back of the truck, and leisurely took a piss in his driveway. He didn't bother to rearrange himself. Holding his sagging britches with one hand, he wobbled out of view to the right of the truck.

I started up the rutted track. House lights appeared through the thick branches that lined the road. I stumbled and nearly went to one knee. I moved from the wheel ruts, which were potholed and uneven, up to the berm of the road where the native grasses had been systematically mowed by the truck's undercarriage. The going got both easier and quieter.

I was nearly to the truck. I walked as quietly as I could. A small cabin, surrounded by a pole fence, sat diagonally across a hacked-out clearing in the forest. The builder had left one tree at each end of the yard. The kid was using them to anchor a clothesline. Several flannel shirts and a couple of pair of jeans moved slowly in the night breeze. One of the shirts was split completely up the back. I wondered why he'd bothered to wash it. No women. No kids. I could see the kid moving around inside the house.

When he came by the front window for the second time, he was stripped down to a yellowed pair of jockey shorts. He left the lighted living room and wandered toward the darkened end of the house. Through the window on the far right, I saw the refrigerator door open, its light casting dim shadows on the ceiling. The door closed. He turned out lights on his way back through the house. The place went dark. He'd gone to bed. I envied him.

I walked back up toward the Fiat. When I reached the main road, I went hunting for his mailbox. No such luck. No mailbox of any kind was to be found within a quarter mile in any direction. Either he didn't get much mail or he had a box in town. I wandered back to the Fiat.

Sleeping in the Fiat was on-the-job training for curvature of the spine, to be avoided at all costs. While trudging up and down the road in search of the mailbox, I'd noticed a small turnout, big enough to hide the little car, about a hundred yards up on the right. I backed her in until the overhanging willow branches folded back over the front end. I forced the door open, grabbed my sleeping bag from behind the seat, and, using the sleeping bag as a shield for my face, rammed my way back out to the road.

About thirty yards short of the cabin, I once again stepped off into the bushes and pushed another twenty yards through the dense underbrush. I was in a small clearing, shielded from the driveway by a thick row of bushes but close enough so that there was no way he could drive by me without waking me up. I spread the ground cloth and then the bag. I took off my jacket and rolled it into a pillow. Fully dressed, I slid into the bag.

A few misguided clouds roamed about an otherwise perfect sky. Somebody once said that living in Seattle was like being married to a beautiful woman who was sick all the time. The lady was feeling fine tonight. I'd probably wake to snow.

MY OLD MAN was strictly an indoor guy. While he was a vapid defender of the natural beauty of the Pacific Northwest, he was not personally inclined to go mucking about in it. He claimed the years of hardship and deprivation had exacted a terrible toll on his body, leaving him with a mysterious collection of bone-grinding ailments that made it impossible for him to survive even a single night in the great outdoors. I'd believed him.

In the fall after my twelfth birthday, he announced one evening over dinner that he had arranged for me to spend the weekend over in Ellensburg, pheasant hunting with a couple of my uncles. They weren't actually uncles. People who came to the house for social occasions had full names. Mr. Handley, Councilman Baines. Then there were the drunks and reprobates, the remnants of the old man's former life whom my mother refused to allow in her home. They were uncles.

A spirited argument ensued. My mother, showing her usual uncanny powers of memory, dredged up each and every foible, folly, and felony readily attributable to the chosen pair. The old man held firm. It was a rite of passage, he claimed. A boy's birthright. An initiation ceremony.

Obviously having anticipated just such an impasse, my father briefly left the room. He returned carrying a brand-new double-barrelled Ithaca sixteen-gauge shotgun and a box of shells, which he presented to me with a flair and flourish normally reserved for visiting potentates.

My mother knew when she was licked. She flounced from the room, her skirt dragging a chafing dish of steamed carrots to the floor behind her. Just before slamming the dining room door, she cast one glance at the old man and another at the carrots rolling about the carpet. The carrots got the better of it.

The next morning, long before daylight, I found myself wedged between Amos Johnson and Buford Patterson as Buford's battered Ford pickup labored over Snoqualmie Pass.

Amos and Buford passed a bottle of Old Crow back and forth in front of my face. About every third pass, one or the other would remember his manners and offer me a pull. I always refused.

While I was intrigued by the heady smell of the amber liquid and filled with an intense desire to be one of the boys, both Amos and Buford chewed while they drank. Between rounds, as the bottle rested in Amos's lap, I noticed about half a dip of wintergreen snuff floating contentedly on the surface like the Spanish Armada. The idea of straining the snuff through my teeth was more than I could bear.

Hunting was fine. Amos and Buford knew what they were doing. By noon they'd both bagged the limit. We made a pass by the truck, where they left the birds and packed up their own shotguns. Now it was my turn.

They led me across two fields to a wooded draw that cut partway down the hillside. They explained the procedure. They'd been saving this particular draw for me. I was to stand at the downhill end of the draw. They would start at the uphill end and work the draw, driving the birds before them. The birds would run as long as there was cover. Reaching the far end, where I'd be waiting, the birds would take flight right in front of my face. I was admonished to keep firing and reloading until I saw Amos and Buford emerge from the bottom of the draw.

Before it was over, I'd emptied both barrels four times and downed two pheasants. One cock, one hen. Oops. The guys weren't finicky. Meat was meat. They led me back to our campsite with a series of hugs and congratulatory claps on the back. Whatever failings I'd shown as a drinker, I'd more than compensated as a hunter. We ate the hen. Nothing had ever tasted better. I'd never felt more alive.

What I remember most vividly was that night around the campfire. Amos and Buford built a huge bonfire at the bottom of the little rocky wash we were using as a windbreak. It was early October, and while the day had been warm enough to raise beads of sweat on my upper lip as I'd trudged up and down the rolling foothills, the minute the sun went down, it got cold in a big hurry.

After depositing several logs bigger than my body on top of the fire, Amos and Buford rolled themselves into their meager bedrolls as close to the fire as they dared and summarily fell into comas.

I lay in my Sears mail-order sleeping bag and watched the stars. There was no middle ground. The front side of me facing the fire threatened to blister at any moment, while the back half of my body struggled to shiver. I'd never known such extremes. No matter how hard I closed my eyes, the lapping flames intruded into my sleep. The glow forced its way under my eyelids. The ripping and popping of the fire poked me from sleep like insistent fingers.

I sat up with a start. Amos and Buford were long dead. I didn't hunt anymore. The kid's cabin was a raging, white-hot inferno. Flames tore through the roof and escaped through the blown-out windows. I was better than a hundred feet away, shielded by a wall of vegetation, but the flames made my face feel as taut as if it were caked with dried mud.

I scrambled out of the bag and ran headlong out into the driveway, branches tearing at my exposed face. I didn't get far.

Forty feet behind the truck the heat became so intense that I couldn't force myself any farther. The fire was white as a welding rod. I raced back and grabbed my sleeping bag.

I put on my jacket, unzipped the bag except for the very bottom, which I draped over my head, and began to inch my way toward the truck.

The cabin was beyond redemption. The roof over the kitchen end had collapsed already. Nothing in there was alive. If the kid hadn't escaped by now, he wasn't going to. That left the truck.

I could smell the exterior of the sleeping bag by the time I reached for the truck. The door handle burned my hand. I pulled my hand back inside the sleeve of my jacket and, using the sleeve like an oven mitt, jerked open the door. The plastic steering wheel was beginning to sweat. The truck would be the next to go. I leaned across the seat.

I opened the glove box and scooped the contents down the front of my jacket, where I hoped the elastic would keep it pressed to my body. One of the tires closest to the house exploded with a pop. The truck settled. I found the seat release and pushed the seat forward. A long Nike gym bag was behind the seat. I grabbed it and retreated without closing the door.

I'd made it halfway back to where I'd been sacked out when the truck went up like a rocket, throwing me to the ground. My lungs empty of air, I forced myself up and, dragging the Nike bag behind me, crawled another thirty yards down the driveway.

My sleeping bag was smoking. The green nylon on the outside had melted, exposing the wispy goose down to the breeze. Feathers, drawn by the chimney of superheated air, rose up into the night and joined the funnel of debris floating sixty feet over the cabin. I realized I'd been unconsciously sobbing. I sat on my haunches, locking my arms around my knees, and tried to catch my breath. The air was too heavy for breathing.

I turned the sleeping bag inside out and stood on it. It was hotter standing up. I unzipped my jacket and let the contents of the glove box fall among the feathers. The zipper was hot to the touch. I threw the gym bag on top, bundled up the corners into a makeshift sack, threw it over my shoulder, and stumbled up the driveway. The little house hissed and popped behind me. I kept walking all the way to my car.

The inferno wasn't readily visible from the road. Only the white glow in the distant treetops suggested that something was amiss. It could just as easily have been mercury vapor lights. Occasional cinders, propelled upward by the force of the fire, broke the tree line, burned themselves out, and fell harmlessly back to earth. No sirens split the air.

I sat back on the willow branches that were draped over the hood of the Fiat and dropped the bundle at my feet. The hood clicked shut.

My heart stopped. I slid carefully to my feet again and backpedaled out to the road, dragging the ruined sleeping bag with me. Maybe I'd hit the hood release on my way out. Maybe I was just being paranoid. Maybe.

By the time I'd liberated the clothesline from the front yard, I could smell my own hair burning. The kid wouldn't be needing the clothes. I left them in the yard. The cabin had sunk in upon itself to form a homogenous pile of glowing rubble, fed from somewhere down inside by the same white-hot jet of flame I'd seen earlier. I'd sweated my way through my leather jacket. The heat from the outside, the water from the inside. By the time I made it back to the car, I was walking along in my own little steam cloud.

I beat my way through the bushes to the driver's door. I unlocked it. I attached one end of the clothesline to the door handle and carefully popped the latch without moving the door itself. I played the rope out behind me as I groped my way through the underbrush. When I ran out of rope, I stepped behind the largest bush I could find, got down on my face, and pulled on the rope. I heard the door squeak open. Nothing. I pulled harder.

I thrashed my way back down the rope. The door was open. So far so good. I untied the rope from the door handle and repeated the whole process on the hood release. This time from behind the car. I heard it pop.

My thick fingers made it difficult to tie a loop in the end of the rope. I managed on the third or fourth try. I tightened the rope over the edge of the hood onto the locking mechanism. The hood opened backward. There was no second release. I dragged the rope out onto the street and gave a tug. The branches were holding it back. I used two hands, and the hood bulged the willow branches up and out as it snapped up on its springs. Nothing.

I walked tentatively over to the driver's door. Trying not to move the car, I reached in the backseat and extracted the black flashlight from my pack. Careful not to lean on the fender, I played the light over the engine compartment.

I didn't need an expert for this one. Two wires, one red, one black, ran from my battery terminals, over the top of the engine, and on through the firewall. I knelt down by the driver's door and looked beneath the seat. The two wires were imbedded in what looked like an unbaked loaf of sourdough bread that was wedged beneath the front seat. My knees threatened to fail me. I sat down on the cold ground.

Only the thought of having to explain my actions to the local authorities got me going again. I retrieved the rope from the hood. With the care of a brain surgeon, I tied another knot around the two wires just behind where they were alligator-clipped to the terminals. I fed the line around the side of the hood.

Once I was at the end of the rope, I gave it one quick, short tug for all I was worth. Nothing. I walked slowly up to the side of the car.

The alligator clips dangled harmlessly over the side. I was careful not to touch them together when I loosened the slipknot.

I repeated the process under the front seat. I jerked what appeared to be two aluminum test tubes from the spongy mass. Carefully, I worked the substance out from under the seat. It was, as I'd suspected, soft to the touch, like an enormous glob of beige Play-Doh. It smelled like nail-polish remover. I gingerly put it in the trunk. I went back to the front of the car, picked up the sleeping bag, and set it lightly on top. I closed the lid.

Back inside the car, I pulled one wire and then the other back through the firewall. I broke off one of the clips, yanking it through. I wound the wire around the aluminum tubes and put them on the passenger seat. I was breathing like a distance runner. I'd been lucky so far. I needed to get the hell out of here. The Fiat started right up.

I jammed it into first gear and blasted out of the little hiding place. The willow branches tore the antenna loose. It dangled, banging, against the side of the car. I got out, tore the wire off, stuffed the wire back in the hole, and threw the antenna to the ground.

I was off the reservation, through Marysville, and halfway to Everett before I stopped shaking. The moment my sanity returned, I realized that there could well have been another device in the car. The one now in the trunk could have been a decoy. The shaking followed me all the way home.

9

"HOW IN HELL can anybody lose a Buick station wagon? You can lose your wallet. You can lose your job. Hell, you can even lose your way, but it's not possible to lose a Buick station wagon."

"We didn't lose it, Leo," whined George. "We just don't happen to know where it is at the moment."

"I thought I told you guys to stay together."

"Jesus, Leo. You look terrible."

For once Ralph had a point. For Ralph, even the most obvious connection to reality was a step in the right direction. Early this morning, I'd had much the same reaction to my face. Something had drawn me directly to the bathroom mirror. I was still wearing my partially fried leather jacket. The stuff I'd collected was down in the Fiat.

I had stood in front of the mirror and run my unsteady fingertips over the collection of scrapes and scratches that crisscrossed my face. Both my eyebrows and the front of my hair were badly singed, the ends rolled up and brown. When I ran my hand over them, small brown whiskerlike ends fell into the sink.

"Never mind how I look. Where's Buddy and the car?"

"He told me to go look for Ralph," said Harold.

"Where in hell was Ralph?"

"I was looking for George," he answered.

"Where in hell was George?"

"I was in the can." Progress of sorts.

They all began to babble at once. I put a stop to it.

"Cut it out," I said. "Let me see if I've got this straight. After I left, you guys followed her back to the Save the Earth building, right?"

"Right," they said in unison.

"What happened then?"

"Nothing," in unison again.

"She just went inside and stayed there." George.

"Then what?"

"We sat outside and waited." George again. I was losing patience.

"Then what?" I growled.

"Then George had to go to the can." Ralph.

"He was gone forever." Harold.

"I had to walk all the way up to the fucking train station."

This started an argument as to other, more convenient venues where George might have been able to meet the call of nature. The guys were experts in this area. I squashed this enlightening discussion in a hurry.

"So, Buddy sent Harold to look for George. Then what?"

"Then he was gone forever too," said Ralph.

"The Mission was closer. I thought George would go over there," said Harold.

"There was a huge line at the Mission," George said, tapping his temple. "Today's Friday, right? Wednesday night's meatloaf night over at the Mission, remember?"

"Ooooh." They all nodded knowingly.

"So he sent Ralph to look for both of you." How desperate,

I wondered, did a man have to be to send Ralph looking for somebody? "Then what?"

George took over. "I ran into Harold on my way back from the train station, and then we both ran into Ralph on our way back to the car."

"Then you all headed back to the car?"

They looked from one to another. George started to open his mouth, thought better of it, and stopped. Harold studied the carpet. Ralph dug around in his ear.

"You fellas didn't by chance stop off for a short one on the way back to the car, did you?" George and Harold tried hard to look offended.

"Just one," said Ralph. The other two stared at him in disbelief.

"Fuck it," said George with a sigh. "Yeah, we stopped at the Lantern and had a few. We were gone maybe forty minutes, no more. When we got back, Buddy and the car were gone. No more than forty minutes, I swear to God, Leo." He held up his hand like a Boy Scout reciting the oath.

"So where are Buddy and the car now?" I asked.

"He's not at our place." Harold.

"The Zoo neither." Ralph. They didn't need to say more. With Buddy, once you'd looked at the rooming house and the Zoo, that was it.

My guess was that when the crew failed to return, Buddy'd gone looking for them among the neighborhood dives, probably having a little pick-me-up at every place he stopped. He was probably sleeping it off in the Buick.

"Okay," I said. "Back to work. You guys get down there and keep track of things. I'll find Buddy." I stopped them before they could pummel me with questions. "When Buddy shows up, I want one of you to call me. Is that understood?" They said it was. They were so relieved that they didn't even grouse about how they were going to get downtown. I followed them to the hall. As I'd suspected, they turned left.

"Take the stairs," I hollered. They instantly reversed directions and disappeared down the hall.

I stood in the shower for a long while, letting the steam wash the smoke from my pores. It wasn't until I stood naked in front of the mirror that I realized I had been partially cooked. My face was considerably redder than the rest of my body, shiny and stretched like after a day of sailing. I took a pair of nail scissors and clipped the remaining burnt ends from my hair and eyebrows. The eyebrows came out fine. Even wet, the hair looked a little ragged. Dry was worse. I opted for a hat.

After slipping into a fresh pair of jeans, an old Carlos and Charley's T-shirt, and my Nikes, I threw everything I'd been wearing last night in the washer. I couldn't imagine how anyone could connect me with the fire, but better safe than sorry. My face was going to make it hard enough to claim I was home in bed. I didn't need a pile of cooked clothes to help anybody out.

The jacket was another matter. The heat had burned the dye in several places, leaving irregular brown patches all over the front. I threw it to the floor behind the front door. The jacket was history.

I jammed a Mariners cap on my head and took the elevator downstairs. The Fiat looked worse than I did. The branches had left myriad scratches all over the body and had torn a small triangular hole in the convertible top next to the rear window. Willow leaves clung stubbornly to every nook and cranny. A car wash was in the offing.

I pulled the bundled sleeping bag from the car and slung it over my shoulder. Grabbing my gear with the other hand, I went back upstairs. On my way to the kitchen, I deposited the reeking sleeping bag on the living room floor. I put the remaining food and drink into the refrigerator and left the cooler draining in the sink. Just for drill, I threw the remaining clothes into the washer with the rest. What the hell. I threw the empty pack in too.

Sitting cross-legged on the floor, I carefully unwrapped the bundle. Everything was covered with feathers. I worked slowly so as not to create any air currents. The loose paperwork I'd yanked from the glove box yielded a name for the kid. Robert Warren was the registered owner. A Marysville address, which I assumed must be the cabin. The rest of it was the usual crap. Old receipts for car parts. A service manual for the truck and a collection of downtown parking receipts. I kept the registration and the receipts and shitcanned the rest. That left the bag.

I hadn't noticed it last night, but the bag was heavy. It was long and narrow, with a zippered compartment for a baseball bat underneath. There seemed to be a bat inside. I fished around. It turned out to be a three-foot metal tube, capped with red plastic on both ends. I pried one of the caps off. The interior was filled with what appeared to be rolled-up posters of some sort. Carefully, I slid them out. Maps.

Unlabeled topographical maps, marked here and there with yellow highlighter. Somebody had neatly snipped the border from each of the five maps, removing the range and section notations in the process. Each of the dozen or so highlighted areas was accompanied by a series of numeric notations, three numbers to each, which made no sense to me. I rolled the maps back up and slid them back in the tube.

A tattered army blanket filled the inside of the bag. The second my hands began to lift it from the bag, I knew what it was. Nothing feels quite as solid and compact as a weapon. I unrolled the blanket. I'd never see this model before. Whatever the hell it was, it was dangerous. It looked like a fancy water gun. Maybe two feet long. Made to use one-handed or two. Fully automatic. Short vented snout. One long banana clip in place, several others folded up carefully in the blanket. They looked to hold about eighty rounds each. The last fold in the blanket turned up an ugly-looking silencer, machined to screw on the front of the little gun. With one of these, Custer could have won the battle by himself.

I rolled and folded it all back the way I'd found it and returned both the gun and the maps to the bag. Gently, I lifted the bag from the feathers that now lined the inside of the sleeping bag and brushed off the bottom. Several missed the sleeping bag and latched onto my carpet. I retrieved them. I fetched a roll of duct tape from the kitchen. I threw in the useless paperwork from the truck, laid the leather jacket on top of the pile, bundled it all back up, and taped the corners together.

Before putting the bundled-up sleeping bag into the trunk of the car, I removed the blob of whatever and fitted it into the bag with the gun and the maps. The wires and the aluminum test tubes went in last. The whole package rode on the passenger seat. I went back upstairs.

I called the restaurant. If you wanted to talk to Floyd, you called the restaurant. Floyd was never there. They'd never heard of anybody called Floyd. Some things don't change. Somebody answered on the first ring.

"Windjammer."

"I need to talk to Floyd."

"Nobody here by that name, buddy."

"Well, just in case anybody with that name shows up, tell him Leo Waterman needs to talk to him."

"Whatever floats your boat, pal." He hung up.

I vacuumed. I dusted. I did everything I could think of to assure that no remnant of last night's debacle remained in the apartment. I had just discovered a loose feather at large in the cooler strap when the phone rang.

"What?" was all he said.

"I need some help."

"You sure you can afford it?"

"I need mind, not muscle."

"That you might be able to afford."

"I need it now."

"Don't you always? A grand."

"Where?"

"You remember where it went down with the Jamaicans?"

"How could I forget?" In my little world, cleaning brains off my car seats was a memorable event. Probably not in Floyd's.

"With you anything's possible. An hour." He was gone.

I'd have to hustle. Floyd was talking about Lincoln Park in West Seattle. It was ten after eleven, between the rush hours, thirty minutes to Lincoln Park. I headed out. I got to the elevator just as the doors were closing. Neither the young couple who lived next to the elevator nor the Pakistani gentleman from the end of the hall made any attempt to reopen the doors. I took the stairs.

Fifteen years ago one of my most prized clients had come to me in a bind. His teenage son Robin, a thoroughly spoiled little boil on the ass of humanity, whom I'd already helped extricate from several minor disasters, had finally gone too far. In a futile attempt to make something of himself, he'd set himself up as the middleman and somehow managed to end up with both the dope and the money after a cocaine deal had been interrupted by the DEA. The other players were not amused.

The mess had come to light when, two mornings later, my client had shuffled out to pick up the Sunday *Times* only to find Chuckles, the family Labrador retriever, eviscerated and nailed to the front door. The handwritten note tucked under Chuckles's studded collar had been quite explicit. Unless the drugs and money were returned posthaste to their respective owners, the rest of the family could expect to meet a similar fate.

My client, having no desire to spend his golden years in Cedar Rapids looking over his shoulder, wanted me to make contact with the aggrieved parties and arrange transfers. I'd refused to have anything to do with the dope. I'd figured this would get me out of it. No such luck.

He wanted me to return the money. Three hundred thousand in large bills. I balked again. Out of the question. Not my style, I said. The client offered a five-percent commission. I did some instant arithmetic and went shopping for professional backup.

I'd heard murmurings about Floyd. Street talk. The kind of larger-than-life stories that tend to circulate about the truly competent. Nothing solid, just a few offhand remarks from the right people to the effect that this guy was the real deal. I'd quietly asked around. Frankie Ortega had told me what number to call.

Two days later, Floyd returned my call. I explained the situation.

"What do you need?" he'd asked.

"I need to get home safe and sound to the wife and kiddies."

"You don't have a wife and kiddies." He'd done some homework.

"Then, who'll feed my cat?"

"You don't have a cat either. Five grand if we can leave them where they fall. Ten if I have to do cleanup."

"I'm hoping we don't have to do either," I said.

"Five grand either way."

We settled on five grand. He was there when I got out of my Mustang in front of Lincoln Park. A big guy, six-four or so, curly hair, little close-set eyes. Big wet lips under a nose that had seen a lot of wear and was flat at the tip. All that was left of his right ear was a withered flap of skin that stuck straight out from his head like a dried apricot. Miss Congeniality this was not.

Without the benefit of an introduction, he started right in.

"This is supposed to be a one-on-one?"

"Supposedly."

"They'll try to make it look that way, then. They'll send somebody harmless-looking. You're responsible for the one you meet. He's your problem. I'll take care of the rest. What are you packing?"

"I'm not," I said. He was disgusted.

"Not very often I get to meet anybody who's actually as dumb as he looks. Just because this is a park don't mean this is just a walk, asshole."

He pulled up his right pant leg and liberated an automatic from a spring holster strapped to his ankle. "Take this."

I dropped the gun in my overcoat pocket. The coat sagged. He shook his head again. His damaged ear quivered. He held out his hand.

"Gimme it back." The gun snagged several times as I fished it out. He set it on the ground at his feet, reached into his left sleeve, pulled out a combat knife, and in one smooth motion yanked up my coat and cut the right-hand pocket out. He retrieved the automatic, thumbed off the safety, and gave it back to me.

"Now just stick your hand down through the pocket and carry it along your leg. Anything happens, shoot right through the coat. You need to get rid of it, just drop it and keep walking. Got it?" I said I did.

We wound our way down the walkway toward the far baseball diamond where the meet was scheduled to take place. Just as we came out of the trees into the field area, he stepped off into the bushes.

"Where you going, partner?" I asked. Wrong move.

"First of all, Waterman, don't pump yourself, I'm not your

partner. Second of all, you just go make the meet. I'll be around. I'll meet you back here when it's over." He stopped. "Remember, the safety's off. Don't shoot yourself. I'm not cleaning up your ass either."

He was gone. I stood for a moment and watched him slither through the shrubbery without making a sound. Impressive.

Floyd was right. There was only one guy waiting for me. He stood right out in plain sight, leaning against the backstop of the distant baseball diamond. I stayed in the trees, skirting the fields until I was behind the first-base dugout. My head was filled with the sound of my own heartbeat.

He was old. Seventy maybe. Black. Immaculately attired in a brown cashmere overcoat and highly polished loafers.

I stepped hurriedly from the bushes, strode across the diamond, and set the briefcase on home plate. Without the weight of the case, my free hand vibrated uncontrollably. I stuffed it in my other pocket.

"It's all there," I said, backing away in the direction Floyd had gone.

"I'm sure it is, my boy, but what say we just have a peek." He had a strange, lilting English accent.

"This is the end of it," I said.

"No hurry now, it's a fine night, is it not?" he said quickly as I started to leave. I had my right hand strangling the automatic inside the cutout pocket of my coat. I kept on backing up until I had the dugout screen between us.

"Tell your people my client did his end. He's righteous in this. From here on, it's not our problem. There's your money. It's over."

"We'll need to—"

From the woods on our left, the sounds of breaking branches echoed across the diamond. The old man waited. Nothing happened. Silence.

"I'll need to count it," he said, trying to buy time.

Before I could answer, a sound like a muffled cough rose out of the thicket directly behind home plate. The old man flinched. His impassive face broke for just an instant. He knew something was wrong.

"Feel free," I said. "Just sit right down there on home plate and count yourself a home run. I'm out of here."

"Wait now," he said, picking up the briefcase and popping the latches.

I stood my ground. He pawed through the contents. A couple of minutes passed. Another cough seeped from the woods.

The old guy kept pawing at the money, sneaking looks around. Silence. He started to speak but had lost sight of me in the darkness. The wind off the Sound suddenly picked up, turning the leaves inside out, filling the air with the smell of pine, drowning out any sounds from the nearby thicket.

I kept backpedaling until I figured I was out of range. He was still fingering the money and looking for me when I turned my back and double-timed it down the walkway.

Floyd joined me right where he'd said he would.

"Three," he said. "Two in the park and one in your back-seat."

We exited the park and crossed the street. I looked in the Mustang. Empty. Floyd inclined his head slightly toward the bushes behind my car.

Peeking out from among the roots of a massive azalea were a pair of shoe soles, the right one worn all the way through to the yellow sock.

"I didn't figure you wanted to ride home with him," Floyd said. Before I could catch my breath, he said, in a voice I'll never forget, "You gonna hold that auto in your hand all night, or are you gonna pay me?"

I handed him the automatic and dragged the five grand out from inside my pants. He didn't so much as look at it. Just put it in his pocket.

"Better do a little cleanup on the interior in the morning."

He turned and walked away. I rode with the windows down. The car smelled of mushroom soup. A little cleanup turned out to be scraping most of somebody's medulla oblongata off the backseat, the headliner, and the carpets.

That first encounter with Floyd made a lasting impression on me. The next morning I bought my first handgun and a new car with no backseat.

In the intervening years I'd called Floyd half a dozen times. The routine was always the same. He'd name his price and meet me there.

He was standing next to the Fiat before I got the motor turned off. I picked the bag off the seat and popped the lock. He struggled in.

"Jesus Christ, Waterman, get a car."

I dropped the bag in his lap. "For me?" he mocked. "You shouldn't have."

He pulled the zipper back and peered inside.

"What's that?" I asked, poking the doughy mass.

He took it out of the bag and felt it over with his hands. Then he pulled off a small piece, rolled it between his fingers and smelled it. Satisfied, he popped it in his mouth and ate it.

"It doesn't have a name, " he said, chewing slowly.

"Everything's got a name."

"Not this shit; it's just your basic accelerant. Been around for years. It's used to burn up things that won't ordinarily burn. The Russians used their own version on the Afghans. They were having a hell of a time burning down the villages. Fuckers live in mud houses. The mud bricks won't burn." He hefted the blob. "Except with this shit. This shit will burn down a stone building. Makes Thermite look like a kitchen match. No explosion either. Just starts burning. Fires up to damn near four thousand degrees. It'll burn underwater. Once you get it going, it'll burn in a vacuum. Really can't be put out; mostly, it just has to burn itself out." He tossed it up and caught it. I winced.

"Totally harmless without the chemical detonators," he said.

I reached over and fished the aluminum test tubes out of the bag.

"The very same," he said. Still handling the material, he looked over at me for the first time. "Where'd you get this, Waterman?"

"It was under my front seat, wired to the ignition."

He shook his head. "Leave town, Waterman. This is serious shit. It's not all that easy to get. A Gomer like you is out of his league here."

Before I could respond, he delved back into the bag. He unrolled the blanket in his lap and whistled. "Nice," he said, hefting the piece. "Russian. KGB stuff. I forget what they call it. Eight hundred rounds a minute, incredible muzzle velocity. Great for shooting through solid steel doors. Nice piece. Not rare though. I can get you fifty. Two thousand a whack. They're big with the local crack-dealer set."

We sat in silence for a moment while he toyed with the piece.

"Anything else?" he asked.

"That's what I wanted to know."

Floyd rolled the machine gun carefully back up in the blanket with the loving hands of a man familiar with guns. He put it back in the bag.

"Tell you what, Waterman. I'll take the Silly Putty and the detonators in lieu of my grand." He waited.

"Done," I said.

He cached the detonators in his pocket, grabbed the stuff like a loaf of bread, and got out of the car. He leaned down.

"You better tell whoever you been brawling with to cut her nails."

"I won't dignify that with a response, Floyd."

"Fair enough," he said. "And I won't ask you who won."

10

FOUR BLOCKS DOWN from the park, I spotted exactly what I was looking for. I wheeled the Fiat up next to the orange Dumpster, opened the trunk, and lofted the bundled-up sleeping bag up through the yawning lid. I walked around to the driver's side, got the bag with the maps and the automatic, and locked it in the trunk. A car wash was next.

Between the washing wand and the vacuum I went through the better part of ten bucks before I was satisfied. I spent a tedious half hour with a Popsicle stick I'd found on the ground, digging willow leaves out of every conceivable nook and cranny. If you didn't count the scratches in the paint, the missing antenna, or the rip in the roof, the Fiat looked pretty good.

I checked my watch. Three-thirty. I was already screwed by the afternoon traffic. Might as well get something done. The paint and the roof would have to wait. I figured the antenna was easy. I followed California nearly to the north end, found the Schucks Auto Parts store right where I remembered it, and bought a replacement antenna and a pair of channel locks.

Forty-five minutes later, my knuckles and forearms now scraped up to match my face, I understood for the first time why reputable mechanics refuse to work on Fiats. I'd always assumed that all the Fix-It-Again-Tony and Failed-Italian-Attempt-at-Transportation jokes had merely been the work of mediocre minds without enough to do. After all, everybody needs somebody to look down on. I resolved to reevaluate that assumption.

The little car must have been built by elves. There was absolutely no room to do anything. Even the final step of unscrewing the old coaxial cable from the back of the radio and screwing the new one on required that I put the top down so that my legs could point straight up as I disjointed my arm into the narrow gap between the back of the dash and the firewall.

At least I had music for the ride. Although the new antenna didn't sit at quite the same angle as the old one, it worked just fine. Unfortunately, there wasn't a single thing worth listening to. The oldies channel was stuck in one of its white-boy sixties grooves, the Dave Clark Five pounding out rock without the roll. Next came "Sugar Shack," for God's sake. KPLU was engaged in heady discussion of the merits of recycling, and everything else I could find either sounded computer-generated or had lyrics having something to do with the singer's skin clearing up in the immediate future. I rifled through the glove box until I came up with a suitable Jimmy Buffet tape, rewound, and eased into traffic to the melodic strains of "Why Don't We Get Drunk and Screw." Ah, culture.

It was after six by the time I rolled into the small lot next to the Embers. I let the door swing shut behind me and stood still until I began to make out shapes in the distance. Carefully, I made my way down to the far end of the bar, ducked under the little gate, and let myself into the beer locker.

I had already stashed Robert Warren's bag behind a stack of Mickey's widemouths when Patsy yanked open the door and stuck his head in.

"How long do I stand to do for whatever you're hiding in here?"

"It depends. How's your past record?" I asked.

"So-so," he replied.

"Eighteen months tops."

"Comforting, Leo. Do I want to know what's in there?"

"Absolutely not."

"Comforting. How long?"

"Until I need it." He didn't like that. "Soon," I said.

He turned out the light and slammed the locker door. I groped my way back to the switch and let myself out. The place was jammed. Patsy was using the speed gun, a compromise of modern bartending to which he resorted only when he couldn't keep up any other way. Patsy wasn't big on help, claimed they robbed him blind. He sneered at my good-bye wave.

My answering machine was full. Three from Jed James, each call offering progressively more profitable work than its predecessor. Jed was like that. Taking no for an answer was not his strong suit. Probably not a bad trait for an attorney.

Two more were from prospective clients, neither of whom gave the slightest hint as to what they wanted. They'd have to wait. The last two were the most interesting.

"Mr. Waterman," the tape hissed, "this is Saasha Kennedy. From the hotel the other day. I was wondering if you'd give me a call at—" She rattled off an office and a home number. "I wanted to—never mind, just give me a call whenever you get the chance." Interesting. I momentarily felt bad about giving her such a hard time. She'd walked into an ugly situation without a clue. I got over it. I'd call her, but she could wait too. The last call was an attention-getter.

"This is Detective Trask of the SPD. Call me the minute you get this message."

I called. They patched me right through. "Trask."

"Leo Waterman."

"You home?"

"Such as it is."

"Stay there. I'll be right over." I didn't like the sound of it. I wanted one last chance to go through the apartment.

"Listen, Trask, I was on my way—"

"Stay there." He hung up in my ear.

I spent ten minutes crawling around the floor looking for any type of forensic evidence that could connect me with Robert Warren. Nothing. I'd spent the night alone, watching television. That was my story. I checked last night's listings so I could be specific, even reading the little blurbs so I'd have some idea of what the shows were about. Trask barged in without knocking.

He stood in the hall with his hands crammed in the pockets of his trench coat. He reached in, grabbed my orange parka from the hook next to the door, and held it out to me.

"You're wanted, Waterman."

"Always nice to feel wanted," I said.

"A guy named Buddy Knox been working for you?"

My stomach rose up and fluttered within my body. My extremities got instantly cold. In that instant, I experienced the same feeling that I'd had when each of my parents had passed away. A feeling of moving one step closer to being absolutely alone. One more of the illusions of connectedness was gone. It didn't matter that Buddy was just an old drunk who worked for me. He was part of the complicated super-structure of relationships which gave me a sense of time and place and kept me getting out of bed every morning. Getting up tomorrow was going to be harder than it had been today.

I remembered standing by my father's bedside that snowy December morning. He'd shrunk down into the covers like a puppet of himself. The cancer was eating him away.

"School closed?" he asked, turning his head slowly toward the snowy windowsill and squinting at the bright reflected light.

"No," I said. "I wanted to be here with you." He smiled.

"We're born alone. We die alone, son. Go to school."

I cut the last two classes, but he was gone when I got home.

Trask interrupted my thoughts.

"Well, Waterman, was Knox working for you?"

"Yeah, why?" I already knew the answer.

"I'm sorry," was all Trask said.

"Where?" I don't know why. *How* or *when* would probably have been better questions. *Where* just came out.

"I'm sorry for the old guy," Trask said again. "But you got no goddamn right to be putting people like that on the street. Goddammit—"

"Tell me," I said.

"The Tacoma PD pulled him out of the bay this morning. He was behind the wheel of a station wagon."

"What happened?"

"Coroner's doing a post mortem right now."

"Duvall?" I asked. He eyed me closely.

"How do you know Ms. Duvall?"

"We went to school together," I said. "Just friends," I added.

"TPD says he took one from a large bore in the forehead." Trask read my mind. "He had a notebook in his pocket with your phone number in it in several places. That and thirty-seven dollars was all they found on him."

"How long before Duvall's finished?"

"A couple of hours."

Before I could speak again, "Let's go," he said. We headed to the elevator.

"Where are we going?" I asked on our way down the hall.

"TPD wants to have a few words with you."

"Am I under arrest?" I asked in the elevator.

"Shut the fuck up, Waterman," was the reply.

I tried again when we got to the car. "If I'm under arrest—"

"Get in the fucking car. Twice in one week with you is more than I can bear."

Using the diamond lane and the siren, we made it to Tacoma in a little over half an hour. I told Trask the story, leaving out Robert Warren. In order to exclude Robert Warren, I had to exclude the rest of the crew. The boys were unlikely to hold up under questioning. I stuck to the story that it was just me and Buddy. Trask didn't buy it. I could tell. He was doing his impression of polite.

We pulled off the Fife exit and wound our way through the heavy industrial district of chemical plants, paper mills, sawmills, and a montage of the filthy industries that formed the economic backbone of Tacoma.

Everything Seattle didn't want in its own backyard had been gleefully passed down the road to Tacoma. Much like San Francisco and Oakland, Seattle and Tacoma share the same bedroom, but not as equals. More like the favored son versus the stepchild. All it took was pricing a major portion of the population out of the local housing market. And take the garbage with you when you go.

We pulled to a stop in the parking lot of a small café. No name. Just CAFE in white letters on a green sheet of plywood. A boat ramp led from the parking lot down into the stinking estuary. The Buick, covered with mud and debris, wrapped in yellow police ribbon like a macabre gift, was sitting sadly at the far end of the lot. A guy that had to be either a cop or a high school football coach got out of an unmarked TPD car and walked over to us. We got out.

He was a typical twenty-year cop. Brawny, running toward fat, with a full head of salt-and-pepper curls. Looked like a perm to get more coverage. Yellow sport coat and tie, brown pants with a grease spot on the right leg.

"Bill," he said.

"Allen, this is Leo Waterman, pain-in-the-ass extraordinaire."

"Where did they find him?" I asked.

"Nose down on the boat ramp. The tide was out so it stuck about halfway in, halfway out. High tide it might have floated out to the middle."

"Nobody saw anything?" We were no more than thirty yards from the café. Somebody must have seen something.

"Café's open from five A.M. to four P.M. You know, breakfast and lunch for the fishermen and factory workers. No dinner. The car wasn't here at four-thirty yesterday when the owner left. It was here when he got back at four-thirty this morning. After dark this whole area is deserted. It's all commercial for two, three miles in every direction. We're checking, but you know how it is. The owner, name's McCarty, he called it right in. You could see somebody behind the wheel." He let it sink in.

I walked across the lot to the Buick. The driver's window was down. The passenger window was a spiderweb of cracks surrounding a single one-inch hole. The water hadn't gotten up past the seats. The interior of the car was splattered with what appeared to be oatmeal. I knew better. I turned away. "What else did they find in the car?"

Allen consulted a notebook from his inside pocket.

"Three empty pints of whiskey. They looked new enough so we—" I assured him the pints were in character. "A case of oil and a blue plastic funnel." He started to say something else, stopped, and snapped the notebook shut. "That was it."

"How many quarts of oil were left?" He checked again.

"Four. Eight empties."

I wandered back to the boat ramp in silence. Trask and Allen followed.

"The car," Allen said, "was turned on. We figured they just popped it into gear and let it drive itself into the slough."

I looked around. Allen was right. Nobody was going to come forward. He kept talking. "We'd have notified SPD sooner, but those plates don't match that car. The old guy had no ID. I called the number in his notebook and got your machine. Then I called SPD. So . . . you want to tell me about it?"

I told him the same story I'd told Trask and got much the same result. He didn't believe it either. They spent most of the time I was talking passing looks back and forth between them.

"So, you've got no idea what he was doing down here?" Allen asked when I'd finished.

"None." More looks.

"Last you knew he was watching this building in South Seattle."

"That's it," I said. He checked his notes.

"Stay around your house, Mr. Waterman. I'll be sending some people over sometime this evening."

Rather than making any promises, I changed the subject.

"Whenever you and SPD are finished with the car, can you arrange to have it towed to this address? On me." I wrote Arnie's address down and gave it to him along with one of my business cards.

"Sure, no problem," he said, slipping the papers into his notebook.

Trask and I said our thanks and good-byes and made our way back to the freeway. Neither of us spoke until we were nearly back to the city.

"Listen, Waterman, this isn't my case. It's not going to be my case. It's probably going to end up with TPD, so it's no skin off my nose either way, but that crock of shit you gave us is never going to float. You know that, don't you?"

"I know."

"This business about refusing to name your client isn't going to float either. You're not an attorney. You don't get privilege."

"I know."

"TPD's going to want to know who you were working for and what in hell you were doing. Any shit about how you were home watching 'The Munsters' last night is not going to be well received."

"I need to call my client," I said.

"What, you need to ask permission?"

"The client just needs to know it's going to come down, that's all."

"You sure you don't want me to turn around and take you back down south to make a statement? I don't mind. I'll wait."

"I'm sure. Thanks."

"The only reason Detective Allen didn't take you with him is that it's not his case either. You're not going to get a night's sleep, you know. Your ass is going to be back in Tacoma before morning."

"I know." We crested the interstate in silence. I could see the Save the Earth building from the car. I'd have to tell the rest of the crew.

"One more thing, Waterman," Trask said through tight lips. "I know about you. You've got a reputation as a cowboy. This isn't the Wild West anymore. You let the TPD handle this. You've got enough problems on this one already. You hear me?"

"I hear you," I said. Trask wouldn't let it go.

"You're in no position to screw around here, Waterman. I don't suppose it's a scoop to you that one of the quick ways to fame and fortune for any cop in this town is to either put you inside or find a way to pull your ticket. I don't know how in hell you managed it, but Captain Henry Monroe's got a wild hair across his ass about you, Waterman. A very wild hair. He'd like nothing better—"

I played my trump card. "Monroe's married to my ex-wife," I said.

Trask thought it over. "That so?" he mused, smiling for the first time.

"You work directly under Monroe?" I asked. He was wary.

"I do. Why?"

"Then I don't have to tell you about Henry Monroe, do I?"

"You said that. I didn't." He quickly changed the subject. "Your father used to be mayor or something, right?"

"City Council."

"Monroe claims you've got no right having a P.I. license. Claims your old man's cronies arranged it for you. That true?"

"It was true twenty years ago," I said.

"But you're deserving now, right? You've earned your spurs."

"You find anybody who does anything for twenty years and doesn't get better at it, then you'll have a scoop."

"Military background?"

"Nope."

"No law enforcement training at all?"

"Nope."

Before he could respond, I went on. "Ask around, Trask, you won't hear many complaints. I've got people who swear by me and people who swear at me, just like everybody else in this profession. Ask around."

"I have, Waterman. I have. After I ran into you the last time, you remember that shooting over in Broadhurst." I nodded. "After that, I asked around. That's what makes this little discussion so interesting. Word is you give honest effort for honest pay. They say you've got a real knack for finding people and things that don't want to be found."

"That does seem to be my niche," was all I could come up with.

"So how come every time we've got some absolutely lunatic situation like the other morning at the hotel, you always seem to be involved?"

"Cream rises?"

"Yeah, either that or the light turd floats."

In spite of my best intentions, I could feel my anger rising.

"What is it with you guys? Is it part of your genuine police department training to give P.I.s a hard time whenever you get the chance? Is it mandatory or something?" He started to open his mouth, but I beat him to it. "It's not like we're competing with one another. All I do is the shit work you guys aren't willing to do. You gonna try to tell me that you guys were going to spend three days looking for little Jason Greer, who's known to be in the company of his father? No chance. Don't bullshit me. You guys would have to find his body before you started asking questions." I'd gotten his attention.

"Hey"—he took one hand off the wheel and pointed a meaty finger at me—"the police department's the last line of defense around here, pal, and we're seriously overburdened. Without us, this whole city would go down the shitter. The scumbags would make it so decent people—" He caught himself. "Maybe you never thought about it, asshole, but people become real cops because they—"

I jumped in. "—want to be in a business where the customer is always wrong."

"Cute, Waterman. More people like you helping out and—"

"You guys can use all the help you can get."

"Not from amateurs. Amateurs are a danger to themselves and others. Ask Buddy Knox."

"Don't flatter yourself, Trask. You guys may have the latest technology at your disposal, you may be able to tap into all the information sources, but it doesn't help much, does it? Yeah, you can send an army of cops out into the streets, but that doesn't help much either, does it? You know why?"

"Why's that, Waterman? Enlighten me."

"Because nobody wants to talk to cops except other cops. On the undesirable scale, you guys run a close second to the slimeballs. That's why you manage to resolve less than half your cases. People are goddamn near as scared of you guys as they are of the criminals."

"So what we need are more helpful amateurs like you out there, is that it? Is that what you've got in mind?"

I laughed at him. "What makes me an amateur and you a professional? You're flattering yourself again, Trask. Don't kid yourself. I can dig up information around this town a whole lot more effectively and a whole lot quicker than you can. I live here. I was born here. This used to be just a big town. Most everybody knew most everybody else. If I didn't go to high school with them, then I played sports against them. If I didn't do either, I've got a friend who did."

"You sure as hell haven't got any friends in the department."

"That's because I don't need any friends in the department."

"Tell that to Buddy Knox," he growled. "And be sure you tell it to TPD when they get here. I'm sure they'll be most anxious—"

"Fuck you, Trask. It was a routine surveillance."

We kept it up all the way back to my place. I wanted to strangle him, but he was right. I had maybe two hours before I got unwanted visitors. They might even be there waiting for me now. That I'd have to risk. There were things in the apartment I needed. Detective Allen would report in and the ball would get rolling. Two hours, at most.

Whoever was in charge down there would assign the case, and I'd be first on the agenda. Trask slipped the Dodge to a stop in front of my building.

"Have you heard any of this, Waterman, or have I just

been talking to myself? 'Cause you sure as hell don't look like you've been listening."

"I heard, Detective. Thanks for the ride and the dazzling repartee."

Trask yelled something at my back as I was opening the lobby door, but I didn't hear that either.

11

"LET ME SEE if I've got this straight, Leo. The police have the Buick."

"Right."

"It's impounded down in Tacoma."

"Right."

"Now you want to borrow the red pickup."

"Right."

Having meticulously cut the sinsemilla bud into pieces with a pair of nail scissors, Arnie scraped the pot off the edge of his kitchen table into a single rolling paper without losing so much as a shred. A lick of the tongue and a flick of the Bic later, he had a joint the size of his thumb fired up.

"Interesting," he rasped while holding his breath.

"You'll have what's left of the Buick back in a week or so."

The pot came back out of his lungs with a rush. Arnie sat back in the chair. He sucked down another massive hit. His eyelids headed south. I waited. He exhaled again, took another toke, then snipped off the end of the joint and dropped it in his shirt pocket.

"Kinda reminds me of the old days, Leo. You remember. People would give your name to other people they met out on the road. Folks you'd never seen in your life would show up on the doorstep wanting to crash for a few days. It was like a perpetual party." He walked over and refreshed his tea.

"Heck, that's how I got the truck. Young couple from back East crashed here for a couple of weeks. They were out of gas money. Then this other dude who was on his way up to the Queen Charlottes showed up and they decided to travel with him. Said I could have the truck.

"Can I borrow it?"

"Is it going to end up trashed and impounded too?"

"Probably."

"Cool." I didn't know people still said that. "Sure, why not? I like it. We'll bury them in their own garbage. Yeah, I like it. We'll have to scrounge the battery out of the Opel."

"How are the tags?"

"What tags? The only tags it ever had were from Iowa or someplace. We'll use the original plates from the Buick. Tags you'll have to liberate on your own."

"No problem," I said. Arnie knew what I meant. When we were younger and couldn't afford to register our cars, we'd become expert at slicing the renewal tags off other cars and gluing them to ours.

"You've got to promise me though, Leo."

"What?"

"You'll take them off a Beamer."

"I promise."

"In Bellevue," he added.

"I wasn't planning on driving that far without tags."

"But off a Beamer."

"I promise."

Forty-five minutes later, I was almost ready to go. I had my gear stowed back in the genuine Caveman camper and the plates bolted on the truck and was tightening up the last battery terminal when Arnie reappeared.

"Here, you'll need these." He was holding a razor scraper and a small tube. "Careful when you go for the tags. I put in a new blade. They're using better glue than they used to. If you're not careful, they just disintegrate." I eyed the tube. "Super Glue," he said. "Waterproof. That way you don't have to worry about them falling off."

I eased myself down in the seat and turned the key. I'd forgotten how good the throaty rumble of an American V-8 sounded. Arnie shook his head dejectedly. "A real ozone ripper, Leo. This baby'll pass anything on the road except a gas station. Did you know—"

I changed the subject. "Where's Nadine?"

"She went out for a walk the other day and didn't come back."

"Really." I tried to sound surprised.

"No sweat," he said. "Pussy may well be the only true renewable resource, Leo. I've got another one lined up for when I get back." I had to admire a man with that kind of insight and planning.

"Listen . . . Sooner or later, when they can't find me, the cops are going to— Back from where?"

"I'm flying down to Eugene in the morning for the Dead concert."

"When's that?"

"Saturday, like always. You want to come along?"

"No thanks." Frightening thought. "When are you coming back?"

"Sunday morning."

"Maybe you ought to stay longer."

"Oh, you mean the cops. No sweat, Leo. The storm troopers don't worry me. I won't be intimidated by the heat." He slipped into character, one hand raised theatrically above his head, eyes on a distant horizon. "I have been to the mountain . . . Besides that"—he winked—"none of these cars is registered to me. I don't know shit." A look of horror crossed his face. "You didn't tell them I owned the wagon, did you?"

"I just told them to tow it back here when they were through with it."

"No problem then. I haven't actually owned a car since seventy-one. These"—he swept his arm around the backyard—"are all remnants of a postindustrial society gone mad. Relics of the age of plenty. The decadent art of the nineties. Did you know that if we'd recycled every American car since nineteen-sixty—"

He seemed to have his end covered. I needed to get down the road.

"Will you get the gate for me?" I asked.

"—*mas es mejor*, more is better. The American Way—"

He was still talking as he walked toward the gate. "—private ownership of the means of production has led us to the brink of ecological disaster." At least he was walking while he was talking. He opened the gate. I drove through.

He came around to the window and stuck his hand inside. We pumped the secret handshake. Arnie always made me feel like I was missing my decoder ring. "Good luck, Leo."

"Thanks, Arn. Have fun down south."

"Oh, I will, Leo. Bettina—you remember Bettina, don't you?" He smirked. Bettina was Arnie's first and only wife. A counterculture diva. We'd detested one another. "I'm staying with her. She's flying back up with me for the party." I made it a point not to ask, but it was to no avail.

"You're coming to the party, right?" Now, I had to ask.

"What party?"

"My fortieth. Didn't you get the invitation? I left a message on your machine yesterday."

"I haven't been home much lately," I said. I hated these

blasts from the past almost as much as I hated Bettina.

"Come on, man, you've gotta come. Everybody's gonna be there. Wendy and her new hubby, Morris, Rebecca, everybody."

"Hey, Arn, you know I'd like to come. But Bettina and I, we don't exactly—"

"You're not gonna let her drive you off, are you?"

"As I remember, you moved to Guatemala in the middle of the night."

"That was different. You call Tom Romans yet?" he asked quickly, changing the subject. I looked blank. "The guy whose number I gave you."

"Not yet. A lot's happened since then." I thought I was home free. No such luck. Arnie was too smooth for me.

"He might be coming to the party." With no escape in sight, I reluctantly agreed to put in a guest appearance on Sunday afternoon.

"Don't forget," he grinned as I inched forward. "From a Beamer."

A promise is a promise. I wheeled out of Arnie's yard, turned left down to Forty-fifth and got on the interstate, heading north. I wanted to do as little driving as possible on the expired plates. I needed a mall. Someplace where I could lift some tags without being seen. It was Friday night. The malls would be jammed. I headed up to Northgate.

It was so easy that for a fleeting moment I considered doing it again the next time the Fiat came up for renewal. Right at the end of my first pass down the first row, there it was, backed up against the fence all by itself, a little gleaming black Mercedes convertible, a full half mile from the mall. The owner had undoubtedly chosen the isolated spot as a hedge against door dings. It wasn't a BMW, but I felt certain that Arnie would approve.

Twenty minutes later, looking legal as hell, I was back

downtown. I had calls to make. Easy one first. I called Hector Guiterrez. Hector managed my apartment building. I could count on Hector. Thirty-five years in Castro's Cuba, sixteen days in a leaky rubber raft, and thirteen months in a federal detention center in Tennessee had left Hector with a deep, abiding distaste for the authorities.

"Hector, it's Leo." Why in hell was I whispering?

"Oh, Leo, Leo," he whispered back. "Chew got prolems, Leo."

"Have I had any visitors?" Stupid question.

"Doan come bach ere, Leo. Dey yoost left."

"Okay, thanks Hector. Did they leave anybody in my apartment?"

"No, but dey coming back. Mudderfokers."

"Listen, Hector, I'm supposed to be watering Mrs. Gunderson's plants while she's away. You suppose you could take care of that for me for a few days? She'll be back in a week."

"No prolem, Leo."

"One more thing, Hector. When you come out in the morning, there's going to be a red Chevy pickup with a camper out in the building parking lot. In Mrs. Gunderson's slot. Don't have it towed. It's me."

Hector giggled maniacally. "Right oonder deir focking noses, eh, Leo? Bueno, bueno." I wasn't sure how bueno it was, but it was a start.

Next, I called SPD Forensics and asked for Rebecca Duvall. For once, my timing was perfect. She was just cleaning up and would be with me shortly.

"Duvall."

"Rebecca, it's Leo." She took an audible breath.

"I just finished up on him, Leo. He was a friend, I understand."

"You could say that. What's the verdict?"

"Cause is no problem. Single gunshot to the head. Point-blank range. A great deal of powder residue. Steel-jacketed, three-fifty-seven, would be my guess. I don't have anything for comparison. As I understand it, the slug exited the passenger window."

"At least it was quick," I said. She took another deep breath. I waited.

She outlasted me. Rebecca Duvall wasn't squeamish. Fifteen years as a forensic pathologist will eliminate one's gag reflex. I forced myself to push.

"Just one to the head?"

"Not exactly," she said.

"Well?"

"You sure you want to hear this, Leo? You tend to be squeamish."

"Tell me." I could hear papers rustling.

"In addition to the entrance and exit wounds, he's got two broken fingers. One a full compound fracture, the other a clean break. He's also got several nonlethal knife wounds on the front right side of his neck."

"Like somebody held a knife to his throat and worked on his fingers."

"That's what it looks like," she said. "Looks to me like he held out for one finger. The left index is really spiraled. The right middle's not nearly as bad." I started to speak; Duvall didn't stop. "I had to clean him up, Leo. He'd . . . ah . . . voided. That's not at all consistent with gunshot wounds."

"So whoever it was worked on him until they got what they wanted and then shot him anyway."

"I'm sorry, Leo, but it looks that way."

"I need a favor," I said.

"What?" She was on guard.

"Hang on to him for a few days, will you? Maybe lose his paperwork until I can arrange something. I don't think he has anybody else."

"Will do, Leo."

"Thanks."

"And Leo," she said as I was about to hang up. "If it's any consolation, he had maybe a year, year and a half, at the outside. No more. Both his liver and pancreas were shot. His liver was the color of—"

I interrupted. "Thanks again, Rebecca. I owe you one."

"No, Leo. This is more like fifty-one. Speaking of which—"

"Yes?"

"Has Arnie braced you about this party of his on Sunday?"

" 'Fraid so."

"You going?"

"Are you?"

"If you do."

"I don't want to."

"Me neither."

"I promised," I said.

"Me too."

"What time?"

"Around two."

"Don't be late."

"See you there." Dial tone.

Duvall had answered one of my nagging questions. Whoever had incinerated Robert Warren and tried to roast me had come prepared for both of us. The Fiat had been well hidden. Somebody had looked hard with the expectation that I was somewhere in the area. Somebody who didn't want me talking to Robert Warren. That meant that whoever it was had already been aware of Warren. I was just a bonus.

I dialed Tim Flood's number. Trask was right. Getting lost was a stopgap measure at best. Sooner or later, I was going to have to answer some questions. Tim might as well know.

No answer. Tim was apparently getting around better than Frankie let on. I headed for the Zoo.

I parked the truck three blocks down and approached on foot. At this point, I was nothing more than a material witness in an out-of-town investigation; I figured it would be a couple of days before anybody wanted me bad enough to start canvassing for me. Wrong again.

I nearly walked into them. If I hadn't spent the last hour liberating license tags, I might not have noticed the tax-exempt plates. There were two of them in a blue unmarked Chevy. They probably thought they were inconspicuous, just sitting there doing nothing, parked half in, half out of a bus stop at ten-thirty at night. I crossed the street two cars behind them and doubled back toward the camper.

Four blocks past the truck, I found a working pay phone and called the Zoo. I asked for George. I guess George didn't get many phone calls. I had to describe him. I waited. One of the cops was out on the sidewalk stretching and casually scanning the street. All I could make out was a well-tailored blue suit and the beginnings of a bald spot.

"Hello." George, tentative and smashed.

"George. It's Leo." It took him a minute to process.

"Oh, Jesus, Leo, have you heard about—"

"I know, George. I need to see you guys. Are Harold and Ralph there?"

"Yep. Oh, God Leo—those sonsabitches," he sobbed.

"Listen to me, George. Are you listening to me?"

"I'm listening, Leo." He sniffled.

"Get Harold and Ralph and—"

"Un huh."

"Walk out the front door and turn left."

"I don't think Ralph can make it, Leo. He's a little—"

"You and Harold help him. It'll look better that way anyway."

"Harold's not so good either."

"It's important, George."

"Okay, turn left—"

"Walk up about four blocks. You'll see a red truck with a camper. Walk around the back and get in the camper. You got that?"

"Around the back to the camper. I got it."

"Make it as quick as you can." I hung up, crossed the street, and approached the camper from the rear. I unlocked the door, stepped up inside, closed all the little flowered curtains, opened the slider between the passenger compartment and the camper, and crawled through the window into the driver's seat.

Cleverly disguised as a spastic conga line, the boys were halfway to the truck. Ralph's arms were draped fraternally over the shoulders of the other two. The trio treated curbs as if they were canyons, pawing with one foot until one or the other located solid ground and then collectively lurching onward. They wandered over the entire width of the sidewalk, occasionally bouncing off the buildings and parked cars, but careening steadily forward, until, just as they drew even with the cops, George, his attention riveted on Ralph, walked smack into a parking meter and dropped to his knees, dragging the other two with him. The nearest cop got out. I started the truck. The party was over.

One by one, he helped them back to their feet. As the crew resumed its journey, the cop stood on the sidewalk and watched, shaking his head. The cop was tall, six-four or so, horn-rimmed glasses lending a little character to his smooth boyish face. His bald spot reflected the overhead lights as he leaned down and said something to the driver, then straightened up and resumed watching. The crew had barely a block to go when, mercifully, he finally lost interest and got back in the car.

They stuffed Ralph in first. He lay across the tailgate with his head and shoulders inside the door and softly began to snore. George and Harold used him as a throw rug as they climbed aboard. Taking Ralph by the shoulders, they yarded him up near the front of the camper and closed the door.

"Sit down fellas, we're going to take a little ride," I said through the window. George and Ralph sat in the built-in booth on opposite sides of the tiny table. Ralph continued to snore. George was livid.

"Did you see that dumb fucker in the glasses run right into me, Leo?"

"Never gave an inch, did he, George?"

"That fucker was solid," he replied.

Instead of continuing up the street past the cops, I backed the truck up, hung an immediate right, and started radically downhill toward the lake. Something bumped against the back of me, rocking the cab. I snuck a look over my shoulder. Ralph, now in the fetal position, had slid all the way up against the cab.

"Ralph took it hard, Leo," said Harold. I was thinking that Ralph took such disasters as sunrise hard, but kept my mouth shut.

I wound down Eastlake and parked in the deserted parking lot of a boatyard. I left the interior lights off. No sense attracting undue attention. I stuck my head through the slider.

"How you guys doing?" I asked.

"Not so good," slurred Harold.

"Me neither," I said. "I'm gonna miss Buddy." They silently agreed.

"Who did it, Leo?" asked George, his anger returning.

"I don't know, but we're sure as hell going to find out." I looked for support but didn't get any, so I kept talking. "How'd you guys find out?"

"A couple of cops, they come in with a picture of Buddy. Jesus, Leo, he had a—" George said.

"There was a hole in his head, Leo," Harold finished.

"Did the cops talk to you guys?"

"Nope," said George. "They just passed the picture around until somebody, I think it was old Bill Knowles, recognized the picture. Me, I had to look again. It didn't look nothin' like Buddy. But it was. . . ." He let it trail off.

"Any idea how they knew to come to the Zoo?"

"The matches," they said together.

"What matches?"

George took the lead. "Buddy was always taking all the matches from the bowl on the bar. He wasn't supposed to, Terry threatened to eighty-six him, but he did it anyway."

"Always had pockets full of them," added Harold.

"What for? Buddy didn't smoke."

"Maybe he just liked to collect stuff," Harold replied with a shrug.

"I think he took 'em 'cause it pissed Terry off. You know how Buddy is . . . was." George caught himself. Never speak ill of the dead.

"What happened down at the building today?" I asked.

"Same old shit," said George. "Regular panhandling rounds, Caroline made the regular trip down to meet the guy, except he didn't show."

"Somebody followed her?" I asked.

"Ralph." George jerked his thumb at the bundle on the floor. "I sent Ralph. What with the construction and all, traffic's so damn bad, even Ralph can keep up. I figured he might as well do something."

"What did he say?"

"He said she drove down like usual. Sat there in her car for almost an hour and then drove off," answered Harold.

"Did she come back to the building?"

"Nope." Together. I mulled this information over.

"I want the three of you at your posts in the morning."

"You mean we're still gonna . . ." George sounded shocked.

"Without Buddy?" Harold asked.

"How much energy do you figure the cops are going to put into somebody like Buddy?" I asked. They looked at each other. I kept talking. "The only way this is going to come out clean is if we do it. Caroline's been meeting this guy around one in the afternoon, right?"

"Between one and two," answered George.

"I'll be there. You guys just keep track of the building, okay?"

I got a couple of weak okays. "For Buddy," I added. The okays got stronger, not exactly a chorus of acclaim, but at least they were willing to try.

I dropped the crew at the rooming house. Ralph first, so Harold could lend a hand. George last, so I could have a word with him.

I counted out seventy-five bucks. "Here's what I owe you guys. Divvy it up in the morning." He stared at the money in his hand. "Looks like you're in charge now, partner." The thought seemed to terrify him.

"I don't know, Leo. I don't—"

"For Buddy, George." He tried to focus on my face.

"For Buddy," he repeated, sticking the money in his pocket.

12

❖

AT SEVEN O'CLOCK on the dot I was awakened by a rapping on the truck door. No great cause for concern. Short of breaking out one of the side windows, nobody was getting inside. I'd put the tailgate up, effectively blocking the door, and then backed the truck right up against the block wall of the parking area. After locking the truck doors, I'd crawled through the slider and spent a miserable night freezing my ass off in the overhead bunk. I needed a new sleeping bag. First thing on the agenda.

I peeked out through the curtains, saw Hector's smiling face, and opened the driver's door for him. He got behind the wheel. He'd brought a steaming mug of coffee, and eggs and something green wrapped in a corn tortilla. The coffee was excellent. The unidentified green substance was so spicy it made my eyes water; I choked it down anyway. Hector crawled through and sat at the table.

He anticipated me. "Dey been back twice, Leo," he said as I slurped down coffee. "Once late last night. Again dis morning. Fockers wake me both times for de key. Dey say dey gonna tow your car off later today."

The sleeping bag slipped to number two on the charts. I poked my head back out through the curtains. Sure enough, two bright orange SPD tags were attached to the Fiat, one on the door handle, one on the windshield.

"Hector, does your brother still own that body shop?"

"Chewer. Got two now."

"You think it would be okay if we took the Fiat over there?"

"No prolem."

"If the cops find out—" He waved me off.

"Yeah, yeah, and eef Geeligan was a Cubano, he'd have gotten off that focking island. Gimme de goddamn key."

I'd offended him. It wasn't hard. Hector was touchy. I'd learned long ago that there was absolutely no way to predict what was and was not going to piss him off. A simple greeting like "Nice morning, isn't it?" could very easily be met with "Waddas chew crazy, chew tink I'm stupid, eets raining like tree bastards out dere." The good news was that he usually got over it just as quickly. I hesitated.

"Chew think I'm afraid of the policia?" He spat noisily on the floor, narrowly missing my shoes. "Chew tink my broder Reuben afraid?"

"Not for a second," I said hastily.

"The last time the policia pick up my broder Reuben, dey keep him nine years. Dey donk his head in de toilet ebery day. Reuben be glad to help. Chew gimme de key," he demanded. "I take it right over."

I fished the key out of my pocket. Hector crawled back through and let himself out. By the time I'd gotten myself organized and was back behind the wheel, Hector had the Fiat started. I jumped out and jogged over to the car. Hector rolled down the window.

"I'll take de bus back. Chew take care of beesnez, Leo," he said with a gleaming gold smile.

"Neither of us is going to be taking care of any business,

Hector, if I don't take these tags off the car." I pulled the two I'd seen off and checked the other side of the car. Sure enough, there was another on the passenger door. I stuffed the tags in my pocket.

"Gimme your keys," I said.

"Chew best not—"

"I'll use your apartment." He fished for his keys.

"Doan answer de phone or de door. Dey been—" he cautioned.

"Not to worry, Hector." He threw the keys at me.

"Worry, I doan worry. Chew tink I yam—"

"Better get this thing out of here."

Hector didn't require further encouragement. Still muttering, he popped the clutch and was around the corner, out of sight before I got back to the truck.

What I needed was to have a talk with Caroline Nobel. Caroline's presence at the waterfront rendezvous on Friday afternoon said that she was unaware of Robert Warren's fate. I was hoping that she'd keep showing up. Frankie Ortega's warnings notwithstanding, Caroline and I were about to get up close and personal.

A shower and change of clothes weren't much help. I had to shave around the scratches on my face, leaving myself with a swirled appearance. The clean clothes I pulled out of my pack were, if anything, more wrinkled than the ones that lay piled by Hector's front door. At least they were clean.

I rummaged through the pile of filthy clothes until I came up with the Post-it with the phone number that Arnie'd given me.

"Environmental." A gruff male voice.

"Tom Romans, please."

"Speaking."

"My name's Leo Waterman. I'm a friend of Arnie Robbins's."

"Any friend of Arnie's—" He let it hang.

"Arnie says you're a good source on environmental groups."

"Depends on the group."

"Save the Earth."

"Nice choice." Silence, then: "What did you say your name was?"

"Waterman, Leo Waterman."

"You that detective friend of his?"

"The same."

"And you want info on the Save the Earth movement."

"That's it."

"Not surprising," he muttered. "I'm kind of busy for the next few days. How about next Monday afternoon?"

"That might be too late." He thought it over at length.

"What are you doing this morning?" he asked finally.

"Not much," I said. Telling him I was presently evading the police seemed a tad too confessional a response for a budding new relationship.

"You know the symposium is going on this week," he said. "Any other time—" If this was supposed to be informative, it wasn't. I waited.

He sensed my confusion. "The Northwest Environmental Action Coalition meets twice a year. A little rhetoric. A little fund-raising. That sort of thing. Gives them a chance to see how little they actually have in common," he added bitterly. "Meet me there at nine o'clock. I'll get you in. We can talk. I'll tell you what I know. It may cost you lunch."

"I can handle it."

"Meet me there."

"Where's there?"

"Seattle Center. The Exhibition Hall."

"See you."

"Later."

I was ten minutes early. An elderly couple had a little card table set up next to the front door. Those with exhibitors' tags were admitted free. Concern cost the general public six bucks. They were attracting quite a crowd. As usual, I was amazed.

My prejudices had expected mostly the granola-and-Birkenstock crowd. I guess that's why they call them prejudices. This crowd was a mixed lot. From well-heeled yuppie couples, kids in tow, to groups of senior citizens, arriving en masse, they filed into the Exhibition Hall.

"You Waterman?" A voice from behind me.

He was tall. Maybe six-six, and remarkably skinny. No more than one-eighty, with the stooped, apologetic posture so often seen in people that tall. Balding, with big expressive brown eyes, he looked more like a retired basketball player than an environmentalist.

I stuck out my hand. He wrapped it with his tendrillike fingers.

"Tom Romans." His badge was a press pass. He handed me one, my name neatly typed under the plastic. I pinned it on.

"What paper do I work for? Just in case anybody should ask."

"Magazine. *Northwest Outdoors*," he said, checking the crowd.

"This happens twice a year?" I asked, trying to get his attention.

"Like clockwork," he said, still scanning the crowd above my head. "Gives them a chance to see if they can separate the general public from a little folding money, raise consciousness a little, check out new products, work out their aggressions, that sort of thing. It's good business."

"Will Save the Earth be here?"

"No way. They think they're commandos, terrorists. They wouldn't be caught dead at one of these. Listen—ah—ah . . ."

"Leo."

"Listen, Leo. I can see you're not familiar with the movement, so let me give you a brief primer. The environmental movement is very wide and scattered. That's a big part of the problem. You understand?"

"No," I said truthfully.

"Okay," he said, looking around. "Ah. You see those three guys over there talking to the woman in the red dress?"

It took a second, but I found the group, backed up to one of the planters on the far side of the mall area, across from the entranceway. Three nondescript guys were engaged in animated conversation with an elderly woman in an ankle-length red wool dress. I pointed. "There?"

"The three guys are with the Foundation for the Homeless. Good group. Provide meals. Do what they can about shelter and medical care. They're here today because there's a rat problem down in Pioneer Square. What with all the people living in the streets, there's been an enormous increase in the food supply and hence in the number of rats. Over thirty people have suffered bites in the last couple of months. Right? So what's the solution?"

"Kill the rats," I suggested.

"You'd think so, wouldn't you?" he grinned.

"Makes sense to me."

"Not to Mrs. Causey there. She's with SETA. The Society for the Ethical Treatment of Animals. They got an injunction preventing the Parks Department from spreading their little cyanide baits."

"She sides with the rats?"

"Can't bear the idea of the little critters rolling around in their death throes. Says it's inhumane."

"Of course it's inhumane; they're rats."

"Not to Mrs. Causey and her constituency they're not."

I mulled this over. He pulled me back from my reverie on rats' rights.

"Listen, Leo, I'm going to trot over and see if I can't rustle up a little copy. Why don't you wander around inside for a while. I'll catch up to you."

The elderly couple at the door ushered me in with a smile and a flourish.

As usual, it wasn't what I expected. It was a trade show. Booths and banners. The public milling around, filling the aisles. I joined in.

It didn't take long for the full scope of my ignorance to become apparent. The first little booth at the bottom of the stairs seemed innocuous enough. Bumper stickers. An American tradition. "Developers Go Build in Hell," seemed to the point, if maybe a bit strident. I was okay with "Rescue the Rainforests." "Muir Power To You" was cute. Things started to get fuzzy at "Pregnancy: Another Sexually Transmitted Disease" and "I'll Take My Beef Poached, Thanks." If "Subvert the Dominant Paradigm" left me scratching my head, it was "Dream Back the Bison, Sing Back the Swan" that turned out the lights. I moved on.

Circling clockwise around the edge of the building, keeping clear of the crowded center aisles, I was awed by the number and diversity of environmentally conscious products being flogged. Organic toothpaste from India. An ayurvedic secret formula of over thirty herbs and extracts. Earthtimes, the environmental game. Fun for the whole family. Made, of course, from entirely recycled materials. Magnometers, low-cost magnetic survey instruments that allow the user to detect the slightest fluctuations of deadly low-frequency electromagnetic radiation, which, according to the instruments' inventor, was slowly but inexorably devolving the entire civilized world to primordial jelly. Supplements, vitamins, oils, unguents, books, magazines, records, tapes. Hell, there were environmental rock groups. It was all there. I kept moving.

The four center aisles were devoted to environmental groups themselves. Forever Green, Save the Japanese Trout, the Eco-Defense Fund, the Wilderness Alliance, Voices of the Rainforest, Save the Salmon, the Natural Fiber Alliance, the Snake River Preservation Society. On and on. Stop wearing furs. Stop animal testing. Criminalize hunting and fishing. Stop reproducing. Adherence to the first aisle alone would have reduced me to an incontinent, celibate, barefoot vegetarian nudist. I trudged on, leaving no booth unvisited.

If Tom Romans's notion as to the disunity of the movement wasn't apparent to me by now, midway down the second aisle I got the message.

Sandwiched between the glitzy offerings of the National Audubon Society and the Sierra Club was a small booth that flagged itself as BARF. Businessmen Against Recycling Forever. The tiny red, white, and blue booth was personed by a thick-necked bald guy, whose aggressively folded arms and scowling visage seemed to be keeping folks away in droves. This man, I decided, deserved equal opportunity.

"Hi," I said. He checked me out from head to toe. I must have passed whatever test he was running. He leaned forward, resting his heavy, hirsute forearms on the counter.

"You had enough of the bullshit? You ready for some facts?"

"Okay," I said. God save me, I thought.

"There's always been a hole in the goddamn ozone layer. All this crap about aerosol cans is batshit. Garbage employs over three million God-fearing people in America. Recycling is economic suicide. There's been a gradual global warming pattern going on for the last ten million years. The darn planet used to be covered with ice, for Chrissake. The greenhouse effect is bullshit. There's more wildlife in American forests now than there was when the pilgrims arrived. Conservation is bullshit. The only goddamn way you can effectively harvest

a forest is by clear-cutting it. If loggers had to go around—"
I lost patience.

"So what do we need to do, instead of all this?" I waved
around me. "What do you propose we do?"

"We need to use everything up as quick as possible."

I boggled. "Why?" was all I could manage.

"Simple." He refolded his arms and rocked on the back
legs of his chair. "It's good business. Business is what America is about. It's what made us the greatest nation on earth.
Business is technology-driven. Technology is a response to
need. The more need, the more technology. About the time
we start running out of things, the rate of technological ad-
vancement will increase beyond belief. Necessity is the
mother of invention, you know. About the time we run out of
oil, well, hell, some fag scientist will figure out how to get
energy out of dirt. When we run out of—"

I backpedaled quickly, hoping to lose myself in the
crowd. I retreated until my butt hit the table across the way.
Mercifully, the stream of traffic picked up and shielded me.
I turned around.

Friends of the Singing Waters. Two elderly women. The
one standing by the counter was diminutive and round. Moth-
erly, creased at the wrists and elbows, hair piled on top of her
head in an elaborate bun. Old-fashioned hairpins holding it
all in place. Looked like Aunt Bee on the old Andy Griffith
show.

"Can I offer you one of our brochures?" she asked
sweetly.

Even sitting in the rocker, the other woman looked remarkably tall and gaunt. A few years younger than Aunt Bee,
maybe. She looked up only briefly as the first one spoke, then
immediately went back to her knitting. She must have been
knitting a tarp. Draped about her feet was a half acre of
something. Yarns of every conceivable color were woven in

random fashion Her red-knuckled hands manipulated the needles and hooks at blinding speed.

I took the proffered brochure, stuffing it into the pile I was already carrying without reading it.

"We protect wetlands," she said in response to my unasked question.

"A noble calling."

"We must all do what we can to prevent the despoilment of the land. It's a sacred duty to." She stopped. "Good morning, Mr. Romans."

"Hello, Blanche. How goes the campaign?"

Tom Romans stepped up to the counter beside me. "If you don't mind, I need to borrow my associate Mr. Waterman here for a moment."

Without waiting for an answer, he led me to the foot of the stairs, out of the rush of the crowd.

"Sorry to be so long."

"No problem," I said. "I'm getting quite an education."

"You see what I mean now? Everybody in this movement has their own little area of interest and isn't too damn concerned about anybody else's area. Since the environment comprises just about everything, the movement comprises just about everything."

"How do they get anything done?"

"They don't. Big business beats them at every turn. Even some of the products there"—he pointed at my bundle of brochures—"if it's a good idea, if it's marketable, Procter and Gamble will be doing it next week. There is no way to beat these guys, unless you're like the Hammer sisters."

"Who?"

"The Friends of the Singing Waters. That's Blanche and Eunice Hammer."

"Where do I know that name from?" I asked.

"They've been around forever. What you probably remember, though, is their father, Willis Hammer."

"Chemicals."

"Right. The man who almost singlehandedly killed Commencement Bay. Had three pulp mills dumping directly into the Sound. Back in the sixties, he was the first guy ever totally shut down by the EPA."

"Right." I snapped my fingers. "This was the guy who tried to shoot it out with the marshals when they came with the papers."

"That's the one. Got himself killed right out at the front gate of his own factory."

"Kind of ironic that Willis Hammer's daughters would be running something called the Friends of the Singing Waters, don't you think?"

"Old man Hammer must be spinning in his grave," he laughed. "Don't be fooled by the lyrical name or the Grandma Moses routine. I only rescued you because Blanche tends to talk forever. Those two are heavy hitters. They're one of the most successful environmental groups around. They started and paid for the entire campaign to recycle used motor oil in the Puget Sound region. Turned it into one hell of a business. After the old man got killed and Eunice—that's the one in the back with the knitting—when she finally got out—"

"Out of where?"

"She had a breakdown after old Willis's death. It was all over the papers. She had to be institutionalized. Tragic story. Anyway, they took the old man's empire and turned it around backward. Turned out Daddy had unwittingly left them everything they needed. The chemical plants, the trucks, the bucks—everything. They've proved to be more successful at cleaning things up than old man Hammer ever was at polluting them. Some sort of family penance, I suppose. They're major players on the scene. Got more money than God. Nowadays, they mostly sue people."

"Who do they sue?"

"Anybody who wants to develop anything, bar none."

"Why?"

"They're rich and dotty. Never married, either of them. Hell, Eunice doesn't even talk. At least I don't know anybody who's ever heard her say anything. What they do now, in addition to recycling a couple million gallons of motor oil a year, is to litigate their sagging behinds off. I can't imagine what their legal bills must be. They may be the only private organization to ever beat a SLAPP suit on their own."

"A slap suit?"

"Strategic Lawsuits Against Public Participation. It's big business fighting back. You get in their way, they slap you with a huge lawsuit. They don't want to win; they just want to break you with legal fees. Most of the time it works. If I remember correctly, they hit Friends of the Singing Waters with a suit for eighty-six million dollars."

I gaped.

"What could those two old ladies have possibly done that was worth eighty-six million dollars?"

"Nothing. All they did was try to block development on a little piece of property up on the Sammamish Plateau. Maybe a hundred proposed new homes, something like that. Nothing out of the ordinary. Friends of the Singing Waters sues and tries to stop every new project. It was just business as usual. That's the point, Leo. There's no correlation between the imagined interference and the response. They just beat people with pure muscle. No rules. They don't care how ugly it gets. They don't care who gets hurt. They sicced teams of investigators on the Hammer sisters. They tried to get them both declared mentally incompetent. You wouldn't believe how ugly it got. The judge had to close the courtroom and then seal the records. I know one of the attorneys. They tried to claim that the old man had been sleeping with both of them for years. When that didn't float, they tried to make out that Eunice was responsible for several unexplained deaths in the institution where she'd been treated. It was unbelievable."

"So what happened?"

"They finally ran into a couple of fanatic old ladies who had damn near as much money as they did. The sisters won five million in damages, which, as I understand it, almost covered their legal fees."

"So there's no way for the public to win?"

"Ah." He held up a long finger. "That's what I was hoping you'd get to. What you wanted to know about was Save the Earth." He shook the finger. "I don't want this to sound like I approve, because I don't. The system may not work, but it's all we've got. Just so you understand me."

I assured him I did. He went on.

"It's easy to look at these militant groups like Save the Earth who go around spiking trees, destroying machinery, sinking boats, and all that stuff and just write them off as the terminally misguided. And to an extent that's true. Particularly with this local group. But to another extent, it's also true that they do more for bringing the problems to the forefront than all the more moderate groups combined. When you think about it, even groups that have grown into institutions like Greenpeace started out by doing some pretty wild things. Now they use their visibility to work more traditionally."

"The ends justify the means?"

"Maybe. Or maybe like in the cases of the Hammer sisters or Greenpeace, it's just important that the powers-that-be understand that you're prepared to follow things to the end. That you're going to do whatever it takes. Nobody, but nobody, sues the sisters anymore."

"So what's wrong with Save the Earth then?"

"What's wrong is that all the actual leaders and founders are in jail. You remember that trawler they rammed a couple of months ago?" I nodded. "It was Japanese. Trying to sink Japanese boats, even if they were illegally fishing, just won't do. Hell, those people could have murdered people and picked up less time than they did. Most of 'em got six years."

He checked his watch. "Anyway, when they went to jail the organization ended up in the hands of this kid Brian Bass, which is ironic, because, as I understand it, they only let him hang around in the first place because he'd inherited a building they could use. He's collected a couple of dozen louts and losers around him, most of them with more money than brains, and has been trying to make a name for them ever since. No focus. They hop on whatever bandwagon made the news last week. They've stood outside the Opera House and thrown blood all over women wearing fur coats. They've torn up fishing nets. They've chained themselves to trees. They've monkey-wrenched machinery. There's even a rumor that—" He stopped. "I better not."

"The lab at the university?"

"You've heard it too?"

I said I had.

"See, now that's the answer to your question. If they were responsible for that, that was stupid. That's a setback. That makes everybody look bad. They're just stupid and badly directed. You get the feeling that if they weren't interested in the environment, they'd be out holding up convenience stores." He checked his watch again. "What's your interest in all this?"

"I've got a client with a loved one who's involved."

"Loved one" didn't exactly roll off the tongue when Tim Flood was concerned, but it was as close as I could get.

"Not good," he said. "I've got a feeling that they're cruisin' for a bruisin', Leo. They're going to do something stupid. I've watched these groups come and go for years. I'd like to think I've developed sort of a feeling for it. This one smells bad to me. They're about due for a disaster, and if they actually got away with torching that lab, all that's going to do is encourage them." He started for the stairs.

"Thanks," I said.

"Gotta run. The rat groups are having a meeting with the mayor to hash this all out. I wouldn't miss it for the world."

13

HAROLD SAW ME first. When I looked up, he was wheeling his Safeway cart madly up the sidewalk beneath the viaduct. I'd never seen him move so quickly. The sole of his right shoe flapped like a feeding fish. The cart's bad wheel spun in a crazy dance as the cart bounced along the ancient sidewalk toward me. He hustled over to the side of the truck.

"Did you see her?" he asked, wild-eyed.

"No. Where's George and Ralph?"

"Back at the building," he wheezed. "She's already made one pass. There's no place for her to park, Leo. What are we going to do?"

I'd been sitting in the truck filling out a report, periodically checking the parking slots for the blue Toyota. I'd probably missed her while I was working on the doors. Harold was right. The Saturday tourist trade on the waterfront was in full swing. As far as I could see in either direction, there was not a single empty slot.

"We'll hand her a place to park, Harold, that's what we'll do. Go up the street to the intersection. Turn around and face me. When you see her coming again, start walking this way. Okay?"

"Okay," he said. "What are we gonna do then?"

I told him. "You think you can handle it?" I asked when I'd finished. I already knew the answer. Harold had gained a certain notoriety among his peers for pulling this same stunt as a last-ditch panhandling ploy.

"Easy," he said, grabbing the cart and wheeling up the street.

I was backed in at an angle, which made it difficult to see back up the one-way street. She was going to be right on top of me before I had a chance to pull out. I'd have to rely on Harold. Not a pretty thought.

Cars crept by, looking desperately for signs of someone leaving. A two-tone brown LeBaron, packed to the rafters with senior citizens, stopped just short of the truck and waited. The driver scrunched down to look up into the truck for signs of departure. I waved him on. A horn blew impatiently behind him. He rejoined the parade slowly inching its way along. When I looked up again, Harold was slowly pushing the cart back toward me along the central divider, his eyes wide, his face a collection of tics and grimaces. I started the engine.

I opened the door and poked my head up over the truck. Caroline was three cars back. Traffic was at a complete stop. Harold was directly opposite me now, headed down to the next corner according to our plan. A burgundy minivan rolled by. Two cars to go. The cars were well spaced for what I had in mind. Every driver was leaving a couple of car lengths, hoping to get luckier than the guy in front. A yellow Toyota pickup eased slowly by. Caroline was next. I nosed the truck out into the flow. Out of the corner of my eye, I could see Caroline Nobel behind the wheel. The pickup moved onward. I settled in behind, moving just far enough forward to give Caroline room to back into the stall. She whipped the little blue car in like a pro.

The street was empty for half a block in front of me. I gunned the Chevy up to the next intersection, turned right, up a block, right again, a block south, and another right. I could see Harold and his cart a block down in front of me. The street was clear. I roared down toward Harold, who stood poised on the corner, his hands white-knuckled on the handle of the cart. We exchanged glances. The light changed. I turned right and rolled down toward Caroline Nobel.

As I eased over the crosswalk, Harold pushed the cart out into the street. I crawled, letting the traffic in front of me move on up past Caroline, keeping one eye on the big sideview mirror. I checked the empty street in front of me. By the time I looked back in the mirror, Harold was well into his act. The cart lay on its side in the left-hand lane, its contents spread over the entire intersection; Harold was flopping around like a beached steelhead in the right lane, apparently in the throes of a seizure. Several people were out of their cars rushing over to give aid.

I had the street to myself. I raced up the street and slid the truck to a stop in front of the Toyota, blocking any chance to escape. I walked around the front of the truck, unlocked the passenger door, and left it open. Whatever she thought I was about, she wasn't having any of it. She leaned her head out the window. Oversize aviator sunglasses covered most of her face. A designer commando. When body language failed to work, she leaned farther out the window of the little car.

"Sir, will you *please* move that . . . that"—she waved a disgusted hand at the camper—"monstrosity."

Something possessed me. I grabbed her by the front of the camouflage jacket and pulled her out through the window. It was a tight fit. I'd planned on easing her to the ground, but lost control as she cleared the windowsill. She hit the pavement hard, landing flat on her back. Her breath escaped in a single rush. The beret bounced off, releasing more blond hair than her pictures had suggested. She groaned and gagged as she fought to find her wind. Appalled at my own behavior, I picked her up by the collar and the belt and half-dragged, half-carried her over to the truck. I stuffed her onto the floor on the passenger side and slammed the door.

I could hear her weakly trying to reopen the door as I sprinted back around the truck. The street behind the truck was still empty. Harold had attracted quite a crowd. Caroline Nobel was still pawing at the door handle and retching intermittently as I wheeled under the viaduct, hung a left, and headed south.

We shot past Harold, who by now was sitting up. I blew the horn three times in the prearranged signal. The good Samaritans didn't know it, but a miraculous recovery was about to take place. Caroline had her head up on the passenger seat, working hard to stifle the dry heaves that racked her body. She was groping blindly for the missing door handle.

"The door doesn't open from the inside, Caroline. Relax and get your breath back. We're going to have a chat."

The mention of her name got her attention.

"Who—" Her body jerked in another series of spasms. A thin line of spittle hung from her lower lip as she rested her head on her arms. Her sunglasses hung from one ear. "Please," she moaned. "Please—I don't know what you—"

"Shut up and catch your breath," I said. She groaned.

I'd spent the better part of an hour this morning scoping out a spot close to downtown where Caroline and I could have our little talk in relative safety. We were almost there. I pulled up to the double gate that separated the street from the heavy construction equipment being used to complete the new I-90 on-ramp. Taking the driver's door handle with me, I got out, unwound the thin piece of wire I'd used to put the chain back together, and slid the gate open.

Caroline made a pathetic attempt to kick me in the face as I got back into the truck. I hit her hard in the shin with the door handle. The leg retracted. She made small whimpering sounds. I drove the truck through. Got out, closed the gate, replaced the chain, and drove the truck back behind a line of cement mixers.

Again taking the door handle with me, I walked around back and let the tailgate down. Caroline tried to kick out the side window but couldn't muster enough leverage. I pulled her out by the coat collar and walked her stiff-legged around to the back of the truck. I sat her on the tailgate. She telegraphed a kick to my groin. I stepped back. Her hair covered her face. Only the eyes of a cornered animal were visible through the blond tangle.

I dug a handkerchief out of my pocket and held it out.

"Here, wipe your mouth." She hesitated, then took it.

Frankie Ortega was right. The pictures didn't do her justice. Even disheveled, white as a ghost, with a line of spit still clinging to her chin, she was beautiful. She swept her hair back with one practiced hand.

"Look buddy," she tried to snarl. Her perfectly clipped diction made snarling sound ridiculous. "I can't imagine what in hell you think you're doing or who you conceivably could be, but this is kidnapping. If you'll let me go, right this instant, I won't—"

"Funny you should say that, Caroline."

"Say what?" She hesitated. "How do you know my name?"

"Buddy. You called me Buddy. This is about Buddy."

"How do you know my name?" she demanded.

"Heck," I said, "I even know your mother's name." She started to speak. "Gene," I said. "Gene Constance Nobel." I had her going.

"What are you, one of those degenerates who follows people around?" She looked me up and down. "I must say, you certainly look the part." Her regal bearing had made a recovery.

"No, actually Buddy's been following you around."

"Who's this Buddy, goddammit?" Her voice wasn't made for swearing either. "Is that how you and this Buddy get your jollies, following people around, or going through their garbage maybe? Maybe you're—"

"No," I said evenly, "all Buddy got from following you was dead."

"Dead?"

"Every bit as dead as Robert Warren."

"Robert Warren. Who is Rob—"

"Young Indian guy. Big red Ford pickup."

"Bobby?" she gasped. "Dead?" I'd made a dent in the veneer.

"Bobby won't be making your little meetings anymore."

"You're full of—how do I know—" She looked at me closely. "You're not kidding, are you?" She got to her feet, wandering in a circle.

"Sit," I said. She leaned back against the tailgate. "No. I'm not kidding."

She combed her hands through her thick hair again as she digested the information. "Dead?" she said again.

"Dead." Traffic noises made their way to the forefront as silence settled in on us.

"How?" she asked softly.

"Somebody burned his house down, with him inside."

"Burned?" She thought about it. "How do you—"

"I'm asking the questions here," I said. Silence again.

"Listen you, please—"

"I'm going to listen. I'm going to listen while you tell me what you and Bobby have been meeting about that was so important that it could get two people killed."

Her mental wheels were turning so fast I could almost

hear them spinning. Behind the curtain of hair, a single blue eye glazed over as if a switch had been thrown somewhere. She gave me her most dazzling smile. Time for Plan B. Plan B always worked.

Still leaning on the tailgate, she slowly shucked off the camouflage jacket, with just enough arching to make her ample breasts strain the yellow T-shirt she was wearing beneath the jacket. She continued stretching with a certain feline grace, gazing out from under her hair to make sure I wasn't missing the show. She slid down to the ground, turned around, and bent over farther than necessary to put the jacket on the tailgate. She lingered, bent at the waist, the seat of her designer jeans taut.

When she assumed that I was thoroughly distracted, she mule-kicked backward and took off running. I tripped her. She sprawled on her face in the gravel. I set her back on the tailgate. She spat on my shirt. "I hate you," she screamed. "You have no right."

"Bobby had a right not to get fricasseed in his own home. Buddy had a right not to have somebody torture him and then shoot him in the head. Those are the rights that we're going to worry about here today, Caroline. You understand me, honey. Your rights, my rights, they don't matter much to me right now. You hear what I'm saying?"

I didn't get an answer. She sat on the tailgate, carefully picking gravel from her palms. She made one last attempt at what had always worked before. She stood and put her arms over my shoulders, drawing her softness up close to me, resting her head on my shoulder. I could feel her warm breath on my neck. "I'm sorry about your friend," she whispered, rubbing her pelvis against me.

I put one hand on her breastbone and shoved her back onto the tailgate. The truck rocked. She tried looking hurt and offended. I ignored her.

"What did you and Bobby have going?" I asked.

"Bobby was my fiancé. We were going to—"

I stuck a finger right up in her face and wagged it back and forth. "Spare me. I'm not buying that crap. Your boyfriend is whoever's standing in front of you at the moment. Now let's get real here, or I'll—" I stopped myself. A mistake. She was quick.

"I suppose you like beating up women?"

"I get hard just thinking about it," I snapped. Another mistake. Immediately, she got feline on me again. She got languidly to her feet.

"Maybe you'd get off from whacking me around a little, huh? Would that do it for you?" She stepped in close again and fixed me with her veiled eyes.

"No," I said quietly. "I like 'em dead. Right after they start to cool off, that's the way I like 'em." She pushed off of me.

"You're disgusting."

She'd tried sex. She'd tried violence. Then she'd tried sex and violence. She was out of ideas. She sat heavily back on the tailgate and ran through her options. The truth was not high on the list. She heaved a sigh.

"We were going to catch them red-handed."

For some reason, I felt less than informed. "Trying to catch whom doing what?" I asked.

"The dumping." My blank expression seemed to exasperate her.

"We wanted to find out where it was coming from."

"Where what was coming from?"

"The stuff they were dumping."

"What were they dumping?"

"I don't know."

If at first you don't succeed. "Who was dumping it?" I asked.

"I don't know that either."

"What *do* you know?" She thought it over.

The girl was persistent, if not imaginative. I figured she'd just seen entirely too many Lauren Bacall movies. She dredged up what she must have imagined was her most seductive look, a hint of a smile, eyes at half mast, lips slightly parted. I shook my head. She pouted, flounced once, and then casually looked up to see if maybe that was working. Her expression suggested that she'd forgotten about pouting. Pouting and flouncing worked sometimes too. She was hopeful. Not this time. She heaved another sigh.

"Bobby knew about some dumping of illegal waste. He knew a bunch of places where they were burying it, up around Marysville." She affirmed herself with a bob of the head. "Can I go now?" I think she was serious.

"Dumping what?"

"He didn't know. Bobby said he was going to check local water samples to see if he could find out."

"What water samples?"

"From one of the towns up by where they're dumping." Impatient.

"What town?"

"I don't know."

"And you don't know who it is that's supposedly doing this dumping?"

"No. I tried to follow one of the trucks yesterday."

"And?"

"I lost it. This goddamn train—"

"Where?"

"Down by Tacoma somewhere."

Now it was my turn to think. A number of interesting possibilities presented themselves. "This was Friday afternoon?" I asked. She nodded.

"How'd you meet Bobby?"

"I met him out canvassing."

"Panhandling?"

"It's not panhandling when you're trying to save the—"

"Earth," I said. "Save the Earth."

Her eyes narrowed. "How do—"

"So you met him out canvassing. Then what?"

"I noticed him hanging around, you know. I saw him at the Locks one day and then down at the Kingdome the next, so I figured he must want something, so I started talking to him." She got more animated as she spoke. "He was real shy at first, but we got to talking about, the planet, you know, and how we're strangling it and all and then, like out of nowhere, he started telling me about this dumping that was going on up on the Indian reservation and how we could catch them at it and how he knew all these places where they were supposed to be planting trees but were really dumping waste."

"So you tried to follow one of the trucks?"

"But this train—"

"Why didn't Robert follow the trucks himself?"

"He tried, but it wasn't that simple. We needed two people."

"Why?"

" 'Cause the truck goes two places." I was hoping that this sounded as ridiculous to her as it did to me. It did. "After they dump, they go down to this yard full of trucks and cars."

"A depot?"

"Yeah, it's right down the street here." She pointed back toward the north. "So they go to the depot and the driver goes inside for a while and then comes out, gets in his car, and goes home. We know, we followed one of them over to West Seattle. He just went home and went to bed."

"What happened to the truck?"

"They hook the part the driver's in up to a different trailer, then they hook the trailer they dumped with up to another—ah—"

"Cab," I inserted.

"Yes, another cab, and then they pull it off."

"Right after the driver leaves."

"Yes—no—well, the cab with the new trailer leaves right away, but the trailer stays in the yard for a while."

"How long?"

"Sometimes it's gone in the morning. Sometimes it's around for a couple of days. That's why Bobby needed someone in the city to follow the trailer. Somebody who had the number and could camp out until it got pulled out. First time, we followed the cab."

"And?"

"It just went back to work with a different driver. Hauling lumber."

"So that left the trailer."

"The trailer turned out to be hard to follow. They all look alike. I mean they're not marked or anything. So Bobby marked one."

"How'd he do that?"

"He climbed over the fence Thursday night and put yellow X's on the trailer, so I'd be able to identify it once it left."

"How long had this one been there?"

"Since Tuesday."

"Why did you guys wait until Thursday to mark the trailer? What made you so sure it was going to be around for that long?"

"Because they hadn't cleaned it yet. They wash the trailers before they go out again. We needed to wait until it was clean before Bobby marked it or they might have washed it off. I camped out in my car for two days making sure the trailer didn't leave."

"And then you followed it when it left?"

"And lost it," she said.

"Why didn't Bobby follow the trailer?"

"*I* wanted to," she said with more emotion than it deserved.

"Why's that?"

She squared her shoulders and stuck out her chin. "It was my chance to do something to save—"

"The earth." No sense asking her how she convinced Robert Warren to let her follow the trailer.

"Yes, the earth. Don't you understand?" she whined. "This was my chance to do something significant, to make a difference, to—" She noticed that I wasn't listening and waved me off disgustedly. "Besides that, Bobby said he had something important to do. He was going to take it to the tribe. He said"—she cocked her head and looked at me—"he said that he sure hoped he was taking this to the right person, because there was no telling who was in on this and who wasn't."

I gave it a minute. I suspected that Bobby's choice of a confidant may have been less than perfect. Only murder held the story together. Bobby and Caroline had barely made progress in their investigation, and already two people were dead. Somebody was abnormally nervous.

Caroline sat on the tailgate and massaged the bridge of her nose. The adrenaline she'd produced while she was being kidnapped had worn off.

"I can't believe Bobby's dead," she said, hugging her abdomen. "I can't believe they're going to get away with it. Bobby's dead and they're going to get away with it."

Her voice broke. It was tough to tell whether Bobby's death or the loss of her big chance bothered her more. My money was on the latter. The latter I could do something about. Bobby was going to stay dead.

"Maybe not," I said under my breath.

"Maybe he's not dead?"

"Maybe they're not going to get away with it."

"Who's going to stop them? The government doesn't—"

"We are."

"We are? How? How are we—"

"Get in the truck."

"I'm not going anywhere with you—you disgusting—"

"Fine," I said. "See you around." I started around to the driver's side. Caroline followed in hot pursuit. "Where are you going?" she demanded.

"I'm going to poke my nose around where it's not wanted."

"I'm coming."

"You're not welcome." I got in the truck and started the engine.

"I'll go to the police. I'll say you kidnapped and raped me."

"Feel free," I said. The sex and violence combo had failed again.

"Please. Bobby's dead." She was doing beseeching now. It worked. I thumbed her around to the other side. Pulling the handle from my pants pocket, I let her in. I handed her the handle.

"There's an Allen wrench that fits that in the glove box. Do something useful and put the handle back on while we're riding."

She rummaged in the glove box. "Where are we going?"

"I'm taking you to a lovely little bar I know of up north."

"Something romantic?" Hope springs eternal in the young.

"Something Native American," I answered.

14

WHOEVER SAID THAT a little learning is a dangerous thing must have spent some time listening to Caroline
Nobel. The kid could talk. As a matter of fact, she never shut
up. By the time we were halfway to Everett, I was prepared
to dispense with the sex and get right to the violence. She'd
already covered the spotted owl controversy and downtown
land use planning and was regaling me on the ozone layer, or
rather, the lack thereof.

"—and soon we'll all have to stay indoors, either that or
we'll all just turn into one mass melanoma." This last image
was too much for me.

I heaved an inward sigh. The sigh must have been more
outward than I'd imagined. She picked up on it. "Does all of
this bore you, Mr.—eh—you know, you never did tell me
your name. If I'm going to be kidnapped by someone, I insist—"

"First of all, you're not being kidnapped."

"I most certainly am."

"You want me to let you out? I'll let you out." I depressed

the brake pedal and angled over toward the shoulder of the interstate.

"You would, wouldn't you? Right out here in the middle of nowhere. In a torrential downpour. You'd leave me."

"First of all, it's only drizzling. Secondly, this isn't exactly the middle of nowhere. Something like a million people live within twenty miles of this very spot. Besides that, you shouldn't have any trouble catching a ride. The day shift at Boeing lets out in about a half hour. Try that stretching and bending routine of yours again." I stuck my chest out and wiggled it around. "I'm willing to bet you get picked up almost immediately."

"You're despicable," she said as I pulled the truck to a stop on the shoulder of the highway.

"Get out," I said. She screwed herself down in the seat. I reached over her and opened the door. "Get out," I repeated.

She shook her head violently from side to side. "I won't!" If her lower lip had been sticking out any farther, I could have used it for a gun rack. I reached back over and reclosed the door.

"Okay, then, I don't want to hear any more of this kidnapped stuff. You're along for the ride. That's it. Just do what I tell you and keep your mouth shut. Is that clear?"

"Perfectly," she said, vivisecting me with her eyes.

Caroline's perfect understanding lasted all the way to the Last Stand.

After wheeling the truck into the gravel lot and pointing it back out toward the street, I shut down and put the keys in my pocket. The drizzle had turned to a light rain, darkening the dirt and gravel of the lot. The bar was humming. Twenty or thirty cars and trucks were randomly strewn throughout the lot. Good, I thought. The more people, the easier it would be to get lost in the crowd.

"Stay here," I said, slamming the door behind me.

I was halfway to the door when I heard the crunching behind me. She was six paces back, wearing her aviator sunglasses in the rain.

"I'm coming in," she said defiantly.

Unfortunately, there was no way to lock her in the truck, and although the prospect of rendering her unconscious held a certain manic appeal, it seemed a short-term solution at best. Wishing I'd left her on the highway, I gave in. I crooked a finger at her. She sauntered over, hands in her jacket pockets.

"Okay, but stay close to me," I said. "This place isn't the Ritz, you understand me?" She said she did. "I'll handle this. You keep out of it." I reached for the door. "And for God's sake, keep your mouth shut," I added as I pulled the door open. The doorway was full.

Most of the patrons were backed up against the front door. Only the click of pool balls rose above the eerie silence.

"Excuse me," I said to the nearest head. Grabbing Caroline by the hand, I prodded, bumped, and excused my way to the front of the crowd.

As usual, my timing was impeccable. The air in the place had the electrically charged stillness of the final moments before a summer squall. Pool balls clicked. The jukebox was silent.

What appeared to be four construction workers lounged around the pool table at the far end of the room. A staring contest was in progress. Most of the crowd was way past middle age, a fairly even mix of men and women, all of whom were giving the guys at the pool table a wide berth. A widebody holding a cue stick spoke to somebody beyond my line of sight.

"You want the table, you put up your quarter. That's how it works, Hiawatha. This here's America. We can come in any place we want. You don't like it, that's tough shit."

He was a dangerous-looking specimen, one of those guys you could mistake for fat if you didn't look closely. Five-eleven, maybe two-twenty-five or so, almost as wide as he was tall. Rapidly thinning brown, curly hair, narrow eye slits over a pug nose, wearing a blue work shirt, red suspenders, and muddy jeans. He chalked his cue so hard it bent, leaned over, and delicately banked the eight ball into the side pocket.

"Next victim," he declared loudly. His three buddies passed smug looks back and forth. His last victim, an older Indian wearing a battered black cowboy hat, returned his cue to the wall rack and slowly walked back to the bar. He was the older of the two guys I'd seen before. A muffled buzz passed through the crowd.

"Who's next?" the guy demanded.

The pockmarked kid I'd seen talking to Robert Warren detached himself from the bar and ambled over to the table. He flipped a quarter out from under the far rail and squatted down, retrieving the balls.

From the far end of the bar, a wavering voice rose above the rest. "You're not wanted here. Why don't you go?"

"We ain't goin' nowhere, grandma. Your brave here just had his chance. What, you want to try next? The way you people shoot, it's no wonder the cavalry kept kicking your ass."

Encouraged by the guffaws of his three-man audience, he waddled over to the older man whom he'd just defeated. Standing in far too close, he said, "Tell you what, I'll make you a deal. You beat me and we'll get the hell out of here. I beat you, I get that hat. What do you say?"

The older man stood his ground. "I don't gamble," he said evenly.

"Well then, just what do you do? Can't get none of these so-called women to dance. Can't get nobody to play a little friendly game."

The kid, who had racked the balls and selected a cue, interrupted the byplay. "You gonna play or what?" he asked to the guy's back.

"I'll play when I'm ready, Tonto. It's my table. Right?" he said, without ever taking his eyes off the old man. He showed a collection of short, worn teeth to the old man.

"You know what you get if you put six of these Indian women together in the same room at the same time?" he asked.

"No, what's that?" said the old guy, still holding his ground.

"A full set of teeth." He swiveled his head toward his pals for more approval and got it. They grinned and nudged one another. He turned his attention back to the old man.

"We played that last game for ten, right, old-timer? Where's my money?" With one meaty finger, he idly played with the pearl buttons on the old man's faded blue cowboy shirt.

"I told you before we started, I don't gamble," he said.

"It's my table. You want to play on my table, you play by my rules. I want my money," he insisted, now using both hands to unsnap the buttons one at a time, exposing the old man's bony chest.

Before I could react, Caroline skittered across the floor and forced herself between the two men. She got nose to nose with the pool shark. She slowly ran her palms up over the guy's chest and rested her arms on his shoulders.

"If you want to pick on somebody, big fella," she said in her Lauren Bacall voice, "why don't you pick on me." The pool shooter slowly smiled and turned again toward his pals.

I began to nonchalantly wander down the length of the bar toward the back of the room.

"Well, look what we got here, fellas." More grinning and nudging. He leaned the cue against the bar, wrapped both arms around Caroline, and pulled her in close. "Well," he said, "now ain't you a hell of an improvement on these other sows."

With a lecherous wink to his pals, he pulled her roughly in and planted an open-mouthed kiss on her. Caroline, of course, responded with passion. I stopped in my tracks. Jesus Christ.

As he ground his mouth against hers, one of her hands crept lovingly to the back of his thick neck and mussed the sweaty curls plastered to the back of his head. The pool shooter redoubled his efforts.

Suddenly, as if overcome by emotion, Caroline went completely slack. As she slid from his embrace, only her teeth, firmly locked on his tongue, kept her from hitting the floor. For a second or two, her entire weight was suspended from his tongue. Purple in the face, his eyes bulging, he forearmed her to the floor and staggered about the room, clutching his mouth, bellowing like a bull.

I used the diversion to walk the length of the room and get a two-handed grip on the cue he'd left leaning against the bar.

"Eee bib mee. Eee bib eee," he howled incredulously as he examined the blood that now seeped through his fingers and covered the backs of his hands. Blood poured down over his chins.

I watched his throat work as he swallowed blood and tried to work his tongue back into the warm, soothing confines of his mouth. No go. She'd torn something loose. His tongue hung from his mouth like a piece of raw, lacerated liver. Gingerly, he tried to push it back in with his thick fingers. Bad idea. The pain nearly took off the top of his head. Water poured from his eyes as he released his tongue and clutched his temples, staggering about in small circles. He howled again and started for Caroline.

His watering eyes opened wide as he lumbered back across the floor, his massive arms outstretched, his fingers reaching for Caroline, who was still sitting on the floor. Using both her hands and feet, she skittered crablike backward toward the door. She wasn't going to make it.

When he got even with me, I tried to conk him on top of the head with the thick end of the cue, but he saw it coming. At the last instant, he stood straight up. The cue hit him directly in the mouth. I cringed.

He went down in a heap, his hands clawing at his mouth, his feet turning him around in circles on the floor as if jet-propelled. If it weren't for the horrible, high-pitched keening sound that was coming from somewhere deep inside his body, he would have looked like he was break dancing.

Mindful of the three others, I turned quickly back toward the pool table. No need. They stood ashen against the back wall. The pockmarked kid had a gleaming Buck knife in his hand. Several other men had formed a loose circle around the trio. Without the big guy, these three weren't shit.

I checked on Caroline. She had regained her feet and was vigorously wiping her mouth with her sleeve.

"Way to stay out of it," I said.

"Somebody had to do something," was her muffled response.

An older woman at the bar reached over and handed Caroline a beer. Caroline used it like mouthwash, swishing and swirling it around in her mouth. Satisfied that she'd gotten the last vestiges rinsed out, she was at a loss as to what to do next. Apparently she didn't want to swallow it. I couldn't say as I blamed her. Equally apparent, spitting was not part of her private-school background.

With her cheeks bulging, she looked at me and raised her eyebrows. I pointed to the guy on the floor. She looked at me again as if to say "Are you sure?" and I nodded. She leaned over and spat the beer on the pool shooter, who by now had stopped circling and was slowly rocking to some internal rhythm. The move was greeted by a standing ovation from the crowd. That left the other three.

I walked to the back of the room. Nobody had moved. The kid still held the knife down by his side, neither brandishing it nor putting it away. As I shouldered my way to the front, the three guys tried to press themselves through the wall.

"You better get him to a hospital," I said to none of them in particular.

They stirred but didn't move. "Don't worry," I said. "I won't let her hurt you." Laughter rippled behind me.

The shortest of the three, a rat-faced guy in engineer overalls and a grease-stained John Deere hat, slowly made his way around me, keeping himself as far from the kid with the knife as possible. The others followed.

As they half-dragged, half-carried the guy from the bar, they were treated to a shower of beer and spittle as the patrons, emulating Caroline, filled their mouths with whatever was handy and sprayed it over their retreating forms. As the door swung shut, a loud cheer erupted.

It was beers all around. Within two minutes, Caroline and I each had four or five beers thrust in front of us; the jukebox came to life, playing an old George Jones tune; a friendlier pool game got underway; the doorway cleared out as people headed back to their seats. In spite of our momentary heroic status, I was at a loss as to how to begin asking people questions.

The older guy in the black hat wandered over. Seeing Caroline surrounded at the bar, he stepped over next to me.

"Thanks," he said.

"No problem," I replied, sipping a beer.

"I didn't need any help," he said quietly.

"Never figured you did," I replied.

He gestured toward Caroline. "That woman of yours—"

"Not mine." I held up my free hand. He nodded.

"Good thing," he answered. "Too young for you anyway." He hesitated, then folded his face into a smile. "Good teeth, though."

"Amen." We clicked beers to Caroline's teeth.

We stood and surveyed the bar together.

"My name's Leo," I said, sticking out my hand.

He took it in his own calloused hand. "Daniel," he said, "Daniel Dixon."

We returned to watching the bar. Figuring that there was never going to be a better time than this, I said, "Actually, Daniel, it's me that needs some help."

"Not as long as you got that little panther with you, you don't."

"She can't help with what I need."

He looked at me closely. "What is it you need?" he asked, showing no visible curiosity.

"I need to know about Bobby Warren."

He took a long pull from his beer. "They say Bobby's dead."

"I know. I was there."

"They say somebody might have burned him up."

"They're right," I answered. "They tried to burn me up too."

He mulled this over at length. "What makes you think I can help you?" he asked finally, polishing off his beer and setting it on the empty table beside us. He didn't give me a chance to answer. "What's done is done," he said, walking toward the back of the bar. I followed.

He leaned against the bar and watched the pool game. The pockmarked kid shot everything like he was trying to blast it all the way through the table. Colored balls scattered like a prison break every time he stroked. His opponent, a squat middle-aged guy with a prodigious gut, merely waited for everything to stop moving and picked his balls off one at a time.

"The kid shoots too hard."

"I keep tellin' him that, but he don't listen," said Daniel, never taking his eyes off the game. "That's my son Henry," he said, nodding at the kid. "Bobby was Hank's friend."

"I know."

"You was in that little green car over in the other lot on Friday afternoon." A statement.

"And here I thought I was well hidden," I said.

"I seen you," he said. I waited. Daniel Dixon spent words the way other people spent money.

Hank Dixon wound up and plastered the eleven ball at the corner pocket. He missed. The ball caromed off two cushions and inadvertently sank the eight ball at the far end of the table. Cheers and groans filled the area. The kid hung up his cue and walked over to where we were standing. He ordered a beer.

Daniel leaned over and whispered in his ear. Hank whispered back and then leaned out and fixed me with an appraising stare before going back to whispering.

Before the fate of my inquiry could be decided, angry voices from up by the door rose above the din.

First a female voice, seriously annoyed. "—the matter with you? We thought you was nice. Where you come from anyway?"

Next a male, also a bit out of sorts. "You some kind of tree hugger or what? It's traditional. Don't you understand?"

Then, of course, Caroline. "Poor defenseless beasts, hunted to the brink of extinction, and for what? So someone can hang their pathetic heads on their pathetic walls. It's barbaric. It's—" I lost the rest in the shouting.

Caroline stood at the center of a closing circle of men and

women, gesturing disgustedly at the collection of trophy heads that adorned the walls. I hadn't noticed before, but a stuffed cougar prowled along a place of honor above the bar, a black bear head growled over the entrance, several excellent deer racks were placed strategically about the walls, and even a couple of skunks served as artwork in the place.

Whatever goodwill she'd created earlier was now a thing of the past. Time to circle the wagons.

Daniel leaned over, his eyes twinkling. "You don't get her out of here, Leo, she's gonna need five friends of her own to make a full set."

"I've heard worse ideas," I said, downing the rest of my beer.

I made my way back up to the front of the bar. Whatever pearls of ecological wisdom she was presently casting before the assembled masses were lost in a sea of angry shouts and curses. A finger-pointing session was about to degenerate into something considerably uglier.

Caroline was attempting to drag a stool over by the entrance, so as to remove the offending bear head from over the door. Several patrons were making sustained efforts to impede her progress by pulling the stool in the opposite direction. True to form, she was still babbling as I slung her over my shoulder and kicked the door open. "—is the twentieth century. How can a noble people, in tune with nature's forces—" Bouncing her head off the door frame put a momentary halt to the diatribe.

"You do have a way with people," I said as I set her back on her feet in the parking lot. The rain had picked up. Driven by a stiff breeze, the small droplets angled in from the west like angry insects.

"Did you see—?"

The door swung open again. Daniel and Hank Dixon came out. I turned to Caroline. "Go get in the truck."

"I most certainly will not. I'm going right back in there and—"

"Get in the truck now, or I'll leave you here when I go," I growled.

She opened her mouth, shut it, started again, jerked her sunglasses from her face, turned on her heel, and flounced over to the truck, slamming the door behind her. We watched in silence.

"What's her name?" asked the kid after the truck stopped rocking.

"Caroline," I answered.

He turned to his father. "She's the one," he said.

The Dixons started across the lot toward the Nova. I followed. Halfway across the lot, Hank turned to me. "We can't help you, mister. Bobby got all moony over that sister you got in the truck there, and look what it got him. No," he said, shaking his head sadly. "We can't help you, mister."

Daniel shrugged and headed for the car. I followed again. They both turned to face me. "Look," I said, "a friend of mine's dead, too. An old man. He wasn't much, and maybe I'm the only one who cares about him being dead, but I don't much give a shit. The same people that killed Bobby Warren killed my friend. That much I'm sure of." They exchanged glances. "I'm not going to threaten you or anything, but I'm not going away either. I'll follow you home. I'll sit in your front yard. I'll come back here every day. I don't much care what it takes, but I'm following this to the end."

Hank started to leave, but Daniel stopped him with a gentle hand on the shoulder.

"He means it," said Daniel. We stood in the rain. Two couples wandered out of the bar, laughing and gabbing. We watched them get into a blue Plymouth and drive out into the street.

The tiny drops were finding someplace on my collar to

mass and form the rivulets that were pouring down my neck. I stood and waited, wishing for a cowboy hat of my own.

Finally, Daniel said, "You need to see Miriam Stone."

"Who's that?" I asked.

"Bobby's grandmother," said Hank. "All Bobby told me was that he had a line on some illegal dumping that was going on on the reservation. He said he was going to take it to the Tribal Council. He wanted my father to go with him. But—" He stopped, looking at his father. Daniel picked it up.

"But I told him that if he was right, then it was probably the Tribal Council behind it. Or at least a couple of them. Have to be. No way to keep that kind of thing quiet 'less somebody on the council was helping."

"So, why his grandmother?"

"Miriam," said Daniel, "is a much-respected woman. She and Bobby were real close. I figure that whatever he knew, she knew. They were close," he repeated.

"What did he tell you guys?"

"Just what I told you," answered the kid. He glanced at the truck. "That and that he'd met this white sister who was going to help him get it out in the open." Anger filled his eyes. "He was all moony for her. I could tell. I never seen him like that before. He was— If it wasn't for her—" He stopped himself.

"Go see Miriam," said Daniel. "She'll know what to do."

"How do I find this Miriam Stone?"

They exchanged glances again, and Hank sighed. "Follow us."

I headed for the truck.

15

CAROLINE WAS CURLED up against the far door, bundled in her jacket, picking at her lower lip, in a full snit.

"Where are we going?" she demanded as I fired up the truck. Without waiting for me to answer, she added, "I insist that you immediately—" I interrupted and told her where we were going.

"Oooh, a medicine woman." She sat straight, her eyes now aglow. "I read a book last year—"

I tuned her out as I bounced the truck out of the lot and followed the Dixons' Nova back toward the freeway. Slowly, as it began to dawn on me that we were taking the same route on which I'd followed Robert Warren the other night, the hair on the back of my neck began to rise. The rain had stopped. The sun poked intermittently through the clouds. The countryside appeared more benign in broad daylight, but the journey was the same.

Caroline was still at it. "—the shamanic tradition of the coastal Indians—"

My suspicions were confirmed when we passed the yellow

police barrier tape strung across the front of Bobby's drive-way. I could see the rear ends of at least two vehicles parked down by where the cabin had been as we flashed by. Caroline took no notice. She was still running off at the mouth.

"—in cedar bark lodges, which believe it or not were really—"

The Nova's brake lights flashed, then stayed on, slowing as we rounded a sharp corner. A driveway angled off, straight uphill from the corner. The Nova nosed in. I followed.

"—even wore cedar bark clothes. I saw pictures. I couldn't believe it. The chafing must have been terrible. I imagine—"

As usual, Caroline was in the right desert but the wrong tent. At least she had the cedar part right. It was a four-bedroom home, two gables off the front, covered wraparound porch on three sides. Maybe a precut, sitting on a little knoll, well-tended grounds and a glassed-in solarium off the near side.

The sight of the house put a momentary halt to her lecture. She started to open her mouth, thought better of it, and, merci-fully, was finally quiet as we pulled to a stop in the driveway.

Daniel emerged from the Nova. I told Caroline to come along. I pulled open the passenger door on the Nova and beckoned Caroline toward the vacated passenger seat. For once, she didn't argue. I closed the door behind her. Daniel arched an eyebrow at me. "Hank going to be all right?"

"In a pinch, I figure he can outrun her," I said.

We walked side by side up the inlaid brick walk. The cracks had mossed in, and the constant rain had created a roller-coaster effect in the once-flat surface. I had to watch my own feet as we walked.

Daniel knocked softly on the front door. From the porch, high above the tree level, Puget Sound rolled in the late-afternoon sunshine. The wind had shifted from the south. I could smell the water. Daniel knocked again. A voice sounded from inside the house. We waited. Footsteps approached the door.

She was tall for a woman. Five-ten or better, about Daniel's age, wearing a well-tailored blue dress with a white yoke. Her hair was artfully arranged into a French braid. At sixty or so, she was an elegant older woman; twenty years ago she'd been a walking heartbreak. I could see the sadness in her eyes. The sight of Daniel seemed to cheer her.

"Why, Daniel," she said, ignoring me. "How nice of you to come."

Daniel had removed his cowboy hat. The breeze pushed a long lock down in front of his face. He brushed it back in place.

"Miriam," was all he could muster.

"Come in," she said, stepped aside. I presumed the invitation included me and tagged along. Miriam Stone led us down the center of the house directly back into the kitchen, where she pulled two coffee mugs down from one of the stark white European-style cabinets that lined the room and filled them with coffee from an automatic coffeemaker on the counter. She handed one to each of us. She waited for Daniel to speak. He tried.

"Miriam—I—we—uh—this is Leo." He waved the cup at me. I stepped over and offered my hand. "Leo Waterman," I said. She took my hand and covered it with both of hers. She reached into my eyes.

"Did you know Bobby?" she asked, still rummaging around somewhere in the back of my head.

"Only indirectly," I answered. She looked to Daniel for an explanation.

He started. "Leo has a friend who—" He stopped. "Bobby was . . ." He stopped again. He handed me the ball. I told her the story.

She listened in silence, her moist eyes bouncing from

Daniel to me and back. Daniel confirmed my narrative with small nods. When I'd finished, she turned away and silently busied herself at the sink. I started to speak, but Daniel waved me off. We waited. She dried her hands.

Without turning, she asked, "So what is it you want, Mr. Waterman? Revenge for your friend? For yourself?" She turned to me, leaning back against the sink. "It can't be for Bobby. You didn't even know my Bobby. What do you hope to gain from this?" I didn't have an answer.

"I don't know," I said. Somehow, for her, this served as confirmation.

"They say it might have been an accident." A statement.

"It was no accident," I said.

"So you say," she replied. There seemed no point in insisting. I waited. She picked it up on her own. "We can't afford to be losing boys like Bobby. Boys like Bobby are the hope of the tribe."

She turned back to the sink, her shoulders shaking slightly. Daniel stepped over and put a gentle hand on her shoulder. She covered it with one of her own, and then turned and put her arms around Daniel. They quietly embraced. I wandered out into the hall, sipping at the strong coffee.

I studied a painting on the wall. A shaman of some kind, disguised under a wolf skin, holding four red sticks in his left hand, his right hand held out flat, parallel with the ground. Maybe . . .

Daniel appeared in the kitchen doorway and waved me back in. Miriam Stone appeared to have collected herself. "Your friend, he was dear to you?"

I thought about it. "Yes, he was," I said. Before she could respond, I went on. "To be honest with you, I don't think too many people are going to mourn Buddy's passing. To most people he was just another old drunk. To me he was—" I was stumped. "He meant more to me than that."

"We have many people who have lost themselves to alcohol," she said. "That doesn't make them less than people. It merely makes them lost. Alcohol can rob a person of his soul, but not of being a person." I agreed.

Her eyes clouded as she remembered her grandson.

"Bobby had not lost his way, Mr. Waterman. He was a good boy. As good as the Tulalips have to offer." Suddenly, her sadness froze over.

"What do you know of our tribe, Mr. Waterman?"

"Not much, I'm afraid. I come up for fireworks once a year," I stammered. I'd confirmed her worst notions. She nodded.

"Well, Mr. Waterman, let me fill you in a little. I don't want to make you the scapegoat for your entire race, but you, like most of your race, are painfully ignorant." When I didn't object, she continued.

"There are no accurate figures, but it's estimated that there were upward of twenty thousand members of the tribe before your people brought your diseases. Before the smallpox, the chicken pox, and all the others were through, we were down to the two thousand or so that we are now." She paused to let the numbers have their effect.

"We occupied many thousand square miles, from Whidbey Island all the way out to Snoqualmie Falls; it was all our homeland. That is what your people have never been able to understand. We are not like the others who have come to these shores. We are not immigrants. We are not transients. We are a land-based people, and this is our land. Not the fifteen thousand paltry acres we are left with, *all* of it." She was blazing now.

"This is why we never melted into your great melting pot. This is why we don't want into your great salad bowl either. We were here. This is ours. We are a land-based people." She caught herself and stopped. She smiled wanly at me.

"I apologize, Mr. Waterman. I suppose I'm overly passionate on this subject, but it's quite important to me and my people. My students often ask me why the native peoples have had such a difficult time assimilating into Western culture. Do you know what I tell them?"

Daniel piped in. "Miriam teaches at the University of Washington."

"I tell them that, first of all, we have no desire to fit in. We have a desire to strengthen and solidify our cultural values and heritage. We have a desire to enhance the continuance of our cultural identity so that it can be passed down to future generations. What we do not have a desire to do is to become lost in the cultural mishmash of the society that surrounds us."

"She has a Ph.D." Daniel again.

"My students often view the treaty of 1855 as the tribe's great opportunity to join the mainstream. They wonder what it was about us that led us to squander all of our supposed opportunities. What cultural character defects can be found to explain our present state. What they're missing, Mr. Waterman, is that there were no opportunities. There was no plan. There never was. We were supposed to move onto the reservation and die. That's what they wanted from us, for us to die and sink back into the earth so that they could get on about their precious business."

"You're still here."

"Yes, and it confounds white society to this very day that we had the unmitigated gall to survive, to prosper even. Bobby"—there was a catch in her throat—"was attending the university, but he was also learning the Snohomish language. Did you know that we were whipped for speaking our language, for dancing our dances? Do you realize what voids are created in a people who are stripped of both their land and their culture?"

"No, but I know about voids," I said.

Her anger boiled to the surface, dragging mine with it.

"What do *you* know of voids?"

"I know that my friend Buddy Knox was every bit as invisible to the society that surrounded him as your people are. I know that Buddy had some kind of massive hole inside of him that he tried to drink full. Maybe the void wasn't forced on him. Maybe in some way it was. I don't know. It was there. The void is there for a lot of us. It's not an Indian thing or a white thing. It's a people thing. I know that you can live smack in the middle of white culture and not be a part of it. All you've got to do is get outside the limits. The minute you become something they don't want to look at, they stop looking at you. It's that simple. You join the void. That much I'm sure of." I decided to shut up before I got myself in trouble.

Miriam Stone heaved a sigh and leaned back against the sink again.

"Perhaps you're right, Mr. Waterman. Perhaps my view is too narrow." We both considered the idea in silence.

Finally, she said, "What do you want from me, Mr. Waterman?"

"I want to know what Bobby told you about some illegal waste dumping that he was looking into." Her eyes clouded over, but not with anger this time.

"I should have listened to him," she said sadly. "I should have—"

Daniel patted her shoulder. Miriam steeled herself.

"Bobby said that he had proof that there was illegal waste dumping taking place on the reservation. He wanted me to go to the Tribal Council with him."

"And you said?"

"I said that he should do his homework on this thing. That he should document his charges. I told him that the Tribal Council would never listen to any vague allegations." She looked me in the eye. "The Tribal Council is both quite political and quite divided, Mr. Waterman. At times," she mused, "we can be our own worst enemies.

"There is a faction—a large and vocal faction—that feels that we should beat the whites at their own game. If the white man values only money, then we should use our legal leverage to beat him at this game. These people are responsible for such things as reservation bingo. They are the ones who opened the reservation liquor store, which, by the way, put the Marysville liquor store out of business, which in turn further inflamed the already tense situation in this area. I'm sad to say that this is the group that presently controls the Tribal Council. They've gone so far as to hire an expert, an outsider, to advise them in these matters. A tribal resources manager."

"Guy named Howard Short," Daniel said. "Had a lot of success back in the Southwest making tribes into conglomerates."

"He's no worse than some of the others," Miriam said quickly. "There are those who wish to return totally to the old ways. No contact whatsoever. These misguided people think time can be made to move backward." She edited herself again.

"The point is, Mr. Waterman, that it would take the proverbial smoking gun to get any action out of the Tribal Council. I told Bobby to document his charges. I didn't think—I didn't know—" Her eyes misted. "How could this be worth such a life? How could—"

"You had no way of knowing," I said. She wanted to agree but couldn't manage it. I tried again. "What was the plan when and if he documented his suspicions?"

"We were going to take it to the council together."

"Why not just go to the law? These people are—"

"Whose law? It's not our law."

I tried a different angle. "Will that still be the plan if I document the charges?" I asked.

"Most certainly, but Robert didn't tell me anything specific."

"He may have done a better job than you imagine."

I told her about the annotated maps. I left out the gun. "The maps have no legends. I'd need someone who knows the land around here."

She turned immediately to Daniel. "Daniel knows the land," she said. Daniel silently agreed.

"You have these maps?" he asked.

"Not with me. I can get them," I said. Daniel was grim.

"Get them," he said. "I'll know the places."

I turned to Miriam. "Did he tell you anything else that might help us?"

She misted over again. "Mostly he talked about this white girl he was fond of. He went on and on. I'd never seen him—'"

"She's out in the car," said Daniel.

"I want to meet her," Miriam blurted.

"No, you don't, I said." Daniel gave me silent support. "We spoke of voids earlier, Miriam," I said. "This one has a terrible void that she's trying desperately to fill. I'm afraid that Bobby was just one of those things she stuffed in the hole." I let it go at that. She looked back to Daniel. He wagged his head emphatically. She took him at his word.

Latching onto Daniel's arm, she walked us to the door. Hank stood outside the Nova. Caroline was back in the front seat of the truck. The rain had followed us. A wind-driven drizzle angled in at about thirty degrees. The Sound was no longer visible. Miriam turned to Daniel.

"Come back more often, Daniel, won't you please?" Daniel promised he would. He didn't mean it. I could tell. She left us standing on the porch exchanging phone numbers. I gave him Hector's number and wrote his number in my notebook. He felt like he owed an explanation.

"Miriam and I, when we were younger—much younger—" He waved a hand. "We went different ways," he concluded.

"It's never too late."

"What's done is done," he said for the second time today. "Nothing we do is gonna bring Bobby back."

"No, but we can sure fuck up some other folks' day."

"Might be fun," he admitted.

"I'll be in touch. I need to go back to the city. I'll call you on Monday, okay? I'll need till then."

"If I'm not there, you know where to find me." He hesitated, looking over at the truck. "Better not bring that one," he said.

"Have no fear."

16

IT TOOK THE better part of an hour and a half to fight the rush-hour traffic back into the city. Five years ago, the rush hour was both limited and predictable. All a guy had to do was avoid the highways for an hour or so in the morning and an hour or so in the evening, and traffic wasn't a problem.

These days, the rush hour was omnipresent. The surrounding suburban territory had filled up at a rate that had exceeded even the most pessimistic long-range plans. Long the butt of local jokes, a series of phantom freeway ramps had for the last twenty-five years completely surrounded the city. Connecting to the extant highway system, but leading off only into space, they had been built to accommodate the traffic of the future. The future had never come.

By the time the highway department had gotten around to connecting these mystery ramps to the existing road system, the traffic of the future had become the traffic of the past and was now equally horrific in all directions. There were as many people trying to get back into the city at six in the evening as there were people trying to leave. Seemingly over-night, the sticks had become the burbs, and the burbs had filled to the brim.

The situation was further exacerbated by the very nature of the local populace. Northwesterners are a curious lot. Maybe something in the genes. Maybe some compensatory response to all the rain. Nature or nurture? Any diversion, however mundane, is enough to slow the traffic to a crawl.

I was always amused when I read stories about how in New York or L.A. or some other urban jungle, heinous crimes were committed in plain view of passing motorists whose conditioned response was to put the pedal to the metal and the problem in the rearview mirror. Not in Seattle.

An abandoned car, even one pulled well off the roadway, elicited a round of gawking and rubbernecking guaranteed to cause a ten-mile backup. An accident was good for at least twenty miles. If it happened on one of the bridges, forget it. Might as well turn around and go back to work.

A crime? God only knew. One thing was for sure. The perpetrator had best beat a hasty retreat. Dallying would in all likelihood lead to being pummeled mercilessly by a van full of hefty Swedes, the whole sorry scene photographed for posterity by the inevitable busload of Japanese tourists. Film at eleven.

Caroline had mostly been quiet. When her initial attempts at conversation had been greeted with a series of low grunts, she'd given up and had spent the time gazing forlornly out the window at the traffic. She didn't come alive until I nosed the truck out of the flow, up the James Street off-ramp. She broke my concentration.

"They've probably towed my car by now."

"Good," I said. "You'll probably get in less trouble on foot."

"Turn down here," she directed. "It's a straight shot down to—"

"We're not going to your car."

"We most certainly are. Right now."

"I want you to show me this truck depot that you and Bobby followed the trucks to."

"They're closed by now. They close at—"

"Good," I said. This got her attention.

"Are we going to break in?" Crime enthused the girl.

"We"—I hesitated—"are not going to do anything together. *You*"—another hesitation—"are going to show me this place, and then I'm going to leave you at your car."

"No way."

"Wanna bet?"

She thought about it. "I know your name," she announced out of the blue.

"Yeah, what's my name?" I asked.

"Leo. Your name's Leo." She was smug. "Hank told me."

I silently cursed Hank. Probably not his fault though. She'd probably worked him like a gearshift lever to get the information. Explained why he'd been standing out in the rain when we came out of Miriam's house.

"Go all the way to the end and then turn down Yesler."

I followed her directions. Ten blocks south of the Dome, she leaned forward with her hands on the dash, squinting out through the filthy windshield. Her jagged nails were bitten to the quick.

"It's right up here somewhere."

We crept along in the right-hand lane, horns voicing their displeasure as we impeded their progress. She pointed. "There."

I pulled to the curb. More angry horns. A little brown two-story, recently repainted, surrounded by a full acre and a half of parking, which in turn was surrounded by a seven-foot chain-link fence. Razor wire on top. No sign or billing. Serious security for a seemingly innocuous truck depot. Advertising was not a high priority.

A picture of the house thirty years ago crept into my mind. It used to be an orchard. I could still see the little red fruit stand they set up out front every fall. This whole area had been essentially agricultural. Small farms and truck gardens, an occasional warehouse, otherwise rural.

My old man and I used to come down here on Saturday afternoons in the fall to get lugs of apples for my mother to can or mash into applesauce. Looking at it now, it was hard to believe my own memory. Wall-to-wall commercial, wholesale, and light manufacturing. Not the slightest hint of its not-so-distant past. I felt ancient. Caroline rescued me.

"Don't get too close," she whispered. "They'll see you."

"Who'll see me?"

"The guards."

"They've got guards?"

"Several. Monsters," she added as an afterthought.

After watching Caroline's performance at the Last Stand, I was immediately wary of anyone who managed to get this much respect from her. "How do you know about the guards?" I asked tentatively.

"They almost caught us."

"When?"

"The night Bobby climbed over the fence." Her attention was still riveted on the truck depot.

"Tell me about it," I said. She turned her attention to me.

"Why?" Nothing was easy with this kid.

"Because it might be important," I sighed. She thought it over.

"Bobby climbed over the fence—"

"Where?" I interrupted.

"Over there in the back, by the shed." She was pointing to an area along the back wall where a hundred-foot-long shed roof ran the full length. Several cabs, two blue, two red, were parked under its protection. At the mercy of the weather, trailers were symmetrically arranged about the lot.

"What happened then?"

"He was supposed to be sneaking in. We wanted to write down the numbers of the trailers." She hesitated. I pushed.

"Well?"

"It was quite disappointing actually." She shook her head disgustedly. "I thought, you know, him being an Indian and everything, that he'd be able to sneak up on them or something. I mean the place isn't exactly Fort Knox or anything, but—"

"But what?"

"But the fool nearly got us both caught."

"How long was he inside?"

"Not long. Maybe two, three minutes. I don't know how they knew, but they knew. Next thing I knew, he was coming back over the fence."

"Where?"

"Right there." She pointed to an area bordering the street, just in front of the truck. If Bobby'd come over there, he'd no longer been interested in being sneaky; he'd been in full retreat.

"You said he was chased."

"A behemoth. He'd only been gone for a second when I saw him coming back over the fence." Her eyes opened wide. "For a second, I didn't think he was going to make it. His shirt got caught in that wire stuff on top. Ruined the shirt. Not that it was much of a loss," she added. "Those shirts he wore were—"

"What then?"

"Then the front door"—she pointed to the house—"opened, and this huge guy came running after him. He was almost to the truck before we got it started and got away." She was reliving the incident.

"Nobody tried to follow the two of you after that?"

She wagged her head. "He just stood in the street and wrote down the license number. I watched him."

"What were you and Bobby driving?"

"His truck," she answered distractedly. "His truck didn't like to start right away. It was a junker like this one. Anyway, for a second there, I thought the guy was going to catch us."

I'd been assuming that Bobby Warren had taken his suspicions to a third party and had been betrayed. That was no longer necessarily the case. Maybe he didn't put his trust in the wrong hands. Maybe just his license number. Anybody with an IQ over forty and a little cash can almost instantly translate a license number into a name. The guy that chased him had all he needed. They didn't even have to worry that they'd rigged the wrong house. Not with that ripped-up shirt hanging on the clothesline out front. The poor kid might as well have hung out a sign. Caroline interrupted my thoughts.

"Well?" She folded her arms over her chest. "Go do something."

"Like what?"

"You're the thug. You're supposed to know things like that."

"Stay here," I said for the third time today.

"Don't I always?" she purred.

The fence was brand spanking new. No more than six months out in the weather. No rust or oxidation on the cut ends of the wires that held the chain link in place. Very little garbage collected at the bottom of the fence.

As I wandered along it toward the front of the little house, something caught my eye. An aberration in the coils of the razor wire destroyed the symmetrical effect. I stood beneath it. I reached up. Too high.

Putting the toe of my boot into one of the links, I hoisted myself up to where I could see better. Sure enough, the wire had captured a two-inch square of blue-checked flannel. I tried to free it. No go. With only one hand to work with, getting it free took the better part of two minutes and the skin off three knuckles.

As I stepped back down, I smugly waved my prize at the truck. Caroline was not in sight. Cursing my own stupidity, I started back. A ham-size hand appeared on my shoulder, welding me to the sidewalk.

There were two of them. One black, one white. All of my rattling around up on the fence must have covered the sounds of their approach.

The hand on my shoulder belonged to a large black specimen. Six-three or so and heavy around the middle, he kept his free hand resting lightly on the handle of an automatic that was tucked into his belt while he tried to push me through the sidewalk with the other. The oily skin of his face was latticed with a collection of pits and scars. His thick right eyebrow was interrupted twice by little highways of horizontal scar tissue. His ears were folded up like new roses. Either this guy had repeatedly been threshed and baled or he'd been the opponent to be named later in a number of wildly unsuccessful prizefights. I was betting on the latter. His hand increased its pressure.

"What you got there, pilgrim?" asked the black guy, nodding at the scrap of cloth in the palm of my hand.

When I failed to answer, the other one stepped behind me. He was younger. Under thirty, taller than the black guy but wiry, with the longest arms I'd ever seen on a human being. They hung down six inches past his knees and ended in a pair of knobby hands so large they appeared to be borrowed. Size three head. A face so narrow it was seemingly grafted together from two badly mismatched halves.

From behind me, "Yeah, pal, what you got there?

Heeeeeeeeee." His giggle was so high-pitched and manic it sounded like a blender. Without warning, he delivered a shattering blow to my kidneys, doubling me over.

I struggled to catch my breath. My lower back was on fire. I slowly straightened up.

"Is there an echo in here?" I asked.

"Never mind Wesley. Wesley likes to hurt people. Let's have it."

"Yeah, let's have it. Heeeeeeeeee."

"Wesley," the black guy boomed.

"Yeah, Frank."

"Shut the fuck up."

Wesley saluted. The black guy sighed.

"Let's have it." He held out his hand. I put the scrap of material in it. Wesley redoubled his efforts on my kidneys. This time the other one. I gagged from the pain and went to one knee.

"Now you got a matched set, asshole," Wesley cooed. "You'll be pissin' blood for a week. Heeeeeeeeee."

They studied the scrap.

Frank turned it round and round with his fingers, eyeing me occasionally.

"What do we have here?" he said finally.

"Looks like flannel to me," I offered, staying down.

"Me, too," said Wesley, stepping closer.

"We're all agreed then, it's flannel," I said. The big guy ignored me. Wesley kicked me in the back. I bounced off the fence.

"What you want with something like this?" Frank asked.

"I'm making a quilt."

Wesley was quick. "I think he's lying, Frank."

"Shut up, Wesley," he boomed again. He leaned down to me. "You better get straight with me, pilgrim," he whispered, "otherwise we're gonna go inside and let Wesley have his fun

with you. Wesley"—he glanced over—"had a very interesting childhood. When Wesley works on people, I leave the
room. Ain't got the stomach for it. Trust me, pilgrim, you don't
want old Wesley working on you." When I didn't answer, he
shook his head sadly.

He used the hand on my shoulder to pick me up and turn
me like a handle back toward the house. "Let's go inside,"
he said.

I ducked out from under the hand and got my back on the
fence.

"I don't think so," I said.

He nodded toward his partner. "Hurt him, Wesley," he
said offhandedly.

"Heeeeeeeeeee." Wesley started for me. There was joy in
his rodentlike eyes and a gravity knife in his right hand. I
could smell his sexual excitement.

The pickup roared to life behind us. Both men turned
instinctively toward the sound. Caroline jammed the rig in
gear and shot directly toward us, bouncing up over the sidewalk, seemingly intent on scraping all of us off the fence. I
climbed like an orangutan. The right front fender passed directly beneath me as the truck took out the post I'd been
leaning on. I vaulted down onto the hood.

Wesley and Frank weren't so lucky. The force of the truck
blasted both of them back into the fence, which, without the
support from the mangled post, collapsed directly on top of
them. A raucous alarm siren bleated out into the night. Automatic
floodlights clicked on and lit the street like a sporting event.
The truck backed up, throwing me to the ground as it bounced
back over the curb. The passenger door flew open. I jumped in.

Without so much as a look, Caroline jammed the truck
into drive and wheeled back into the street. My door closed
on its own.

"Oh yes," she said. "Very manly. I especially liked the

way you didn't even know those two goons were there. If it wasn't for me—"

I was too busy ministering to my badly scraped left knee to pay any attention. A flap of skin hung out from the tear in my jeans. Gingerly, I pushed it back in and folded the ripped fabric over it. It was already beginning to throb. My back was killing me.

Caroline turned left without slowing, throwing me over into her lap.

"Hang on," she grunted and turned left again. I hung on.

When the truck straightened again, I sat up. We were headed back toward Pioneer Square. Caroline was muttering to herself.

"What's your problem?"

"Problem? Why would I have any problems? Just because I hook up with the only guys in the world who couldn't sneak up on Stevie Wonder, why should I have any problems? A simple little thing like—"

I had the urge to make excuses. I had the urge to inform her that I hadn't been making much noise, that I'd been out of sight from the building, that the place had some type of motion or sound detectors or something, but I resisted. "Screw you," I said, probing my knee.

"You wish," she said with a sniff as we cut back under the viaduct and headed uptown toward her car. "I especially liked the way you just stood still while the skinny one was trying to puree your kidneys. Very manly," she repeated, before I could respond. "And you just gave the other one that piece of Bobby's shirt. You just handed it to him. I mean really, couldn't you at least have—"

"Have what?" I growled. "Have gotten myself killed? Those guys were armed. What was I supposed to do?"

She sniffed once and jerked the rig to a stop in front of her car. Leaving the truck running, she hopped out and walked over, leaned in, and pulled the keys from the ignition, bouncing them up and down in her hand. As I slid across the seat, she restarted her monologue.

"If you'd had any balls at all, what you would have done was to—"

She was still talking as I drove off.

17

REBECCA DUVALL USED an oversize slotted spoon to poke gingerly at the rubbery surface of the casserole.

"By the way, Leo, I'm assuming that it wouldn't be news to you were I to tell you that a number of seriously annoyed law enforcement officers have been inquiring as to your whereabouts."

"I've been traveling incognito."

Again, she tried unsuccessfully to pry one of the white geometric cubes loose, failed, and turned to me. I shrugged.

We'd managed to avoid talking about Buddy. Instead, we shook hands, patted backs, and reshaped old times until we were certain we'd be the last people to make a pass at the table. Everyone was spread throughout the house, eating off their laps. The party was in remission.

Bettina's esoteric entrees remained untouched; Rebecca was concerned. "Somebody has to at least take some of this stuff," she whispered from behind her plate. "Her feelings will be hurt."

"Go for it," I suggested.

Dispiritedly, she gouged the casserole, which this time broke apart. A quivering blob came loose with a wet sucking sound. Shaken loose from the spoon, it vibrated obscenely on her plate.

"I hope the boys in blue didn't give you a hard time," I said.

"No, no. They're always the soul of discretion. Dr. Duvall this, Dr. Duvall that. They always act like it's a clerical mistake for me to be listed among our known associates."

Ed and Tina Reynolds passed us on the right and headed directly for the easily recognizable food on the far side of the table. This was all the encouragement Rebecca needed. We hustled over, absconded with the last mortal remains of the real food, and found a couple of seats on a battered brown leather sofa. We munched Maryland crab cakes and peeled shrimp.

"Arniie." Bettina. Knickknacks wobbled on the shelves. No response. "Arniiiiie," again.

"Where is the birthday boy anyway?" Duvall asked between bites.

"Probably out having his stomach pumped."

"Seriously."

"He's out on the back porch getting people who haven't been stoned in years wasted out of their minds."

"We better leave before they come back and start to talk."

I silently agreed. Bettina spotted me and clanked over, spilling white wine all the way.

"Where's Arnie?" she demanded.

"He's out back trading recipes," I said.

"Whatsamatter, Leo? You got a problem? Did we wake up on the wrong side of the futon today or what?"

"If *we* woke up on the wrong side of anything together, Bettina, trust me, it wouldn't be a problem. I'd immediately kill myself. No problem."

Duvall elbowed me viciously.

"You should get so lucky, Waterman. You don't have what it takes."

"You're right, Bettina. I'm missing both a lobotomy and a bookmark." Another pistonlike elbow threatened to break the skin.

"Fuck you, Leo," was the best Bettina could manage before stumbling off on her search for Arnie. Rebecca shook her head sadly.

"What I can't figure, Leo, is why you came. I thought for sure I'd have to do this one alone. You and that woman"—her eyes followed Bettina—"and believe me, I use the term loosely, have always detested one another. Why bother?"

"I was already here," I said.

Duvall arched an eyebrow. I told her the story.

I'D SPENT THE night in Arnie's backyard. After unloading Caroline Nobel, I'd swung by Kmart, picked up a cheap sleeping bag, and rolled over to Arnie's place. Deserted. Then I remembered the Eugene trip. Even better. I let myself into the backyard, closing the gate behind me, and backed the truck against the fence. The house was locked.

As I stood on the back steps deciding what to do next, the wind suddenly shifted out of the south, and a hint of salt joined the air. The thunderheads that had stood at attention all day slid across the sky from the Sound, filling the air like cannon smoke, blotting out the last of the sun. The trees took on a strange green cast as though I was looking at the world from underwater. I sprinted back to the truck.

It rained hard, blistering the truck and the camper with a deafening ten-minute drum solo. I checked for leaks. Everything shipshape. Just as quickly, the rain ended. The truck looked clean. The backyard had been transformed; the once-dusty thatch now had a black sheen. I walked up to the Avenue and gorged myself on Ezell's chicken, picking up a sixer of Portland Ale on the way back. Somewhere between ale number three and four, I slipped into my new bag and slid off the end of the world.

I slept in. Around ten, when I poked my head out of the camper door, music was wafting from the windows of the house. Arnie was back. I dug out some fresh clothes, located my dop kit, and headed for the shower. Thank God I knocked.

Bettina opened the door. I'd forgotten all about Bettina. Barefoot, she was wrapped in a flowing blue robe whose thirty-odd yards of material were covered with crescent moons, stars, and assorted mystical symbols. With her barbed-wire hair sticking straight out from her head, she could have been used to repel boarders.

I tried to look humble. I was prepared to be nice. I was, after all, uninvited. She started it. She took me in from head to toe, slowly working her small lips.

"Very stylish, Leo," nodding slightly. Bettina had a way of squeezing words out through her lips without moving them. The sound came from somewhere deep within her cheeks and angled down toward her angelic lips to be finally extruded through her pastry bag of a mouth.

"Sorry," I said. If she'd closed the door, I'd have gone gently into that good morning. But no. No, she had to start. More nodding.

"Very chic. I especially like the rip in the knee of the jeans. Very trendy. It's all the rage with the kids, you know. But, Leo"—she leaned in perilously close—"the crusty stuff around the tear is definitely optional, and that flap of skin hanging out could, in some circles, be considered overkill, if you know what I mean."

Like the rest of the known world, I couldn't get a word in edgewise. Bettina filled silence the way air fills a vacuum.

"The scratches on your face and the three-days' growth are a nice touch though. Definitely lends a plebeian touch."

I started to speak. She held up a chubby hand. "No, no, let me guess. You went out looking for cigarettes, and somebody stepped on your face."

She gave me her most unctuous smile, the one I hated most. It looked a lot like the grille on a fifty-seven Chevy. If you missed the feral little eyes, you could easily mistake this particular grimace for genuine warmth. I knew better.

I barged past her into the small foyer. "Arnie up?"

"The party isn't till two, you moron."

"I'm going to take a shower," I said, heading for the stairs.

"Wait a minute," she bleated. "You can't just—" I was gone. Arnie was rolled up, cocoonlike, in the bedroom at the top of the stairs. He raised his head. I waved.

"Gonna hit the shower," I announced. He weakly waved back. Two fingers. The peace sign.

"Have at it, old pal," he croaked, sagging back into the covers.

I stayed in the bathroom for hours. I stayed until she had long since given up banging on the door and was threatening to call the fire department. Arnie's insane laughter was a constant source of strength. I hung around for the rest of the day, just to piss her off. Just like old times.

"THAT, and I figured Wendy was sure to show up for the party," I finished.

"Wendy, eh. And what would you be needing from Wendy?"

Wendy Harris, former cheerleading captain and present real estate mogul, was engaged in animated conversation with a bald guy who looked vaguely familiar.

"Who's that guy she came with?" I asked, pointing to the far side of the living room. "Is he the one that works for the EPA?"

"That's her new husband. Ed or Ted or something, and

no, the EPA guy was that short guy with the good hair. He was number three, I think." I remembered. "Ed or Ted is a bond broker of some sort," she added.

"What number is this?" I asked. Wendy got married the way some people changed underwear.

"Four, maybe five, but who's counting?"

While my attention had been diverted, Duvall had slipped her plate down under the sofa. I shook my head sadly.

"What if one of Arnie's cats finds that stuff?" I asked.

"We have a pet overpopulation problem, Leo, or don't you read the papers? Just doing my part. What say we go meet Wendy's new hubby while we still have the chance."

"Great idea," I said.

She started to rise. I stopped her. "Listen. When we get over there, be charming. Talk about cadavers or something. Keep the hubby busy long enough for me to get the number of the EPA guy from Wendy."

We smiled, backpatted, and handshook our way across the room. The party was thinning out. The eat-and-run types had done so. Those with small children had made the appropriate baby-sitter excuses. I hadn't seen Arnie in two hours. Wendy and Ted or Ed were more or less keeping to themselves over by the front windows. It took Rebecca and me ten minutes to cross the thirty feet. Wendy pulled us the last eight.

"Leo, Rebecca, come here, I want you to meet Ted." She handled the introductions. Within a minute, Rebecca had managed to separate Ted from Wendy. I made my move.

"Wendy," I said.

"Yes, Leo." She twinkled. Flirting was a way of life with this woman.

"Before Ed—"

"Ted," she corrected, moving in closer.

I searched for a delicate phrase. "Before Ted, there was that guy who worked for the EPA—"

"Charles."

"Yeah, Charles."

"He was two before Ted."

I ignored her. "Whatever." So much for delicacy. "What exactly was it he did for the EPA?"

"Regional director for enforcement."

I tried to look impressed. I shouldn't have bothered.

"Sounds good, but doesn't pay. I tried to steer him into consulting, he could have made a fortune, but the boob was fixated on public service. Can you imagine? He thought—"

"Do you have a number for him?" I interrupted. She was taken aback.

"Whatever would *you* want his number for?"

"I need to talk to somebody in the EPA. I figured he'd be a good place to start." Her eyes glazed over.

"You're not still doing that security guard thing, are you?"

There was no point in correcting her. " 'Fraid so." Her expression screamed regret, but at least she was polite.

"I think I have one of his cards in my purse," she said, reaching behind her to the windowsill. She rooted around and came out with a business card. I reached for my notebook. She handed me the card.

"Keep it. And Leo," she whispered, "be careful of that little jerk. A bureaucrat from the top of his head down to his tasseled little shoes, if you know what I mean."

I figured this meant that she'd been only moderately successful in separating him from all his worldly goods.

Wendy, as was her custom, expected an immediate return for the favor. "Do you still own that big old house up on Queen Anne?" she asked.

"Sure do."

"You live there?"

"No. I rent it out."

"For goodness sakes, why?"

"It was my parents' house. I don't know; I just wouldn't feel right living there. I'd always hear my mother telling me to clean the place up."

Now we were on Wendy's turf. I could see the wheels turning.

"Leo," she said, moving closer, "do you have any idea what we could get for that place with the market the way it is? It must be worth at least—"

"I can't sell it."

"You can buy a lot of sentiment with a half a mil—"

"The old man left me the place in trust. I can't sell it until I'm forty-five." I'd ruined her day.

"What a pity."

"Annette sure thought so." To my ex-wife's dismay, the house and my trust had not been part of the community property settlement.

"Your father must have been quite a—"

"Good judge of character," I finished for her.

The timing was perfect. Just as Wendy was about to respond and almost certainly piss me off, Ted and Rebecca inserted themselves back into the conversation. Ted began to speak.

"So, Leo, Rebecca tells me that you're a private investigator."

"It pays the bills."

Wendy couldn't resist. "If it paid a few more, he could make an honest woman out of Rebecca here," she explained to Ed/Ted.

I could see Duvall's temple veins throbbing.

She smiled sweetly. "I think, therefore I'm single," she said. At that moment, Maureen Hennesey, with all of the usual manic effervescence that made her the chairperson of every committee in the city, lunged out of the back room.

"Bettina's reading everyone's cards on the back porch. You all have to come." Grabbing Wendy and Ted or Ed by the elbows, she herded them toward the back of the house. Rebecca and I appeared to trail along.

The minute Maureen and her prisoners rounded the corner in front of us, we made our escape. Great minds do think alike.

"I'm outta here, Waterman," Duvall announced.

"Me too. I'll walk you to your car."

Rebecca, with her usual sense of good timing, waited until we were outside to talk business.

"The *Times* made arrangements for Buddy. Seems it was part of his retirement package," she said as I opened the door for her. "They picked him up yesterday. Funeral Tuesday, at ten o'clock at McLannahans."

18

"SCREW THE POLICE department," said Jed James.

"In my past experience, it usually works the other way around, Jed."

"You haven't been served with a warrant, right?"

"Nope. I don't know what's waiting back at my place. I haven't been home in a few days. I'm over at—"

"No. Don't tell me," he snapped. "Under the circumstances, it's best I don't know where you are."

"They want me for—"

"Screw 'em," he repeated. "You've got a right to be anywhere you want to be. They've got nothing to say about when you go home and when you don't. Until such time as you're officially notified that you're wanted for questioning, you don't owe them a thing."

"Rumor has it that the TPD is looking for me pretty hard."

"Indubitably," he said quickly. "They called here Friday looking for a line on you. I had a few messages on your machine. I, of course, as an officer of the court, cooperated fully."

"Of course."

He switched gears. "I've still got that matter I needed—"

"Sorry. I've got too many loose ends right now, Jed."

"So it seems, Leo." He hesitated. "You've got all of my numbers, right? The office, the car, my home number. You got all of them?"

"Yup."

"If and when the Gestapo catches up with you, call me, day or night, and I'll come to the rescue."

"Will do."

"Remember, no statements. Just make your call."

"I'll remember."

"Later." We hung up simultaneously.

I was camped out on Arnie's back porch. Yesterday's card-reading room was Arnie's version of a home office. Probably a tax dodge.

Arnie had left early to take Bettina to the airport. I'd promised to lock up. I called Hector.

"Hector, it's Leo."

"Steel at large, eh?" He giggled maniacally. "Bueno, Leo, bueno."

"How's things around the ranch, Hector?"

"Jew was right, Leo. Dey was plenty pissed off about de car."

"I figured."

"Dey been comin back once a day to check for you. Yesterday, dey wanted to know eef I remembered eef de car had an antenna or no."

"What did you say?"

"My eeenglish no so goood, Leo. Jew know how I mean? 'Antenna? What ees dis antenna?' " He cackled wildly.

"You been watering Mrs. Gunderson's plants?"

"Got eet covered, Leo."

"See you soon."

"Not eef I see you first." He was still laughing when I hung up.

Next, I called Charles Hayden at the number Wendy had given me. Mr. Hayden was in conference. As much as it pained me, I had to use Wendy's name to get through. He was not pleased.

"What?" he demanded, without benefit of an introduction. "Let me guess, she's got a new lawyer. I don't know what she told you, buddy, but if you're working this on a percentage, you're in deep shit. They already picked me clean."

"I'm not an attorney, just a friend," I said, hoping to slow him down.

"Wendy doesn't have any friends, only victims."

"An old friend."

"What was that name again?"

"Waterman. Leo Waterman." The line was silent.

"Are you that investigator she knows from high school?"

"The very same," I answered.

He growled into my ear. "Let me guess, I'll bet this is choice, she's hired you to—"

"I'm not working for Wendy," I interrupted again. More silence.

"Sorry," he finally said. "I guess I get a little overwrought whenever that woman's name is mentioned. I didn't mean to— Anyway, what can I do for you, Mr. Waterman?"

I told him the story. I kept it vague. He listened, interrupting me only twice for clarification.

"Have you personally been to any of these sites on the maps?"

"This afternoon," I said. He tried hard to convince me not to go, but I kept talking. Later in my story, he broke in again.

"Do you know precisely what it is that they're dumping?" he asked.

"All I'm sure of is that it's worth killing over."

He mulled this over. I was hoping he'd take me seriously.

It was worse than that. He seemed genuinely concerned.

"Bring the maps on down here, Mr. Waterman. We'll handle it from—"

"No. This is something I've got to do."

"Listen, Waterman. If you don't cooperate, I can have a team of U.S. marshals—"

"You and your marshals need probable cause, don't you?"

"So?"

"Probable cause takes too much time. My guess is that whatever is going on is about to cease, at least temporarily."

"Why's that?"

I told him of my encounter with the guards at the depot. He sighed.

"What makes you think they're going to stop?"

"They were nervous already. Nervous enough to kill people," I added. "Saturday night's little encounter will probably push them over the edge. My bet is they'll go to ground."

"You may be right," he admitted. Lowering his voice. "Maybe it would be best if you could get us something solid first. With the fucking red tape the way it is around here, maybe . . ." He trailed off.

"Call me first," he said finally. "Not the police. We don't want them mucking about in anything toxic either. Call me." He rattled off a string of numbers where he could be reached. I wrote the numbers down.

"I need something from your end," I said.

"What's that?" He didn't like the sound of this.

"Can you check recent water samples from that whole section of Snohomish County?"

"Easy."

"Do it."

"Why?"

"Just might give you part of the probable cause you need."

"All right, I'll start on it as soon as I get off the phone."

He lowered his voice. "Listen, Mr. Waterman, get us something solid here. This is a governmental agency. I don't know how much attention you pay to politics, but the last couple of administrations have not been wildly supportive of our efforts. They've tied our hands in ways you wouldn't believe. These days, we need a smoking gun before we can actually do anything. Unless we actually catch somebody with his dick out, our hands are tied. Suspicions won't do it. By the time we're allowed to take action, the damage is long since done."

"I understand," I said.

"And, Mr. Waterman—"

"Yes?"

"Two things."

"Go ahead."

"One, stay away from whatever it is you find. If it's serious enough to kill over, it probably has negative long-range health consequences. Don't touch it; don't breathe it; stay away from it."

"I understand." Silence. "And two?"

"You're about to disappear from today's phone log. We never had this conversation." He hung up.

I went looking for the boys. Not at the rooming house. Not at the Zoo. They hadn't been seen at the Zoo for a couple of days. I headed downtown.

It didn't take long. On my first pass, I spotted George lounging in the doorway of a furniture warehouse three doors down from Save the Earth. He had the door open before the truck had come to a complete stop. His eyes were clear. He smelled of bay rum.

"Jesus, Leo. Where you been?" he demanded.

"Laying low, George."

"No shit," he said grimly. "I sent Ralph up to your place

to look for you yesterday morning and the cops nabbed him. Questioned him for an hour before they finally let him go."

"He's okay, I hope."

"Yeah," George smiled. "Good thing it was Ralph. If he did know anything, he probably forgot." The smile widened. "He went into Harold's seizure act; did it almost as good. Scared the shit out of them. They drove him all the way home. Even walked him upstairs." Before I could comment, he continued. "There's something going on, Leo. Something big."

"What makes you say that?"

"Lots of activity around the building. They didn't panhandle at all this weekend. Every night a whole bunch of them have been getting dressed up in dark clothes and going out."

"How many's a whole bunch?" I asked.

"Four. Five. Caroline's been going with them."

"Interesting. Any idea what they're up to?"

"Whatever it is, it takes gasoline."

"How's that? They been driving a lot?"

"Nope. They been buying gas cans at every surplus store downtown."

Now I *was* worried. Two deaths later, I was finally getting into what Tim Flood had hired me to do, and I didn't have time for it. Whatever they were up to would have to wait.

First thing this morning, I'd called Daniel Dixon and made arrangements to pick him up at the Last Stand at one o'clock. Maybe I should have let Charles Hayden and the EPA handle the map work. Maybe . . .

George bailed me out. "We got it covered, Leo. By tomorrow, we'll know where they're going every night." A shiver ran down my spine.

"I want you guys out of it, George. We don't need another killing."

"Too late, Leo. There's too many guys involved now."

"What guys? Harold and Ralph—"

George stopped me. "All the guys. We've got all the street people mobilized. They heard about Buddy and want to help. One more night and we'll know where they've been going." He hesitated. "Which reminds me, we need some more money. Me and Harold and Ralph already gave away all the cash you gave us—" He stopped again. "Buddy's share too," he said quietly. "We need more money." He held up both hands. Scout's honor. "Believe me, Leo, ain't nobody spending it on booze, but folks gotta eat, especially when they ain't drinking. Lots of bus fare too."

"Tell me about it."

"We followed 'em the first night as far as up to the market."

"On foot?"

"We only had twelve guys the first night."

"Only twelve? How many have you got now?"

"If you count Mary and Earlene, thirty-seven."

"Thirty-seven? Who in hell told you to go out and hire thirty-seven—" George reached for the door handle.

"It ain't about you no more, Leo. It's about Buddy." He eyed me levelly. "Keep your money, Leo. We don't need it." He started to get out. I stopped him.

"Okay, okay, tell me the rest of it." He left the door open.

"Well," he said, "Saturday night we had maybe twenty guys. We stationed them from where we lost them at the market all the way up to Denny. But they didn't go that far. They cut down toward Westlake."

"How do you know they're not driving all the way to Canada, for Chrissake? This is the dumbest—"

George looked hurt. "Hey, Leo, we may be drunks, but we're not stupid. All these years working for you, we learned a few things. Soon as they started acting weird, we checked the odometers in the vans. It's the same every night. First night when they came back, they left the van unlocked. We checked the mileage. Ten miles round trip." He looked sheepish. "Second night, that was Saturday, they locked up all the vans. We couldn't see in. Norman had to kick in a window." He shrugged. "Ten miles again."

"Go on."

"Anyway," he continued, "last night we had a whole shit-load of people. We started up on Westlake and stationed everybody all the way up over the University Bridge."

"And?" He had me going now.

"And they crossed the bridge and turned right. That's where we lost them. I used the last of the money this morning to get a shave and a haircut so I could take a cab along the same route. I made the driver check the mileage. It's four and a half miles from here to the other side of the University Bridge. Wherever they're going can't be much more than half a mile away."

He folded his hands in his lap and waited. I noticed then that he had a minor case of the shakes. He picked up on it.

"We're okay, Leo. A little shaky maybe, but we'll live. Hell," he added, "Ralph's beginning to form complete sentences. Who knows, another week on the wagon, he might even make sense."

"Close the door," I said.

George pulled it to. "Where we going?" he asked. "I told Norman I'd meet him and some of the others. We were gonna start walking up there early. It's a long ways. We're out of bus money, so I figured we'd better—"

"We're going to get you some money," I answered. "Where's the nearest phone booth?"

"Far end of the second lot." He pointed south. I wheeled us down to the pay phone and left George in the truck. I called Tim Flood. Frankie answered.

"Frankie, it's Leo."

"It's about time we heard from you. Tim don't like to be

paying people he don't hear from." I didn't have time for the speech.

"The shit's about to hit the fan, Frankie." Always professional, Frankie cut the shit. "Wadda you need? You need the twins?"

"Maybe later on the twins. Right now I need money."

"How much. Where to?"

"Two grand. I'll send somebody."

"Gimme a half hour."

"His name's George Paris."

"One of your bums?"

"You should hire such good bums, Frankie. He'll be there in a half hour. He needs it in cash."

"No problem."

"Something else, Frankie."

"What's that?"

"I'll do what I was hired to do, but—"

"I know you will, Leo." I could feel his smugness through the phone.

"This thing has branched out. I'm attracting some serious heat."

"Professional or official?" he asked quickly.

"Official."

"No sweat."

"I may have to tell them who I'm working for."

"Do what you have to, Leo. It's not a problem."

"You may be getting some visitors."

He stopped me. "Fat chance, Leo. You just take care of the girl."

"One more thing."

"What now?"

I told him what I needed done and why.

"It's in trust. We can't take it back."

"Can you tie it up?"

"I'm sure the legal eagles can arrange something."

"Do it," I said.

He hung up in my ear.

Once back in the truck, I fished a twenty out of my wallet and handed it to George. "Cab fare," I said. I wrote Tim's address on a piece of paper and handed it over. "Go to this address. Ask for Frankie. He's got two thousand dollars for you." George eyed the address.

"This Frankie wouldn't be Frankie Ortega, would it?"

"In the flesh."

"You have interesting friends, Leo."

"Look who's talking." We yukked it up together.

I checked my watch. Noon, straight up.

"I need to go, George." He started to get out. I stopped him. "First off, George, don't let anybody take any chances. Stay safe." He nodded. "Secondly, be careful with the money. Some of these people, you know," I stammered, "when they've got their pockets full, you know . . ."

"I know," he said sliding out the door. He stopped. "This is for Buddy, Leo. But"—he held up a finger—"whenever this is over, there's going to be one hell of a party." I didn't doubt it.

19

FIFTY YARDS FROM the crest, we went out of control.
I kept it floored. Letting up would have meant backing the
rig two miles down the mountain. The roar of the big V-8 was
lost in the cacophony of shuddering and vibrating going on
in the camper behind us, as everything that wasn't screwed
down shook loose and blindly obeyed the laws of gravity.

Again the truck desperately fought for traction, the tires
spinning wildly in the loose dust, nearly grinding us to a halt
one moment, then suddenly finding a purchase and pitching
us randomly forward the next. I fought the wheel, trying to
keep the truck centered on the narrow dirt road.

With only the left rear wheel providing intermittent
traction, the truck refused to run true. Instead, as if
remote-controlled, it angled us steadily toward the steep,
wooded gully ten feet to our right. Daniel's boots indented
the dash as he braced himself for the seemingly inevitable
ride down the gully. His hat had fallen to the floor. He left
it there. He kept his eyes straight ahead. We surged forward again, bouncing off the cut bank, showering the hood

with earth and debris, crawling upward toward the top.

Thirty yards from the top, after a particularly nasty fish-tail, the right rear wheel slipped completely over the edge. For an instant, the camper was still as it rocked and squeaked on its springs and then, in slow motion, began the inexorable slide into the dark woods.

Mindlessly, both Daniel and I shifted our weight to the left, as if that was going to help. The sound of rocks scraping on the frame filled the cab. I kept it floored.

Suddenly the drive wheel, as it passed over the berm of the road, found solid ground and again rocketed us up and forward.

"Go. Go. Go," Daniel chanted as the truck picked up speed.

The speedometer read fifty-five. We were going maybe ten. The temperature gauge was pinned in the red.

"Go. Go. Go—"

I kept the wheel crimped all the way to the left as we lurched forward. It was like driving on ice. The road leveled out. We picked up momentum. The last part, backlit by the sky, was straight up.

In the last ten yards, the forest disappeared. Blue sky and fast-moving high clouds filled the windshield. I could hear my gear against the back of the camper. We bolted over the top.

We were three rows into the new planting before I slid to a stop. I didn't have to turn the truck off. It stalled on its own. The rapidly cooling engine ticked and groaned. My hands were cramped to the wheel. I broke them loose and shook them out. A mantle of dust settled around us.

"Trees," Daniel said through the silence.

"Little trees," I confirmed.

We sat stupidly staring at a narrow forty-acre clear-cut. Symmetrical rows of four-foot Douglas fir seedlings stretched like a scar across the ridge toward the northern horizon. Only the ridge had been cut and replanted. The nearly vertical sides of the mountain shimmered blue-green, untouched.

Daniel, needing a way to control his shaking hands, stretched one of Bobby Warren's maps tightly across his lap. He locked his index finger on the yellow highlighted area. I leaned over. The notation read "6-9."

Several days in Patsy's cooler had loosened the bond between the yellow ink and the paper. Most of the yellow had transferred itself to Daniel's finger. He was concentrating too hard to notice.

Slowly swiveling his head around at the surrounding country in all four directions, he finally announced, "This is right. This is what's marked."

We got out together. The wind from the south flapped and wrapped the huge map up around Daniel's torso, forcing him to stuff it back inside the truck. He walked over to the nearest tree. I tagged along.

Taking the nearest branch in his hand, he ground the needles between his thumb and his yellowed forefinger. "Healthy as hell," he said. "Maybe four years old."

I tried it myself. He was right. No signs of disease. The needles were pliant and firmly locked onto the branches. Confusion settled over me. I don't know what I'd been expecting. Maybe steaming open pits of noxious waste bubbling to the surface. I wasn't sure. Whatever I'd had in mind, this pastoral example of excellent land use sure as hell wasn't it.

Before I could collect my thoughts, Daniel said, "Let's walk it."

He took one side. I took the other. The cut was maybe two hundred yards wide and half a mile long. We methodically walked the perimeter, each of us occasionally venturing a few rows into the planting, our solitary footprints the only blemishes in the neatly furrowed rows. Each little tree had the biodegraded remnants of a plastic tape around its base. A couple were in good enough condition to make it obvious that they'd once said something, but none were good enough to read.

I had about given up when Daniel and I met up at the far end.

"Nice planting job," he said. "One of the nicest I've seen."

"That's what I was thinking."

"Planted in June of eighty-nine," he said casually. I was in no mood for Holmesian deductions. My fear and frustration boiled to the surface.

"Did you sniff the dirt or something, Daniel? Is this some miraculous dating technique known only to indigenous peoples?"

He smiled and reached in his pocket. "Naw. I found this piece of the *Everett Herald* half buried in the ground a ways back. It was between two rocks. Kept it out of the weather."

He produced a yellowed piece of battered newsprint from his pocket and handed it over. Sure enough, barely legible, at the top of the page. June sixteenth, 1989.

"So, maybe the notations are dates."

"That's what I'm thinking," he replied. We were hell on the obvious.

We mulled this over in silence, as we picked our way back to the truck. By the time we'd gotten all four maps unfolded, the inside of the truck was full; we could no longer see one another.

"What's the oldest date you've got on yours?" I asked.

"Four-dash-eight," he replied after a great deal of rustling.

"I've got a seven-dash-seven," I said.

"What's the newest?"

We rustled, folded, refolded, and cursed for several minutes. Finally Daniel announced, "I've got a nine-dash-one. That's last month."

"Newer than anything I've got," I said finally.

"New or old?" he asked.

"I don't know. What do you think?"

"New's only a few miles up the road."

"Let's try that one," I said, starting the truck.

It took another five minutes of folding, cursing, and re-folding the maps before I could see out the windshield.

Everything was the same. Logging road twenty-eight-dash-two-five was, to all intents and purposes, the same rutted track from which we'd just descended. Not as steep, but nearly as ugly. The truck, burdened by the top-heavy weight of the camper, lurched alarmingly over the ruts, at times threatening to topple completely over. No sweat. After our last ride, this one was a walk in the park.

Everything was the same. Newly planted ridge. Smaller trees.

"Well," started Daniel, "we were right about the dates."

"Still got the little orange tapes around the bases."

"Just planted," he confirmed.

"Be right back," I said as I walked over and liberated one of the little orange plastic tapes from the base of the nearest seedling. I handed it to Daniel. "Greenside Up, Everett, Washington," he read.

"It's a start."

"THAT'S ONE OF ours all right," he said, turning the little orange ribbon over in his fingers. "I hope you didn't damage the tree getting it off. They're quite delicate when they're this young."

I assured him we hadn't damaged the little buggers. His name was Herb Stratton. Sole proprietor of Greenside Up. He was short and slim. Not skinny, but incredibly wiry and athletic. A pared-down pile of bone and sinew. He'd compensated for his totally bald pate by growing a black, bushy Smith

Brothers beard. Four earrings in his right ear. His age was anybody's guess. He could have been twenty-five or he could have been fifty-five. There wasn't enough of his face showing to tell. Only the twinkling blue eyes.

"What else can you tell us from the ribbon?" I asked.

"Everything. I keep it all on the computer." A Macintosh flickered gray on the desk behind him.

"Would you look this one up for us?"

"Don't need to." I thought maybe he was smiling behind all the hair.

"It was the last job we did. Only finished about three weeks ago."

"Nice work," said Daniel.

"A no-brainer," Stratton replied.

"Why's that?" I asked.

"We only had to replant the ridge. The tribe's one of the few timber owners who have any sense of decent land use. Unlike most of them, they've got more sense than to screw up the drainage and the fishery. They leave the slopes alone. It's the slopes that are a killer to replant."

I started to speak, but he anticipated my question. "You've never lived till you've hand-planted some of those slopes, man. A dozen men can barely manage four acres a day." He shuddered visibly. "This one"—he waved the orange ribbon—"we did the better part of forty acres in a day and a half. It was like that on all of them."

"All of them?"

"Sure. We've done seven or eight of them in the past couple of years. All of them perfect. Great access. All graded flat. Not even slash piles to work around. Neatest sites I've ever seen."

I pulled the maps from the tube and spread them over the counter.

"These?" I asked, pointing at the highlighted areas.

Without answering, he pushed a few keys on the computer. The screen filled with a list of names and numeric notations. Stratton methodically worked from the maps to the screen and back.

Finally, after several rechecks, he ran his fingers through his thick beard and said, "You've got one too many." He pulled at his beard again.

"Which one?" I asked.

"This one." He pointed to a yellowed spot on the center map. "We haven't done this one."

"You sure?" I asked. He breathed a sigh of exasperation.

"Of course I'm sure. These were the best damn sites I've had to work with in twenty years. I'm sure as hell not going to forget one of them."

Silence settled over the little office as the three of us stared at the spot on the map. Finally Stratton said, "Check with Winthrop Logging. Maybe they'll know something. They get there before we do. Maybe it's new."

"Thanks," I said.

"Glad to help. If we could just get more companies to be—"

While Daniel and I rolled the maps up, Stratton rambled on. Without being asked, he wrote down Winthrop's address on a pink Post-it note. My hands were full. He stuck it to my coat.

"Listen, Mr. Waterman," he said as I opened the door, "if you get a chance, thank Winthrop for the cleanup job. It's so seldom that anybody bothers to—" I assured Stratton that I'd convey his appreciation.

"BULLSHIT," was the first word out of his mouth.

"What's bullshit?" I asked.

"You're bullshit." I was glad we'd cleared that up. He wasn't through. "Who the fuck do you think you're fooling?

You're just some kind of goddamn inspector." With one brawny arm, he swept the maps to the floor. They covered my feet. "Take those fucking maps and get out, before I shove 'em up your ass. You got any complaints about those sites, you go see the tribe. We got it in writing. It's in the contract. It's all there in black and white. If they'd wanted cleanup, we'd never have taken the job. Barely turned a profit as it was. Shitty little sites. Damn near not worth dragging the equipment up there. Fucking regulations."

His eyes narrowed. He reached out quickly and grabbed my shirt front, pulling me halfway over the counter. "Let me tell you something, pal. My family's been logging this area for forty-five years. Used to be lots of families around here made their living logging. We're damn near all that's left. You understand that? Huh, do you? Rest of them are working in some stinking factory somewhere. You come in here with that bullshit about—" Disgusted, he let go and straight-armed me back two steps. "Get out." He pointed toward the door. Daniel crumpled the maps to his chest and backed out the door. I wasn't far behind.

Daniel and I sat in the truck as he refolded the maps.

"Did you catch his name?" Daniel asked.

"We never got that far. Sounded like a Winthrop, though."

"Planters were a lot friendlier than cutters."

"Considerably," I agreed.

"Was interesting, though."

"Very," I agreed again.

Daniel read my mind. "If the loggers aren't cleaning up the sites, then who is?"

"Good question, Daniel. A mighty good question," I mumbled absentmindedly. "Be right back," I said. I headed back inside.

The little bell over the door tinkled my arrival. He came

out from the office in the back, took one look at me, and started around the corner for me, fists clenched at his sides. I began to babble.

"Look, Mr.—" I held up both hands in front of me. "I'm not here to make trouble. I'm not with the EPA or the Forest Service or any other agency." He kept coming, his eyes pinched down to slits.

"You got big balls, pal," he muttered, still advancing.

"A friend of mine's dead," I blurted as he stepped up to me. He stopped. "Dead?" he repeated.

"Murdered." He momentarily relaxed, then tensed again. "If you're some kind of insurance—"

"No insurance," I said quickly. He again relaxed slightly.

Before he could regroup, I told him as much of the story as he needed to know. He listened without interrupting. When I'd finished, I handed him a business card. He studied it.

"So who are you working for?" he asked. Good question.

"Myself, I guess." He stuck out a hand. I flinched.

"Winnie Winthrop," he said. My hand disappeared into his.

"Leo Waterman."

"Busted his fingers and then shot him in the head?"

I nodded. He shook his head sadly. "An old guy, you said?"

"Sixty-six."

"Jesus Christ." More head shaking. "My dad's sixty-six."

He leaned back against the counter, folding his big arms across his red suspenders. "Who did the replant?" he asked.

"A company called Greenside Up."

"Bunch of goddamn hippies." He pulled at his ear. "But they do a good job," he added grudgingly.

He massaged the problem for a moment. "Wait here," he said and stalked back into the office. His cutoff pants ended six inches above his work boots.

I walked back out to the truck and retrieved the maps. Daniel seemed surprised that I was still in one piece. I went back inside. Half of a muffled phone conversation leaked out of the back room. I waited.

Winthrop reappeared, shaking his head again.

"Good thing you're a detective."

"Why's that?"

" 'Cause you got you a mystery here, Mr. Waterman."

"The cleanup?" I ventured.

"No shit."

"So you guys aren't cleaning up the sites."

"Cleaning up?" he laughed. "We aren't even burning the slash. We're just cutting, bucking, and yarding them out. It's like I said, the only reason we took the job was because we didn't have to clean 'em up. Got it in writing. Couldn't even do it except it's on the reservation. The tribe don't have to live by all the fucking government regulations. Stratton at Greenside says the sites are stumped and graded when he gets there. No burn piles. Says they look like football fields."

"A third contractor?" I suggested.

"No fuckin' way. Wouldn't begin to pay for the gas. No way."

I spread the maps out again, covering the entire counter.

"Could you check these against your records?" I asked.

Winnie wasn't computerized. He pulled an enormous ledger book out from under the counter and spent the next five minutes cross-checking with the maps. The door tinkled. Daniel had either gotten tired of waiting or was concerned for my safety. Winnie looked up briefly and went back to his checking. "That's all of them," he announced, shutting the book with a bang.

"No extras?" Daniel asked from behind me.

"Nope."

Daniel stepped forward, pushed the maps around until

he found the right one and pointed to the spot. "What about this one?"

Winnie leaned over. Confused, he turned the map around to face him, reopened the book, and checked again.

"That's the new one. Finished it last Friday."

Daniel and I exchanged glances.

"How come Greenside doesn't know about this site?" I asked.

"No reason for them to know until we settle up with the tribe."

"How long does that take?"

"Terms are net thirty."

"Who pays who?" I asked.

"We pay the tribe. We scale the logs, figure board feet, the tribe sends somebody down to check, and after we agree on a figure, we pay the tribe."

"Who exactly do you pay?" asked Daniel, close and interested now.

"Tribal Resources. Guy named Short." Daniel looked grim.

Winthrop slammed the book shut again. Daniel retrieved the maps.

"Thanks, Mr. Winthrop," I said without offering my hand up for slaughter.

"Get 'em," he said. "Sixty-six. Who in hell would—? Get 'em."

20

❖

THE BIG FLATBED burst out of the trees into the roadway. Startled, I stood on the brakes. The pickup skidded to a halt. Everything loose in the camper slid to the front.

The truck driver punched the air horn angrily as he roared by, headed back the way we'd come. The truck was empty. The only cargo was a green tarp, neatly folded and tied down on the bed, close up to the red cab.

Dust hung suspended in the air. Daniel checked the map. "That's the one," he announced.

The thick red dust settled on the windshield. I turned on the wipers. The washer was empty. The dry wipers dragged and scraped the dust, clearing two fans of visibility. I eased the truck forward.

Sixty yards up the road, I spotted what appeared to be a small turnout on the opposite side of the road and rolled the truck in.

The overgrown gravel road had once been a driveway. The carcass of a moss-covered cabin sagged and leaned forlornly in a ragged clearing, the broken ends of its collapsed roof pointing skyward like bleaching ribs. The doors and windows turned to dust, the brown unpainted siding buckled under the strain of a wicked lean to the right.

I U-turned the truck in the front yard and got out. Daniel followed me around to the back of the truck as I unlocked the camper.

Leaning in, I pulled the seat cushion from the dinette seat, reached way down into the wheel well, and fished out Bobby Warren's bag. I dug out the nine-millimeter and turned to hand it to Daniel. No Daniel.

He stood just inside the front door of the cabin, kicking around in the rubble with the toe of one boot. He squatted and peered up under a lean-to-like area formed where a section of roof clung tenaciously to the wall, defying gravity.

Using the makeshift roof for support, he leaned down, reached in, and came out with a half-full two-liter bottle of Coke. He swiveled his head, caught my eyes, and said, "Classic Coke." As usual, I was lost.

"If you're thirsty," I started.

"Nobody's lived here for fifty years," he interrupted.

"So?"

"Bottle's brand-new." He agitated the liquid. "Still got the fizz."

"Bums—campers—who knows."

He grunted in return, carefully replacing the bottle where he'd found it. He ambled over. I held out the nine-millimeter. Without a word, he took it, noiselessly working the slide, checking the load. "Nice piece," he said quietly and tried to hand it back.

"Keep it. You might need it," I said, pulling the rolled-up blanket from the bag. Daniel peered over my shoulder as I unrolled the blanket and exposed the wicked little automatic and the four banana clips.

"Looks like a toy," he commented.

I pulled the wire shoulder brace along the top of the gun and snapped it into place, transforming the pistol into a rifle.

"The Indians are outgunned again," Daniel said, as I held the weapon up to my shoulder and checked the feel.

"You can have this one if you want," I said, offering the gun.

"No thanks." He bounced the nine-millimeter in his palm. "This little baby will do me just fine. I do appreciate a man who comes loaded for bear though," he added with a wink.

I unclipped the shoulder strap from both ends of Bobby's bag and fed it through the automatic's handle, clipping the ends together to form a loop. I took off my jacket and slipped the loop over my shoulder. The gun hung down to my belt. After tearing out the right-hand pocket, I put the jacket back on. The elastic at the bottom of the jacket held the gun firmly in place. My right hand had easy access to the trigger guard. I filled the left-hand pocket with the three remaining clips. Floyd would have been proud of me.

"Ready?" I asked Daniel.

"Ready," he said. "You expecting trouble?"

"This stuff," I said, patting the gun through my coat, "is purely for defensive purposes. Just to make sure we get out of here." He nodded.

We started up the road. When we reached the bottom of the logging road, I instinctively started toward the low side. Daniel stopped me with a hand on the shoulder.

"Let's stay high," he said. "It'll be easier going. They push all the road debris downhill."

I took his word for it and followed him up the little bank to our left. For the first five hundred yards the going was slow as we traversed a series of brush-filled gullies. The road builders had used up the whole ridgeline, leaving us with only a tangled roller coaster of loose sidehill to walk on. For another quarter mile we trudged on, Daniel in the lead.

The loose dirt was taking a toll on my legs. My calves were in knots. Daniel seemed unaffected. I tugged at the back of Daniel's jacket. "Maybe you should stop for a minute," I wheezed. He grinned.

"I'm fine," he said, the grin getting bigger.

"Well, I'm not."

"You gotta get in shape, Leo."

"I thought I was."

"It's that city life." I couldn't disagree.

We sat together on a downed pine. I started to speak. Daniel held a finger to his lips. "Listen. You hear it?" he whispered.

I listened. All I could hear was the blood pounding in my temples. I shook my head. "Listen," he repeated.

I listened. Slowly, as the sounds of my own body quieted, I became aware of the faint sound of machinery in the distance. More than one machine. Idling, then laboring, then the whoop, whoop of backing up.

"Not far," he said quietly. Without another word, he rose from the log and started uphill. I followed, using both hands to grab the pine saplings and pull myself up the slope. Without my hand to hold it in place, the automatic banged incessantly against my right hipbone, rubbing it raw. I ignored it. Compared to the cramping in my calves, the chafing of the gun was barely noticeable.

The machinery was louder now. Neither the scraping of my feet nor the sound of my labored breathing could drown it out. Daniel was ten yards in front of me, off to the left, moving easily through the tangled underbrush.

I put my head down and tried to gain ground. The loose earth sent me skiing six feet back downhill. Only the top of Daniel's head was visible above the brush. He seemed to be stopped.

Gathering myself, I gave it all I had and sprinted up the

hill. My hip joints threatened to fall out of the sockets, but I kept my legs going. Daniel was ten yards to my left. He hissed and held up a hand. I lowered my head and thundered on. No stopping now. Daniel hissed more urgently. Ten more paces. I only got two.

Fifteen feet to my left, Daniel had a ringside seat as I lumbered uphill and stepped off into space. The last picture my mind snapped was that of Daniel shaking his head sadly as I turned a complete somersault in midair and landed flat on my back. The air whooshed from my body. My throat seemed to close.

The clearing was much the same as the others. A narrow strip along the ridgeline. All similarities ended there. A hundred-foot-wide trench had been gouged twenty feet deep through the center of the cut. They'd worked their way about halfway down the length of the clearing. At the far end, the trench had already been filled.

Two flatbed semis were backed up to the trench, adding their cargoes to the hundreds of fifty-five-gallon drums that already filled the trench. Two bulldozers, rumbling at idle, their black diesel smoke staining the air, stood ready to cover and smooth the area.

Three hundred yards away perhaps a dozen men were working the area. Three rolling barrels off each truck, four or five standing around the trench, the dozer operators at the ready. Or at least, they had been working. Frozen in time, they all stood stock-still and stared at me as I slowly slid to the bottom of the hill. For an instant, no one moved.

I saw but didn't hear a shout as one of the men standing by the side of the trench opened his mouth wide and pointed at me. All heads turned. The shouter sprinted for one of the green pickups scattered around.

I rolled to my stomach. My lungs were still empty. Getting to my knees seemed to take an eternity. I looked helplessly toward the top of the bank. Daniel was nowhere to be seen. I cursed him.

Willing my legs under me, I tried vainly to scramble back up the bank. The ground was too soft; the hill too steep. Instead of propelling me upward, my feet sank into the hill, filling my sneakers with the loose dirt. I slid back to the bottom.

I looked to my left. The top of the logging road was eighty yards away. Behind me, in the clearing, one of the trucks screamed to life. I'd never make it to the road. Silently cursing Daniel again, I tried to control my shaking fingers and unzip my jacket, groping spastically for the automatic.

I was fully exposed, silhouetted against the red dirt of the hillside. Waterman's last stand was going to be brief and bloody.

I rolled onto my back, pointing the automatic back toward the clearing. A tree hit me in the face. Cursing again, I rolled to my right. Daniel was on his knees at the top of the bank, holding the butt end of the uprooted tree.

"Grab on," he yelled.

I let go of the automatic, grabbed the dead tree, and started hand-over-handing myself up the bank. Daniel stood and began to back up, yarding me up the eight-foot embankment.

Halfway to the top, all hell broke loose. Although I couldn't hear the sounds of gunfire, slugs began hissing into the bank on either side of me like angry bees. I looked back. The green pickup was halfway across the clearing, bouncing insanely across the furrowed ground, the driver firing out the window, bearing down on the base of the embankment. I pulled and climbed.

As I threw my right leg over the top, a sudden sensation of heat told me that a slug had passed within inches of my head. My right ear buzzed. Releasing the tree, I grabbed both hands full of the thick grass that carpeted the top of the knoll and rolled up and over the edge.

Daniel, who had been leaning back into the tree at a forty-five-degree angle, fell heavily onto his back amid the scrub brush. The green pickup skidded to a halt at the bottom of the bank. Another bullet sailed perilously close to my head.

The driver, no longer impeded by the bouncing of the truck, braced his left arm on the window frame and showed me a mouth full of yellow teeth. The bore of his chrome automatic looked as big as a sewer pipe. My chest ached as he brought his face right down into his shooting hand and sighted in. He grinned again. I was paralyzed.

Then the windshield of the truck exploded. Daniel had righted himself and lay prone on the ground beside me, using two hands, calmly squeezing off rounds at the driver, who, unexpectedly faced with the prospect of return fire, went wide-eyed, threw the truck into reverse, and bounced back more or less the way he'd come.

The remnants of the windshield slid down over the hood as the truck picked up speed. The driver, his attention welded to Daniel and me, steered with one hand and fired repeatedly out through the gutted front window with the other. He was still firing wildly when the rear of the truck struck a large stump, spun wickedly to the right, and toppled over on its right side into the open trench.

"Look at 'em scurry," Daniel breathed.

He was right. The other workers, having witnessed our encounter with the truck driver, had abandoned pursuit and were hunkered down behind the trucks and machinery.

I wiped the sweaty side of my neck. My hand came away red. I stared idiotically at my hand, rubbing the oily blood between my thumb and fingers. I scraped more blood off my neck and stared some more.

"You lost an earlobe," Daniel said.

Before I could comprehend, the passenger door of the green pickup, now pointing straight up in the ditch, opened, and the driver's head appeared through the window.

I pulled the automatic up, flipped off the safety, and tried to rake the truck. The automatic pulled violently up and to the right. The first few rounds were low, puffing the dirt in front of the trench. The next five or so hit the truck, shattering the passenger window. The rest could have been considered out-of-season goose hunting. By the time the clip was empty, the little gun was pointing nearly straight up. All heads had disappeared.

"We better get out of here," I panted.

"Good idea."

We lunged back down the mountain a hell of a lot faster than we'd come up, picking our way among the maze of roots and snags that littered the ground, keeping as far away from the road as the terrain would allow. Halfway down, running out of control, I tripped over an exposed root and fell headlong into Daniel's back, slamming us both to the ground.

I scrambled up and offered Daniel a hand. His nose was bleeding. Wiping it with the back of his index finger, he shook his head and put the bloody finger to his lips. We listened together. Nothing.

"They're not coming after us," he said finally. I silently agreed.

"It looked like maybe only the guy in the truck was armed."

"You think we discouraged them?"

"What you mean *we*, white man?"

I couldn't argue. Instead, I pulled him to his feet and pointed him back down the mountain. Under control now, I watched my feet and followed.

We hadn't gone a quarter mile when the road, now two hundred yards to our left, overflowed with the sounds of straining vehicles. We hunkered down in the bushes, listening intently for sounds of pursuit.

While we listened and counted vehicles, I fumbled the exhausted clip from the automatic and reached for one of the spares. There was only one in my pocket. I'd lost the other two. Cursing myself now, I snapped the clip into place, swinging the gun in a wide arc as if to frighten off would-be attackers.

"They're running," Daniel announced. I listened. He was right. I could hear the trucks moving up through the gears as they hit the main road, their labored roaring fading slowly into the distance.

"How many went by?" I asked as the silence settled in upon us.

"Four."

"How many were there?"

"I was too busy saving your ass to count," he answered. "But the one in the ditch ain't goin' anywhere."

I changed the subject. "We need to get to a phone."

"No phone anyplace around here. We'll have to head back to that store we passed about six miles back."

"It's time to call in the cavalry."

Daniel got to his feet and brushed himself off. When he got around to his hair, he noticed that his hat was missing. I couldn't remember whether he'd had it on when we'd started down the mountain. Daniel was disgusted. "The cavalry, huh. You do have a way with words, Leo. You truly do."

Moving slowly now, we picked our way carefully back down the mountain, until we came to the edge of the road. Daniel stepped into the ditch, poked his head out between the bushes, and surveyed the road in both directions. Nothing. We were directly across from the abandoned driveway where we'd parked the truck.

We trotted across. As Daniel disappeared up the drive, something beckoned me to turn and take a last look at the hillside. The sight stopped me in my tracks.

"Daniel!" I shouted.

I heard the sound of his feet on the loose gravel beside me. I couldn't drag my eyes from the enormous plume of black smoke that was trying to rise from the top of the hill. The plume shot up a couple of hundred feet and then flattened out, refusing to drive with the wind, as if pulled back to earth by its own opaque density.

"Jesus," I heard Daniel mutter.

"They set the woods on fire."

"That ain't wood smoke. Woods are too wet to burn." He scratched his head. "I never seen smoke looks like that."

This last comment snapped me to attention. I remembered Charles Hayden's warnings. Involuntarily, I held my breath.

I squeezed "Let's go" out from between my teeth.

My tone got his attention. Exchanging as little air as possible, we hustled back to the truck, rolled up the windows, and bounced back out onto the paved road.

A mile up the road, driving far too fast for a particularly nasty corner, I had to swerve to avoid crashing into three blue chemical drums that, having burst on impact, were now spewing their gleaming, black, tarlike contents onto the road.

"Looks like one of the trucks lost part of its load."

"Hurry," he said. "We gotta report this."

"Then we're gonna have a talk with this guy, Howard Short," I said.

"After we report it," Daniel insisted. "This is bad stuff, Leo."

He was right. First things first.

21

"FIRST WE HAD a deal and you tried to screw us. Then we give you the benefit of the doubt, cut you another deal, and now you try to screw us again. I'm beginning to wonder about you, Hayden. I'm beginning to think Wendy was right." The last part fried his brain.

"The deal didn't include murder, dammit," Charles Hayden snapped. "I'm way outside my umbrella of authority here, Waterman. My ass is in a sling. Not only is this guy Short found sitting there, big as life, in his office with a bullet in his head, but he's an Ind"—he remembered Daniel—"a Native American. The local authorities ... I'm a public serv—" He threw up his hands.

"A deal's a deal," I insisted.

"Another broken promise by the Great White Father," Daniel solemnly intoned, shaking his head sadly. I tried not to laugh.

Hayden turned his back to us, running both hands through his thinning razor-cut hair, staring out the front window of the little store as yet another fire engine raced by to join the melee up the road.

Daniel bobbed his eyebrows up and down, grinning at me behind Hayden's back. I forced my face to stay still. My ear throbbed. We waited.

It was now nearly ten at night, the purple sky straining its way toward complete darkness. I felt as if I'd been sitting in the store for days.

It was a little after three-thirty when I'd first burst through the door of the Lucky Seven Mini-Mart demanding to use the phone. I must have been a sight. One look at me and the woman immediately bent down behind the counter. In my confused state, I thought she was going for a gun and raised the automatic to waist level. She came up with a baby.

"No, mister, please," she wailed. Two big tears plowed furrows down her round cheeks. "Take whatever you want, but please——" She stopped. "Daniel?" she said tentatively.

Daniel stepped around me. "Winona," he said, "take the baby and go on back to the trailer. We got trouble here. Go." He pointed.

Winona needed no further encouragement. Clutching the baby to her chest, she turned on her heel and hustled out the back of the store. I called Charles Hayden.

He must have left my name with the receptionist. She immediately slipped me through the system.

"What is it, Waterman? I've got a meeting."

"I've got your smoking gun."

"What? Christ. Who?"

"I don't know. They got away."

"What were they doing?"

"Dumping waste."

"What waste?"

"I don't know," I said again. "Barrels. They set them on

fire. You told me not to get anywhere near it." I could hear him gulp air.

"Where are you?"

"I need a deal."

"What deal? This is no time for that crap. Don't you realize—"

"You'll keep both of us out of the hands of the local authorities."

"How in hell am I going to arrange that?"

"Arrest us. You Feds have authority over the locals. I don't give a shit. Do whatever it takes. When this is over, we go with you, or we just go."

"I can't— Where are you?"

"Deal?"

He expelled the air he'd gulped earlier. "Deal," he said.

I put Daniel on the phone. He calmly gave Hayden directions. Daniel handed the phone back to me.

"He wants to talk to you again." Mindlessly, I jammed the phone onto my injured ear. I reeled around the store in pain. Transferring the phone to my good ear, I said, "Hurry."

"Make sure you stay there," he said. The line went dead.

Honor was not Charles Hayden's strong suit. He called the cops. A pair of Washington State Police were the first to arrive. Young and edgy, they came in crouched, SWAT-team style, one in the front, one in the back, guns at the ready. I was glad I'd remembered to return the automatic and the nine-millimeter to their hiding place under the seat cushion.

"Don't move," the front door cop growled.

Daniel and I were sitting, side by side, on the counter.

"Who's moving?" I asked.

"You see anybody moving?" Daniel deadpanned, scanning the ceiling.

"Maybe you should try 'stay where you are,'" I suggested. "That would make more sense, under the circumstances."

From behind us, "Put your hands up. Now."

"No," I said calmly. "Our hands are in plain sight right here on the counter. Your partner can see them." Partner moved his head up and down.

I could hear their labored breathing. The academy hadn't covered this.

"Didn't they tell you about the spill?" Daniel asked.

"What spill?" From behind us again.

"There's a toxic spill five miles up the road. Somebody needs to block the road. God only knows what's in those drums."

"God only knows," Daniel parroted.

"You said that call was from the EPA?" From behind the ice cream freezer in front of us.

"Yeah." From the back of the store.

Still combat-ready, they emerged from the cover. "Hold your arms out."

This seemed reasonable. We complied.

Even after patting us down, they listened to the rest of our story over the sights of their revolvers. The big one, whose name tag identified him as Probationary Trooper Derek Coffey, stayed with us, while his partner raced off to set up a roadblock.

Trooper Coffey was a man of little faith and even less humor. The dust from his partner's exit was still in the air when he reverted to type.

"All right, you two, over there"—pointing at the north wall—"assume the position. Let's go, move it. MOVE IT," he bellowed.

"No," I said again. "And hold the command voice, will you?" Daniel reamed an ear with his pinkie. "You've frisked us. We're not armed. Besides that, Daniel here is a Native American. A Tulalip. This is the Tulalip Reservation. You have no authority over Mr. Dixon. Only the Tribal Police

Force has jurisdiction here." Daniel silently agreed.

Rebuffed and unsure, Trooper Coffey kept his slitlike eyes glued to our chests and his hand on the butt of his revolver, uncertainly waiting for help to arrive.

Charles Hayden and an eight-man toxic disposal team arrived forty minutes later. The clock on the wall read four-twenty. On his way through the door, he flashed his credentials at Trooper Coffey and then fumbled the badge to the floor when he spotted Daniel and me. "What—" slipped out.

He turned on the cop. "I thought I told you to—"

"This is the reservation. Only the Tribal Police Force . . ." the cop blurted.

"There is no goddamn Tribal Police Force."

Disgustedly, Hayden snatched his identification from the floor.

The young officer reached for his piece again. Hayden stopped him.

"No, no—never mind," he sighed.

He turned to us. "One of you will have to show us the place," he announced without enthusiasm. "First we need to identify the specific agent. We need to know exactly what we're dealing with here."

"There's several drums of the stuff spread all over the road about five miles up," I said.

"My partner's got a roadblock set," announced Coffey.

Hayden ignored him, dashing back out the front door. His white-overalled team, which had already begun unloading its gear, flung everything back into the sparkling unmarked white truck and disappeared up the road. We waited.

At five o'clock straight up, the truck returned. The guy in the passenger seat was out and sprinting toward the door before the vehicle was fully stopped. He was wearing the spaceman hat that zipped into the overalls.

"Liquid PCBs," was his muffled shout from behind the plastic faceplate.

"Damn," muttered Hayden.

He collected himself. "Okay, first clean up the road; we're gonna need it."

Spacesuit nodded. Hayden continued, shouting his way through the headgear. "I'll get us a lot more help up here." More agreement.

Hayden jerked his thumb toward Daniel and me. "One of these guys can show you the site that's on fire," he shouted at spacesuit.

Spacesuit shook his helmet. I couldn't make out the garbled phrases leaking out from the suit. Obviously, Hayden could.

"Good, good," he said finally. "Okay, get to it."

"They can see the smoke," he said to no one in particular.

Charles Hayden trotted for the phone. Daniel and I leaned back against the counter and waited. When he finished mumbling into the phone, Hayden turned his attention back to me and Daniel.

"This is reservation property, right?" I shrugged and turned to Daniel.

"Sort of," Daniel replied. "This whole end is land that the tribe sold a few years ago for a couple of golf courses and housing developments. That's how come nobody lives out there."

"So where's the houses?" Hayden demanded.

"It's all tied up in court," Daniel said. "Lots of the property turned out to be under the Wetlands Act. A bunch of environmental groups stuck their faces in. The developers can't get permits to build anything." He stopped. "Gonna be years," he added with a trace of a smile. "Maybe never."

Hayden pulled out a little notepad. "Who handles this sort of thing for the tribe?" Daniel silently looked my way. So much for our little talk with Mr. Short.

"Might as well tell him," I whispered. "They'll just bust everybody's balls until they find out." He thought it over.

"Howard Short," he said after a minute. "Resources department. He's got a little office out by the highway. Right behind the liquor store."

Hayden crooked a finger at the impassive Trooper Coffey. Coffey reluctantly separated himself from the pop cooler, the contents of which he was making a serious dent in, and shuffled over. Hayden tore the page from his pad and held it out to the officer.

"Round up your partner and get this guy down here."

Coffey eyed him sullenly, a silent challenge to Hayden's presumed authority. He stared blankly at the piece of paper without making a move to take it. Charlie Hayden shook it in his face.

"You want to call your superior? Is that it?" No response. Hayden's ears were bright red.

"Feel free to use the radio in the aid unit out front. Check with anybody you can think of, but get your ass in gear unless you want to finish your career as a school crossing guard. Is that clear, Trooper Coffey?"

Coffey took the page as if he were holding a dog turd, stepped around Hayden, and made his way out front.

"Fucking locals are such a pain in the ass," Hayden said after the door had swung shut. "Every time we—"

His tirade was interrupted by the scratching of his handheld radio, which rested on the counter between Daniel and me. Somehow, from all the squeaks and burps, Hayden could tell it was for him. He turned his back, held the radio to his ear, and screeched back and forth for the better part of five minutes, then signed off and headed for the phone again.

After that, things really got rolling. Within an hour, no less than four fire engines, their crews wearing full respirator units, had roared past the Lucky Seven on their way to the site.

Fresh out of people to call, Hayden turned his attention to us.

"It would have been better if you'd just called me and not gone blundering in there yourselves." Daniel shot me a knowing grimace.

"You wanted a smoking gun," I said.

"What I didn't need was a smoking pile of PCBs. Do you have any idea how toxic PCBs are?"

"Not really," I answered.

"Lung cancer, skin cancer, lymph cancer. You name it, you can get it from that stuff." Daniel shuddered. Hayden continued. "If the wind were from the west, we'd be evacuating Marysville right now, but we got a break." It was his turn to shudder as he ran that movie. Local bureaucrat evacuates entire city. He shuddered again. "Thank God, the smoke cloud is blowing out over the Sound." He shook his head. "What I can't figure out is how they got that stuff burning at all."

"Why? Is it hard?" I asked.

"Damn hard," he replied. "Incineration is the only approved method for getting rid of PCBs, but it takes twenty-one hundred degrees and a kiln to incinerate the stuff. That's why it's so expensive to dispose of. It all gets sent out to Kansas to be incinerated in a wet-walled slagging kiln. It takes—"

He was interrupted by the return of Trooper Coffey. The young cop stood in the doorway, his hand once again resting on the butt of his gun, gesturing with his head for Hayden to step outside. Resignedly, Hayden went onto the porch.

Coffey had company. In addition to his partner, who fidgeted nervously behind the wheel of the cruiser, two Snohomish County cops stood by an unmarked Chevy.

Charles Hayden was running his hands through his well-tended hair again. The cops seemed unimpressed. Hayden turned to come back inside. The troopers made a move to follow. Hayden held them off, closing the door behind him. He fixed on Daniel.

"Your friend Mr. Short—"

Uncharacteristically, Daniel interrupted. "He's not my friend."

Hayden regrouped. "Fellow tribe member—"

"He's not a tribe member either. He's a Cree."

"Whatever he is, Mr. Dixon, he's dead." Hayden mindlessly massaged the bridge of his nose. "The officers found him sitting in his office, with a bullet wound to the head."

"Suicide?" I asked.

"The officers don't seem to think so. He's been dead a couple of days, they say. They want—" He hesitated, squared his shoulders, and turned his attention to me. "They want to take you two with them for questioning. They say it's just routine. Why don't you two just—"

"What about our deal?" I said. Hayden had been waiting.

"You didn't tell me you were already wanted for questioning. That wasn't part of the agreement, Waterman. I can't possibly keep a lid on this. If I'd known—"

"If I'd known you weren't good for your word, I would never have called you to begin with and you wouldn't be sitting on the biggest bust of your career. But that's all water under the bridge, isn't it? Let's deal with the present. Think about it, Hayden. This is a lot cleaner deal without Daniel and me. We're not looking for any publicity in this. You can have this one to yourself." His eyes widened at the thought.

He started to respond, thought better of it, sighed, and turned pensively back toward the window, rocking slowly on his feet. "Okay," he said finally, and then fell back to thinking. I felt as if I'd missed part of the conversation.

"Okay," he said again. "Here's what I'm going to do—"

He never got to the rest of it. The white van in which he'd originally arrived slid to a stop in front of the store. One of the spacemen, his helmet in hand now, got out and started across the lot. Something about the white suit, stained now with soot and tarlike residue, gave the officers the urge to keep their distance. The minute he started toward them, they backed quickly toward their respective vehicles. He opened the door and came inside.

He was about thirty, his black curly hair plastered to his head, two black streaks running down along his right cheek.

Without preamble, he started to speak. Hayden gestured him toward the center of the store, away from the door.

"Well?" Hayden asked.

"It's under control," he said. "We got it out."

"How much was there?"

"Hard to tell. A lot's covered over already."

"An estimate?"

"At least a thousand, fifteen hundred drums, maybe more."

"Jesus. Must be a recycler then."

"Oh yeah. No way it can be a user. Way too much of it."

"Jesus," Hayden repeated. He rubbed his hands together. "Okay, here's what we're going to do. First of all, we're going to evacuate all civilians in the immediate area."

"It's under control. We got it out," the guy protested.

"Trust me on this, will you, Larry?" Larry looked dubious.

Without giving Larry a chance to respond one way or the other, he continued. "I want to leave a fire team there all night, just to make sure we've got it out. We'll start cleanup in the morning. No sense taking chances in the dark." Larry agreed. "In the meantime, clear the area."

Larry looked out over his shoulder toward the parking lot.

"Nobody out there except a few cops," he noted.

"Exactly," said Hayden.

A thin smile crossed Larry's lips. "Oh. It's them you want to—"

"I didn't say that," Hayden corrected quickly. "I merely want to protect the public from the deleterious effects of these materials." The smile got bigger.

"I don't know—" Larry started.

Hayden threw an arm around Larry's shoulders. "Larry, what we've got here is probably one of the biggest toxic waste cleanups in history. If Waterman here is right, we've got eight of these sites beyond this one, to clean up. There are promotions to be had here, lad. You hear what I'm saying?" Larry nodded gravely. "We don't need any meddling by local authorities, now do we?"

"No, sir."

"Do you suppose those gentlemen have any idea of the possible health effects of these materials?"

"Probably not."

"Do you imagine they know what PCBs can do to a man's reproductive organs?"

"Probably not."

"What do you suppose would happen if you were to put your helmet back on and explain the various health effects to them?" Larry smiled again.

"I'd bet they run like hell."

"Exactly."

It didn't take long. I don't know what spacesuit told the officers out front, but whatever it was had the desired effect. Within two minutes, both patrol cars were burning up public property back the way they'd come. I took the opportunity to ask a few questions.

"Excuse me, as much as I hate to be dim, I still don't understand what is going on here that's worth killing people over."

Hayden turned quickly. "Are you kidding me? Didn't you

hear what Neville said? Maybe fifteen hundred, two thousand drums." He turned back toward the window.

"So what?" I said to his back.

"So?" He swiveled again. "So, it costs about a thousand dollars per drum, minimum, to legally dispose of that type of material. A thousand times fifteen hundred is—"

"A million and a half or so," Daniel piped in. Hayden nodded.

"Eight sites. Over a million dollars a site. Jesus," he muttered, overwhelmed by the enormity of his own figures.

The little parking lot was quiet for the first time in hours. Even the radio had stopped its infernal squalling. The humming of the coolers had suddenly become audible. Hayden heaved a sigh.

"Okay," he said. "You two get out of here."

We started to move; he stopped us. "This is it, Waterman. This is the end of the deal. As much as I appreciate the help you've been, I can't—I mean—I need to put some—"

"Distance."

"Yes, distance. I need to put some distance between us here. I'm sure you understand."

"Distance is just what Daniel and I had in mind," I said.

"I mean distance," he said solemnly. Ever since he'd run the numbers by me, I'd been waiting for this part. I'd offered him a cookie. He wanted the whole jar. Wendy had been right. He was a bureaucrat to the core.

"You're out of this," he continued. "You're not going to see your names in the papers tomorrow morning. You understand what I'm telling you? I never heard of you. Understood and agreed?"

I understood completely. This treat was too good to share. There might even be a cushy Washington, D.C. job in here somewhere.

"I understand," I said.

Daniel stretched and flexed, working out the kinks on our way out to the camper. The sky was bruised, a layered molten gray, holding the promise only of something different.

"I noticed you didn't say you agreed," Daniel noted as soon as we were well out of earshot.

"Most astute of you, Daniel. I try not to lie."

"That's good, Leo. Lying's bad for the spirit."

22

PERHAPS IT WAS intended as a cautionary peek at purgatory. Maybe that's what he had in mind. Or maybe the guy was just having trouble orating himself all the way to any sense of moral resolution. Considering Buddy's lifelong slide from grace, this was a definite possibility. Either that or the priest was just long-winded and didn't have sense enough to come in out of the rain. He droned on.

A westerly gale mixed the icy, slanting rain with the last remaining leaves into a blenderlike frappe that swirled around heads and down collars as we stood dripping by Buddy's grave. The water that had entered my collar had, by this time, found its way all the way down my sleeves and was now dripping off my hands. Buddy was the only one present who was dry and comfortable. He'd have liked that.

The crowd was divided into sections. Hard by the right of the grave, Buddy's three somewhat interchangeable ex-wives jockeyed for position. Each veiled in black, each with an umbrella-toting limo driver who stood respectfully one pace to the rear, bending forward, struggling to keep the umbrella functional in the swirling maelstrom as his stout charge elbowed and upstaged her competitors shamelessly, like a well-oiled finalist in a bodybuilding contest, posturing through one last collective attempt to impress the judges.

None of that reserved, stiff-upper-lip, WASPish mewling into hankies. No sir. What we had from the ex-wife section was the Super Bowl of sorrow, as each writhed, moaned, mumbled, and tore desperately at herself in an all-out attempt to outgrieve the others.

The most substantial of the three women zealously held down the central position. Her periodic spasms of lamentation were invariably punctuated by an imploring tilt of the head toward the heavens, followed quickly by a violent thrusting of her substantial elbows outward and toward the rear. This position both lent a martyrlike quality to the pose and, not coincidentally, served to keep her smaller rivals bobbing and weaving about in a manner that would have been the envy of many NBA centers.

Buddy's actual friends, as usual, occupied the low ground. They had been relegated to a spot at the foot of the grave, where a pile of sodden earth waited for the return of the backhoe. Only their soaking, rain-plastered heads were visible above the mound. As the unpredictable wind spiraled around the grave site, an occasional whiff of something akin to a pack of wet hunting dogs assailed my nostrils, reminding me of their presence.

George, Harold, and Ralph had been joined in their vigil by an eclectic assortment of the city's more colorful street denizens. Three or four I knew. Earlene and Mary sobbed together, arm-in-arm near the center of the group, the green army blanket thrown over their heads offering scant protection from the elements. The Speaker, who for this special occasion had traded in his omnipresent sandwich board for a Hefty Bag parka, seemed to be quietly conducting his own service, his lips mouthing their own silent benediction, his hands punctuating the salient points. Nearly Normal Norman looked better than usual. His enormous mane of untamed red hair, which usually stuck alarmingly out in all directions, had been plastered onto his head, gentling his otherwise fiercely bearded countenance into something vaguely cherubic.

Five minutes into the ceremony, while hunching up and swiveling my neck in a futile attempt to channel the rain away from my armpits, I'd noticed the guy under the laurel tree.

No need to wonder. This was the cops. Fifty yards of glaucomalike downpour and blowing leaves wasn't sufficient cover for this guy. All the signs were in place: worn overcoat, one epaulet unbuttoned and moving with the wind, partially covering twelve acres of fire-sale sport jacket, polyester pants—that baggy look they all develop over time. The face was a stew of melancholy and bored cynicism. This one had started out skinny, but twenty years of lingering over pie and coffee had pasted a gross paunch beneath his bony chest. If he'd had a chin, it would have been a triple model. As it was, his neck seemed to be sprouting layered goiters. I ignored him.

As if by magic, four workmen appeared from the surrounding mist and began slipping the four ends of rope through their gloved hands, lowering the coffin into its final resting place. I lost my bet.

Restrained by their beefy chauffeurs, the ex-wives, in a touching show of self-restraint, limited themselves to showering the rapidly descending coffin with a hail of wilted floral matter. As each in turn stepped forward, sniffed dismissingly at the others, and wailed into the wind, my mind heard laughter.

I watched them go, resisting the powerful urge to scratch the soaked bandage that covered the former home of my right earlobe.

George appeared at my elbow. He seemed to be impervious to the weather. His slicked-back white hair, although showing a bit more pink scalp than usual, was still in place. The rain had loosened and washed away the layer of dust that generally covered his shoes and outer garments, leaving behind a temporary sheen of cleanliness and respectability.

"Seemed like the wifies was all broke up about it," he said.

"Shattered."

"These are the same three broads who used to jail him regularly for nonpayment," he added with a snarl.

"I miss him already," said Ralph. His eyes were full.

"Seemed like Buddy was forever," muttered Harold.

"Buddy would hate us getting mushy over him," I said.

"Fuck him." Harold snuffed through a filthy handkerchief.

We lapsed into silence.

George filled the awkwardness of the moment by slipping his arm through mine and leaning in close.

"We found out where they're going," he whispered.

"Where?" I whispered back. He went leaden, not answering.

"Leo Waterman." A sandpaper voice from behind me.

Without turning, I said, "That's me." George grimaced.

A bony hand appeared on my shoulder, trying to turn me like a top. I went with the flow. No more than a foot separated our noses. His breath spoke of a titanic struggle between garlic and Binaca. Garlic was winning.

"You're coming with me," he said evenly.

"Am I under arrest?"

"If you want to be."

I remembered Jed's advice on the phone last night.

"If you want me to go anywhere with you, you're going to have to arrest me."

Harold, Ralph, and the others had wandered closer, forming a loose semicircle around the cop and me. He checked his back. His eyes narrowed.

He reached inside his coat. Everyone tensed. He pulled out a folded piece of paper and handed it to me. It was a material witness warrant.

"I can get all the backup I need," he said.

"No need." I said it loud enough for everyone to hear.

I reached into my inside pocket. It was the cop's turn to tense. I came out with my notebook, tore out a page, and handed it to George.

"Call this number. Ask for Jed James. If you have any trouble getting through, tell the lady you're calling for me." He nodded. "Tell him I've been arrested. He'll take it from there."

I checked my watch. Eleven forty-five. "You guys be at my place at four o'clock," I added.

The cop openly smirked. "If he's not there, you boys make sure you start the meeting without him. Waterman here won't be—" I cut him off.

"I'll be there," I said. "Four o'clock."

23

I MADE IT home by three.

As we rounded the corner, the cop now paternally propelling me by the elbow, the expression on their faces told me all I needed to know. Either they were simultaneously passing kidney stones, or Jed was already here.

The three of them stood impatiently in the hall, leaning back, holding up the stained pea-green walls, arms defensively folded. Detective Trask, Detective Allen from Tacoma, and a skinny little lamb-to-the-slaughter who turned out to be Assistant D.A. Van Pelt.

Before I even got seated, Jed started on them.

"Now as to these cretinous charges," he began.

They looked from one to another. The D.A. cleared his throat.

"At the moment, Mr. James, there are . . . er . . . no formal . . ."

Jed scooped at his papers. "Let's go," he said to me. I froze.

"If and when you fellas get your shit together, my client

will be, of course, anxious to assist you in any way possible."
Big smile. We started out.

"If he's so anxious, where's he been for the last three days?" Trask.

"Is Mr. Waterman charged with something?" Jed repeated, halting.

"As I stated, Mr. James, there are no charges," said Van Pelt.

"Then Mr. Waterman's movements are of no concern to any of you. This isn't Nazi Germany, you know." Jed was big on the Nazi analogies.

The two cops looked to Van Pelt for assistance. Van Pelt, hooking a finger into his collar for relief, looked like he'd rather be peddling time-shares in Beirut.

"We had assumed that Mr. Waterman, as a public-spirited citizen, would be willing to cooperate in our—"

"And your notion of cooperation includes a trumped-up material witness warrant"—Jed wristed his copy of the warrant into the air. It floated back to the stained table, bounced once, and slipped over the edge onto the worn linoleum floor—"served upon my client at a time of great bereavement? This is your conception of a reasonable manner of asking the public for help?" Silence again. "Well?" he demanded.

Trask jumped in. "We've been attempting to locate Mr. Waterman for several days."

"Let's," snarled Jed, "deal with one abuse of power at a time, shall we? What do you say? We can take up the matter of your illegal entry of Mr. Waterman's domicile after we settle the matter of this—this"—he used the toe of his hiking boot to kick the warrant over toward the assistant D.A.—"toilet-paper travesty."

Before they could regroup, Jed seized the initiative.

"Now," he began, "so as to neither waste any more of my

time nor inflict any further damage on Mr. Waterman's already mutilated civil rights, specifically what crime is it that Mr. Waterman's testimony might conceivably be material to?"

"The murder of Beaumont Knot," said Detective Allen immediately.

Jed cast me a glance. "He worked for me," I said.

"I want to confer with my client alone."

They took their time. Van Pelt had to take a quick little skipping step to keep the heavy door from hitting him in the ass when Jed kicked it shut.

"Toilet-paper travesty?" I winced as the door clicked.

He grinned. "I'm a little off my feed this morning. Have no fear. I'll warm up." I never doubted it for a second.

"Who in hell is Beaumont Knox?" he demanded.

"Buddy."

"The old guy who—you mean—"

"Yup."

"Somebody offed him?"

"Yup."

"While he was working for you?"

"So it seems."

"You know who?"

"If I did, I'd be there."

Jed thought it over. Finally he asked, "Can you work around these assholes?" tilting his head toward the hall.

"That's what I've been doing. It's getting hard."

"Then we better answer their questions."

"You sure?" I asked.

"Have you come up with anything substantial?"

I started to answer, but he cut me off. "Never mind, don't answer that."

He paced about the little room, finally coming to rest at the far end of the table. "Sit here," he said. I walked over and deposited myself in the chair. Jed slid one cheek up on the table and leaned in close.

"Listen, Leo, just because they're incompetent doesn't mean that they can't eventually stumble upon the proper paperwork. Even a blind pig will get an acorn once in a while, if you catch my drift."

He glanced derisively over his shoulder.

"The only way to get these guys out of your hair is to at least partially cooperate, so here's what we're going to do. I'm gonna invite the Three Stooges back in here. Out of the goodness of our hearts, we're going to help them out. I'm going to stand right behind you. I'll hold on to the chair like this." He bounced off the table and walked around to my back, slipping his fingers between my back and the chair. "If they ask you anything you don't want to answer, just lean back against my fingers, and for Chrissake be subtle. Don't have a grand mal or anything. You got it?" I said I did.

"Tell me about it. Just the facts, none of your suppositions. Nothing you've found out. Just what you were hired to do," he said.

I did. He listened intently, stopping me several times at junctures where I was rolling over into areas he didn't want to know about.

"You're going to have to name your client, you know."

"I know."

"Is Mr. Flood aware of this?"

"Yes."

"Really?" He rubbed his chin. "Amazing. We can let them take it up with the ubiquitous Mr. Flood, then." He hesitated. "You're sure he's willing, now? Rumor has it that sending him a surprise package of cops would not be the recommended procedure for living a long and fruitful existence."

"What I'm sure of is that they're going to have a hell of a

time getting anywhere near Tim. He's had lots of practice."

"That's their problem. Let's go for it."

They filed back in. Van Pelt, using prescribed interrogation technique, dragged a chair from the far end of the table, getting as close to me as he could. The two detectives held up the far wall. Van Pelt started.

"Is it correct that Mr. Knox was in your employ at the time of his untimely death?"

"Yes," I said. The D.A. eyed Jed warily, as if expecting an anvil to fall from the ceiling. Relieved, he continued.

"Do you have any knowledge whatsoever as to the identities of the perpetrators of this act?"

"No," I answered truthfully.

From the other side of the room, Trask made a noise like he was choking on a fishbone. Van Pelt carried on.

"What specifically was Mr. Knox doing for you?"

"Surveillance."

"Of what?"

"A building."

"What building?"

I gave him the address. Trask and Allen already had it. Van Pelt wrote it down anyway.

"Why did you have Mr. Knox watching the building?"

I unobtrusively leaned back in the chair. Jed jumped in.

"Any answer to that question would constitute not only bad faith regarding Mr. Waterman's duty to his client, but, more to the point, would be merely hearsay. Mr. Waterman has only his client's word as to the particulars of the circumstances."

I moved off his fingers. Van Pelt leaped.

"He has no privilege. He's not an attorney. As I'm sure you're aware, Mr. James—" Jed poleaxed him.

"If you want the particulars of Mr. Waterman's employment, take it up with the employer. As I'm sure *you* know,

Mr. Van Pelt, you have a legal obligation to pursue all primary sources of information first and not to rely on hastily harvested hearsay." I winced.

"He's—" Van Pelt stammered, looking back at the two detectives. "Mr. Waterman is prepared to name his client?"

"Of course."

"Well," said Van Pelt.

"I was working for Tim Flood." I recited the address. Nary a soul bothered to write it down.

"Doing what?" Allen asked. Trask looked confused.

"Ask Mr. Flood," Jed shot back. "He's the primary source for this information. Do your job. Stop asking us to do it for you."

Allen started to speak, but clamped down.

They kept at it for over an hour, without getting anything else. Halfway through, obviously disgusted by Van Pelt's pitiful lack of progress, Trask strode the length of the room and slid a paper onto the table in front of me.

Jed snatched it up. "What's this?" he asked without curiosity.

"An arson report," Trask snapped.

"Snohomish County is a tad out of your jurisdiction, isn't it, Detective? You seem to be having enough trouble handling even your own meager responsibilities." Trask ignored the rip.

"Snohomish County arson's got a cabin burned to the ground, and what do you suppose they find in the vicinity?" He didn't wait for an answer. "A car antenna. From a Fiat. Not your most common car."

"So?" Jed inquired.

"So your public-spirited client here drives a Fiat."

Jed waited for me to lean back. When I didn't, he continued, rapid-fire.

"Have you, in some way, connected these pastoral pyrotechnics with the death of Mr. Knox? Have you forensically linked this *alleged* antenna to Mr. Waterman's car? Have you asked Mr. Waterman if you could examine his car? Have you accomplished anything other than this pathetic fishing expedition?"

Trask lost his temper. "We tagged Mr. Waterman's goddamn car, but the fucking thing disappeared." Jed looked down at me quizzically.

"I'm having it serviced," I said.

"We're the ones getting serviced around here," Trask thundered.

"How many Fiats do you suppose there are in the state?" Jed asked.

"Screw you," said Trask.

"No need for that type of unprofessional behavior, Detective." Jed in his most annoyingly calm tone. "I'm sure a review board, especially in light of our cooperation, would find your demeanor——"

Van Pelt wheedled things into a calm. He tried, I'll give him that, but the poor guy was a lion tamer in a pork-chop suit. Jed ate him for lunch.

We were back on the street at one-thirty.

"You owe me one," he said as the revolving door deposited me on the sidewalk. "Get this cleaned up, so I can get you back to doing something socially useful."

"Right now a shave and a shower sound socially useful."

He looked me up and down. "In this case, I agree." He got serious for a moment. "All we accomplished here today, Leo, was to get you a little breathing room. As soon as they find they can't get to Tim Flood, they're going to circle back to you."

"A couple of days is all I need. If I don't have it by then, I'm not going to. By the way——"

"What?"

"Hastily harvested hearsay? Spare me."

"I just couldn't get on a roll this morning." A gleam appeared in his eye. I knew what was coming. "I was up all night worrying about this case you won't handle for me."

He started off. I yelled after him.

"Don't lose sleep over it, Jed. Only the mediocre are at their best all the time."

24

BETWEEN THE CAREFULLY combed rows of George's white hair, his scalp was bright red. "You callin' me a liar?"

"No, George, I'm not calling you a liar. I'm just—"

"I'm telling you, Leo, these little jerks are planning to burn down a fucking boat shed."

"No way," I said.

"Earlene seen 'em. Sounded weird to me too, so I followed up like you told me. I went down there last night myself. She's right. That's where they been going. No goddamn doubt about it."

"Nobody'd go to this much trouble to burn down a plywood boat shed. It just doesn't make sense."

"I'll show ya, goddammit," insisted George.

"They got it stuffed full of gas cans," Earlene said. "Been bringin 'em in one at a time every night for a week. One of 'em just strolls up the street like his car run out. Natural as can be. Ask Mary. She come with me." Mary nodded. "She was with me when the cops chased us off."

"The cops?"

"Said my big ass had better find some other place to hang out. Told me to get back downtown where I belonged. Said if he saw me down here Wednesday night, I was going to do county time. The bastards," she added as an afterthought.

"Why Wednesday night?" I asked. They gave a communal shrug.

I should have been more specific with George. When I told him to show up at four, I'd meant him and maybe Harold and Ralph. He'd brought everybody. My apartment looked like the circus was in town.

Thirteen damp, disreputable-looking characters were scattered around my apartment, perched on every available surface, fingering anything that wasn't nailed down and a few things that were. A half dozen of them were sacking my kitchen at this very moment. I made a mental note to take inventory after they left.

"You know what's going on, Leo?" asked Harold.

"Not the foggiest. Maybe—"

My explanation was interrupted by Nearly Normal Norman, who came shambling out from the kitchen. His massive, knobby hand was holding a blue Tupperware container. The cover was in his other hand. My stomach rolled. To the best of my recollection, whatever was in that container had been there for well over a year. Norman held it in front of my face.

"What's this?" he demanded. I held my breath and peeked inside.

Whatever it had been, it wasn't anymore. A metamorphosis had taken place. A forest of purple and green cilia sprouted from the original pile, lending a soft, furlike texture to the substance. It looked like it was about to moult. I grunted and waved it away, unwilling to expend any of my precious air.

Norman straightened up, stuck his rubicund nose nearly

into the contents, and inhaled deeply. "A bit piquant," he pronounced, heading back toward the kitchen.

"For God's sake don't eat any of that," I hollered after him.

"Why? What could happen?" asked Ralph. A mistake.

Norman's head reappeared from around the corner.

"What could happen?" he bellowed, striding into the center of the room, fixing everyone with his maniacal stare. "I'll tell you what could happen. Two days from now, I could be down on the Square when suddenly my tongue could swell up to the size of a snowshoe. Then, with my luck, I'd get it caught in the zipper of my jacket. My eyes would bug out of my head and hang down, you know, like on springs." He gazed about.

Satisfied he had everyone's undivided attention, Norman began to augment his gruesome recitation with a robust pantomime, clutching his throat and staggering bug-eyed about the room. "I'd be flopping around on the sidewalk like a beached tuna, puking my ethereal fluids all over my shoes," he rasped. "Then—then—"

He gave it a pregnant pause. "The whitecoats would come and take me. They'd finally have their way with old Norman. They'd use me for their accursed laboratory experiments. I'd end up on a cold steel table, with my guts pinned all over—"

George gently interrupted. "Never mind, Norman," he said soothingly. "That's a fear we all have to live with."

Norman, seemingly appeased, disappeared back into the kitchen for further research. George turned to me.

"Norman's kinda runnin' his own movie," he explained.

Even though the Mexican lunch I'd treated myself to on my way home was now moving around alarmingly, my brain had been slapped into consciousness by something that Norman had said. I was talking to myself out loud. "The boat shed sits on Ship Canal, right?"

"Good, Leo," giggled Earlene. "Good thing he's a detective, huh fellas. Not much gets by old Leo. Yeah, Leo, boats work better if they got water."

They yukked it up. I let them have their fun.

Things had been pretty tense ever since George had tried to tell me that Save the Earth was planning a terrorist campaign on a boat shed. The relief was welcome. It gave me time to regroup my thoughts.

"What's on the road side of the shed?" I asked.

They had to think about it. Finally, George said, "A construction site."

"That's right," remembered Earlene, "some university building."

"They was puttin' carpets in all day yesterday," said Mary. "Me and Earlene watched 'em from the bridge, didn't we?" It was Earlene's turn to agree.

"Interesting," I said, reaching for the phone.

I called Duvall. She answered before the end of the first ring.

"Pathology."

"Rebecca, it's Leo."

"Be still my heart."

"Are you still on the University Medical School faculty?"

"Why? Thinking of changing your career path? If it's Med School you've got in mind, this is going to take significant alterations of your school transcripts. I'd recommend sanitation work as a more realistic choice."

"Are you?" It came out harder than I'd intended.

"A little testy today, aren't we?"

"Sorry," I said.

"No and yes."

"No and yes what?" I tried to keep my voice modulated.

"No, you're not actually sorry, and yes, I'm still a faculty member."

"You remember that animal research lab that somebody torched?"

"How could I forget? I'd like to get my hands on whoever—"

"What are they doing to replace it?"

"Not doing—done. It's opening Wednesday night. Big dedication ceremony. A ribbon cutting, all of that." She misread my silence. "Don't worry. I weaseled out. I figured you'd be under lock and key by then. You won't have to put on a suit and take me."

"Okay, well—" Something in my hesitancy put her on alert.

"Why?" she asked. "Is there something— Leo, if you know anything about who—"

I broke the connection, leaving the phone off the hook. Rebecca wasn't inclined to let questions hang. She'd be calling right back.

I was so immersed in thought that it was a full minute before I realized that there were a dozen pairs of eyes boring holes in me. Even the scavengers in the kitchen had stopped their marauding long enough to tune in.

"You got it, Leo?" asked Ralph.

"Yeah, Ralph, I think I do. It's insane, but I've got it. It's not the boat shed. It's that construction site out by the road. They're just using the shed for storage. They're going to burn down the research lab, either before or during the dedication ceremony."

"What are we gonna do?" asked Ralph.

"Let's call the cops," suggested Earlene, cackling madly.

"We can't," I said.

"Why not?" asked Harold.

"Because that's not what we're getting paid to do. Caroline's going to be with them. The cops will get her too."

"So what?" asked Ralph. "Burning buildings is not nice. Maybe she'd be better off with the cops." In the abstract, he had a point. Unfortunately, this wasn't the abstract. This was Tim Flood. I turned to George.

"You want to go back to where you picked up the cash and explain to those folks that we didn't get the job done?"

He didn't bother to answer.

"Maybe you could make a deal with the cops," suggested a little guy wearing about twelve sweaters. The bulk, when combined with his round, cabbagelike face, made him look a bit like the Michelin Man. As I remembered, his name was Waldo.

"We tell them what's happening and they let the girl go," helped Mary.

"They'll never go for it."

"Why not?" she asked.

"Because, from what I hear, this is maybe not the first time they've burned the goddamn thing down."

"You mean—" George.

"You got it. They're dedicating a new building because the last one got burned down. This Save the Earth bunch are the prime suspects in the last fire. No way the cops are going to let anybody skate on this thing. Besides that, there's probably state and federal raps involved here too. No way."

"So, what are we going to do?" asked George.

"We have to stop them ourselves."

"What does this have to do with finding out who killed Buddy?"

For Ralph, this was a most astute, if somewhat ill-timed, question. A moment of silence came over the group.

Daniel's admonition notwithstanding, it was now time to lie.

"The girl we're going to keep away from the cops was the last person to see Buddy alive. We need her. She's the key."

While the first part was the truth, the second part was, at best, highly suppositional. I changed the subject.

"How many of them have been going out there every night?"

"Five," said George. "Caroline and four guys."

"Same five every night?"

"Yup."

"You said you guys saw a dry run."

"Waldo and the Speaker saw it," corrected George.

Waldo spoke again.

"The four guys go in first. Caroline stays outside keeping lookout, then follows them in, maybe five minutes later. They went through the whole thing night before last, before the doors were on. Did it twice."

"Chances are that they plan on burning it tonight," said George.

"Why not tomorrow during the dedication?" asked Waldo.

"Sure would make a lovely picture in the papers," mused Mary. "All of them muckety-mucks standin' around while the damn thing burns to the ground. What a picture. Can you see it?" Her eyes glowed at the thought.

Pyromania became pandemic. The crowd was universally enthralled with the prospect. They all joined in, each adding a few more details and victims to the bonfire of authoritarian doom and destruction until, as nearly as I could tell, everyone in the city who wasn't presently in my apartment had been consumed by the flames. It had even begun to sound good to me until, having run out of victims, they began to cast furtive glances in my direction. This brought me up short.

The phone was now making horrible sirenlike noises in an attempt to tell me that it was off the hook. I replaced the receiver. Silence settled in like fog. The sound of scraping plates filtered in from the kitchen. I tried not to think about what it was they might be eating.

"George is right. It's got to be tonight," I said finally. "The site will be crawling with cops tomorrow night. They may be crazy, but they're not that stupid."

"You sure?" asked Harold. "They looked pretty stupid to me."

"It's either tonight or it's a kamikaze mission. Tonight there's some chance of walking away. Tomorrow night, they'd be better off going up with the building. No, it's gotta be tonight."

I was talking more for my own benefit than for theirs. It was now ten after five. Whatever we were going to do, it had to be soon.

"What time have they been going out?" I asked.

"Between ten and ten-thirty," George answered quickly.

"Who's watching the building now?"

"Bob and Leroy and the Speaker," George said.

"We gonna take her before they go?" asked Ralph.

"Won't work," I said. "They'd just call it off. We're going to have to separate Caroline from the others after they get there. We need to get them into a position where there's no turning back."

"What then?" asked Mary.

"Then we separate Caroline from the others."

"Then?"

"Then we call the cops." A collective groan went up.

The idea held very little appeal for the assembled multitudes. Very few of their own problems had ever been satisfactorily resolved by the powers that be, and they were loath to believe that the system could be of any use here.

Finally, George broke into the discussion, waving everyone to silence.

"Okay, Leo, suppose we go along with the program. Maybe you're right. If we don't call the cops on the little shits they'll just do it some other night. What I still don't see is how in hell are we going to separate Caroline from the others. I'm lost here."

I told them. They listened intently. When I'd finished, the room erupted in a chorus of complaints.

"You mean we're going to wait around for the cops?" demanded Earlene. "We'll all be busted."

"Not busted, heroes."

I'd learned years ago, when I'd first started using street people as operatives, that in spite of their meager circumstances, they were no more immune to the hopes and dreams of our society than anyone else. Nobody aspires to be a bum.

As I'd hoped, they massaged this scenario to death. Before they were finished, Ralph was mayor and the rest of them were inventing new city ordinances when George lost his patience and put a stop to it. "Shut up," he yelled above the din.

"I don't see it, Leo. I just don't see it," he said after they'd quieted.

"What don't you see, George?" I asked patiently.

"I don't see her acting the way you say. People just ain't like that anymore. Ten, twenty years ago maybe, but not anymore. They got that flat look in their eyes these days. They won't even look at you."

A buzz of agreement sailed around the room. "You could fall dead right in front of them on the sidewalk and they'd just step over you. And you're tellin' us that she's gonna—"

"She will," I assured him.

George wasn't ready to quit.

"If she's such a goody-two-shoes, how come she's hangin' out with these Save the Earth assholes? Huh, tell me that?"

"She's not a goody-two-shoes," I said. "She's just incapable of minding her own goddamn business."

25

❖

"I WISH I still smoked," said Saasha Kennedy, as she nervously fidgeted about in the front seat of the camper. The mercury vapor lights surrounding the buildings across the street reflected off her oversize lenses, making it impossible to see her eyes.

"The waiting is always the hard part."

"I think the police would be a better option."

"The craving for certainty is a vice, Ms. Kennedy. Didn't they teach you that in school?" She ignored the dig.

"What if she refuses to come with me?"

"Then I'll take her back to her grandfather."

She fidgeted some more. "I don't know how I let you talk me into this fool's errand, Waterman," she said disgustedly.

"Guilt," I suggested. "You think you owe me. Your brain is telling you that if it wasn't for me, Thomas Greer would have splattered himself all over Third Avenue. You feel guilty. That dubious emotion combined with your highly cultivated sense of professional duty has brought you here, to the very brink of disaster." She was too nervous to rise to the bait.

"It's the unprofessional nature of this that causes me concern."

"Why?" I asked. "This is what you do, isn't it? I looked you up in the book. It says you specialize in adolescent therapy."

"My patients don't generally come in under this sort of duress."

"Don't kid yourself. Their parents just do it with a tad more subtlety, that's all. None of those kids wakes up one day with an intense desire to see a shrink. Trust me."

Before she could come back at me, I changed the subject.

"You did a nice job on Earlene, by the way. She looks great."

"That's another thing." She wagged a finger at me. "When you asked me to bring a change of clothes and my cosmetics case, I thought it was for the girl. If I'd known—"

"Don't worry, you'll get the clothes back."

"I don't want the clothes back," she snapped.

"Hey, Earlene's good people. A little crusty maybe."

"A little crusty? There was moss growing on that woman."

We were interrupted by a tapping on the window. George was tight-lipped. "Here they come," he said.

"Everybody in place?" I asked.

"For all the good it's gonna do."

I turned to Kennedy. "We'll be back." She responded by frowning and locking the door behind me.

I slipped from the truck and followed George through the parking lot toward the eastern end of Pacific Avenue.

In the space of four hours, it had turned bitter cold. The winter storms that usually kept the Northwest in a perpetual cloud bank had unexpectedly blown to the north.

The night was clear, and a multitude of randomly scattered stars seemed to hover no more than a couple of blocks above us. In the curb-lined beds surrounding the dormitory lot, the rhododendrons protectively curled their leaves, hunkering inward against the cold. My breath swirled around my ears, leaving a vapor trail as I walked. George's wing tips scuffed scratches in the rapidly forming sheen on the asphalt.

We stood in the artificial shade of a massive walnut tree as the black van, driving well within the speed limit, rolled slowly by.

"They'll park over by the stadium and walk back."

"Only smart thing they've done," I commented. "Gives them three possible ways out of the area."

We stood in the shadows until the light at the end of the street changed and the van turned left, then we hastily crossed the street, jogging into the driveway of the new lab, all the way to the back of the lot.

Forty yards of new sod separated the back of the laboratory from Ship Canal. The water slid silently by like a piece of moving black glass. A thin blanket of fog floated inches above the sliding water.

The new laboratory was surrounded by ancient yew hedges, which had somehow managed to survive both the fire and the ensuing construction. The twisted, interlocking bramble, now bare of leaves, formed a solid wall, separating the back of the laboratory from the grass bank leading down to the water.

I was counting on the fact that Caroline would be able to hear, but not see, what was going on in the little park next door.

Covering our faces with our sleeves, George and I pushed our way through the hedge and skied down the icy embankment into the park, angling toward the farthest corner, hard under the bridge. There was no need to look for the crew; their collective breath rose into the air like smoke signals.

Norman, Waldo, and Earlene were huddled around a one-piece metal picnic table, silently rubbing and hugging themselves in an attempt to stave off the cold. I stopped by the table, using a finger to signal for silence.

I watched as George crossed the open area to the farthest edge, parted the top of the hedge, and forced his body through the tangle. Satisfied that he was in place, I turned to the crew.

"You guys ready?" I asked.

"I'm freezing my ass off, is what I'm doing," whispered Earlene. "No wonder those businesswomen are always in such a shitty mood; I'd be in a bad mood too if I had to walk around with my twat freezing off like this all the time."

I waved her off. "Let's stick with the business at hand." As I continued, Earlene folded her arms over Kennedy's blue wool coat and sulked. "That bitch threw my clothes out, Leo," she muttered.

"George will tell us when they're on the way," I said. "They're going to pass right behind us here, on the bank by the water, so we're going to have to be quiet. Any last-minute questions?"

There were, but the moment had come. From the far side of the little park, George squeezed out a "Sssssst." He pulled himself back through the hedge and, as we'd arranged, hurried diagonally across the park to the front corner, by the street.

Norman, Waldo, Earlene, and I lay down on the brittle grass, listening intently. I crawled over to the hedge, peering out between the twisted stems, looking for feet. Nothing.

I tried to control my breath. I didn't want it to signal my presence. A block away, the overhead lights lit a gray-blue science-fiction moonscape. I breathed down the front of my jacket and listened. Nothing.

The crew was looking anxiously my way. The urban commandos should have been here by now. When we'd run through it earlier this evening, George and Harold, a pair not renowned for great dispatch, had been at the boat shed by now. Something was wrong. Maybe George had been mistaken. I decided to have a look for myself. I was halfway to my feet when Norman slashed the air with his arm. I ducked.

They came silently, only the muted sound of crunching grass announcing their presence. Five pairs of closely grouped feet passed before my vantage point, moving steadily downhill toward the shed. I couldn't identify which feet belonged to Caroline. The squeaking of the door told me that they were inside the shed.

When I heard the scraping of cans, I duckwalked up the length of the hedge to the corner nearest the lab, burrowing into the branches. I squinted up toward George and waved my arm. He pushed his way through the hedge to the front sidewalk and was instantly out of sight.

Save the Earth tiptoed within three feet of my position as they came up the bank to the back of the laboratory. I was well below their level, with an unobstructed view through the twisted trunks.

Three of the guys were carrying a gas can in each hand. One guy hefted a three-foot pry bar. His tall, geometric hair gave him a profile like a felt-tip marker. Must be the Bass kid. Caroline was empty-handed and pissed off. I knew the look well.

Bass wiggled the bar into a crack in the door and heaved. Nothing. He stepped back, then reinserted the bar and leaned his scrawny back against it. Still nothing. For the first time someone spoke. Of course, it was Caroline.

"Let Bob keep watch, I want to come in," she whispered. A smile crossed my lips. Some things don't change.

"Just do it the way we practiced it," Bass grunted, putting his full weight behind his efforts. "Give it five minutes on your watch and then meet us in the basement."

"I don't see why—" Caroline started.

With a sharp sound of snapping metal, the door popped open, swinging slowly, its pneumatic guide hissing softly.

A full minute of silence followed as they held their breaths and waited for the alarm that never came. Satisfied that they were undetected, Bass motioned the other three guys inside. They entered, single file. He turned to Caroline. "Stay here. Do your job," he whispered urgently.

She folded her arms over her chest and turned her back on him, staring out at the canal. I heard him heave a sigh as he followed the others inside, pulling the door shut behind him. Everything was blue and quiet.

I signaled the crew. In unison, they rose from the grass. Earlene began picking at the bits of grass and litter that clung to her coat. As they were about to begin, I heard the door to the lab hiss open again.

Caroline was following the guys in. Five minutes, my ass. She hadn't even given it a full minute. So much for the plan. Time to call the cops.

Earlene saved the day, emitting a quavering wail that shattered the freezing air like a plate-glass window. "Nooooo. Noooo, please," she wailed.

Caroline's head popped back out the door. She seemed to be sniffing the air like a retriever, wary but sorely tempted.

"Oh, God pleeese, no—" another scream split the air, followed by a series of horrific grunts and groans.

I looked over my shoulder. Norman and Waldo held Earlene down on the frosty picnic table, the borrowed burgundy dress riding high around her hips, Waldo at the head, working on a full nelson, Norman down by her feet trying vainly to control Earlene's wildly pumping legs.

"Oh. Oh. Oh," she hollered.

Three feet to my left, the hedge parted. I looked down; I could read the label on Caroline's black Reeboks. Her indecision was palpable. I slid deeper into the corner of the hedge. The feet disappeared. I waited, barely breathing. I heard her feet snicking on the asphalt.

The lab door hissed open again. We'd lost her. Son of a bitch. I couldn't believe it. Dejectedly, I got to my knees.

Suddenly, six feet to my right, Caroline Nobel, doing her best Wonder Woman impression, burst through the hedge, landed with both feet on the frosted grass of the hillside, fell directly on her ass, and slid all the way to the bottom. If she hadn't fallen, she'd have seen me for sure. I was behind her now. She came up running. I followed.

I could see now why Caroline had hesitated. The charade was not going as planned. I'd chosen Waldo and Norman because, to the naked eye, they appeared the most menacing. The afternoon rain had left Norman's hair sticking up like Don King's, adding an extra six inches to his already gargantuan stature. Waldo, nearly as wide as he was tall, always looked like a particularly malevolent troll, so he was perfect. Together, I'd figured they'd make the perfect pair of rapist-muggers. The problem was that Earlene was in the process of kicking both their asses.

Having for some unknown reason regained her feet, she now delivered a roundhouse uppercut to Waldo's groin. Waldo staggered about clutching his privates and groaning pitifully. Norman looked terrified.

"Stop that this instant, you animals," Caroline yelled, as she ran across the clearing toward the fray. I followed at a dead run.

Waldo continued his moaning; Norman backpedaled steadily.

"You fucking pervert. If you ever—" Earlene was screaming now.

Caroline waded in. "What were these pigs doing?" she demanded.

That was as far as she got. Earlene, now in a full rage, brought one up from her knees and planted it flush in Waldo's chin. He went down in a heap. Norman, hemmed in by the hedge, held up both hands in surrender.

I tackled Caroline from behind, rolling her to the ground, clamping my hand over her mouth. As I rolled over onto my back, Caroline now struggling frantically on top of me, Earlene hauled off and kicked the prone Waldo, who was trying desperately to scramble out of harm's way.

"The little son of a bitch grabbed my boobs," she snarled, scooting after him, aiming another vicious kick at his head. "I'll kill him." Waldo, perfectly built for the task, rolled just out of reach.

"Stop it, goddammit," I yelled. Everyone stood still.

Caroline was tattooing my shins with her heels. I wrapped my legs around hers and flopped over, using my weight to pin her to the frozen ground. I heard her breath escape as my full weight came down on her.

"Norman," I grunted. "Get over here and take the girl."

He complied, affording Earlene a wide berth. I rolled us back over. Caroline managed only one brief monosyllabic screech before Norman engulfed her in his massive hands and arms. He held her under one arm like a load of books, using his free hand to keep her mouth covered.

I pulled the roll of duct tape out of my jacket pocket and taped Caroline's hands and feet, while Norman held her down. Just for good measure, I gave a couple of wraps around her mouth. She frothed and mumbled through the tape.

"Take her out to George," I said when I'd finished.

He lumbered off toward the street, seeming to take no notice of the extra weight.

"Earlene," I said, rising. "Help Waldo over to the street."

"I'll help his ass to hell," she said. "That little pervert."

"Then help Norman. I'll take care of Waldo."

Waldo looked like he thought this was a swell idea.

George was waiting with the camper.

"Hurry, Leo," he said. "You guys were slow as shit back there. Cops must be real close by now."

"I don't hear no sirens," muttered Earlene, trying to work her way around me to get at Waldo.

"They'll come in quietly," I said.

Norman deposited Caroline on the floor of the camper and closed the door. Through the window, Kennedy's eyes, for once, looked bigger than her glasses.

George could handle the crew. At least, for Waldo's sake, I hoped so.

I hopped into the driver's seat, slipped the truck into gear, and floored it, bouncing out into the street, heading east toward the Montlake bridge.

"What about your friends?" Kennedy inquired.

"They're going to stick around and be witnesses," I said.

"Why would they—"

She stopped, openmouthed, as three police cruisers raced full-bore over the bridge toward us. I watched in the mirror as they slid left through the intersection, screaming down Pacific toward the lab.

I could hear Caroline's muffled sobs from the rear of the camper. She was taking out her frustrations by kicking madly at anything she could reach. I knew the feeling.

"George and the others are going to stick around and claim they saw the breaking and entering. Makes the case stronger. Otherwise, some smart lawyer will have those jerks back out on the street day after tomorrow."

Kennedy sorted this information in silence as we wound up the hill toward Broadway. Caroline kicked harder.

I wheeled all the way to the top of the hill, chicaned through the neighborhood streets, and pulled to a stop on Tenth Avenue, two blocks down from Tim Flood's house, right where this disaster had all begun last week.

I shut the engine off and turned to Kennedy.

"You ready?" She grimaced in reply.

"Stay outside until I get her unwrapped."

"Was all that tape really necessary?" she asked.

"You're about to find out."

I walked back to the camper, checking the street on the way around. Few lights showed in the windows. It was an old neighborhood. They turned in early. I unlocked the camper door. Caroline was lying on her side, with her knees drawn tightly up to her chest. She tried to mule-kick me, as I stepped up onto the camper. I caught her feet under my arm and kept walking forward until her legs pointed up toward the ceiling, her shoulders pinned to the floor. She stopped struggling.

"Okay, Caroline. Here's the drill. I'm going to take the tape off you here in a minute." I used my free hand to point back out through the door. "We're about two blocks from your grandfather's house."

Her eyes widened. More wild struggling and gurgling.

"It's a quiet neighborhood. It's late. You start waking people up and I'm going to march you down the street and turn you over to Frankie and the twins. That'll be the end of it. You got that?"

The struggling momentarily stopped.

"You got that?" I repeated. She nodded, banging her head on the floor in the process.

I unwound the tape from her ankles. She stayed put. Probably trying to lull me into a false sense of confidence. I yarded her over and unwound the tape from her wrists. She was up in a flash, tearing the tape down from her mouth, wearing it like a dull silver necklace.

"You work for my grandfather? I knew it. I *knew* it. You son of a bitch, Leo. You son of a bitch," she repeated over and over as she struggled vainly to find the overlapped end of the tape.

"Right now, I work for you." She wasn't buying.

Giving up on the tape, she came at me with both hands and feet. I ducked my head and body-blocked her into the front of the overhead sleeper, keeping my head down, allowing her to vent her spleen on my back.

I stepped back suddenly, putting the length of the camper between us.

"That's enough," I said.

She was breathing heavily, her hands involuntarily curling and uncurling as she looked for an escape route. I felt the camper lurch as Saasha Kennedy stepped up inside and sat down at the small table. I reached back and closed the door behind her.

"Who's this bitch?" Caroline sniffled.

"This is a friend of mine," I said. "Her name is Saasha Kennedy. She's here to see if maybe she can't help you out of this mess you're in."

"I don't need your fucking help. I wouldn't be in this fucking mess if it wasn't for you, you asshole."

"Caroline—" Kennedy began.

"Fuck you," she screamed. What followed was several minutes of unintelligible cursing, mostly nouns and adjectives, very few verbs. Among other things, the girl needed work on the artful use of profanity.

Eventually she ran out of gas and turned her back on us, resting her arms up on the sleeper, resting her head between them. I laid it out for her.

"Here's where it's at, Caroline. Your friends at Save the Earth are on their way to jail now. They're going to be doing some serious time. In a few minutes, that building you guys hang out in is going to be crawling with police. Whatever you've got down there is history. You've—"

Caroline turned quickly. "All my stuff is—"

"It's gone," I said. "It'll be in a police evidence locker by morning."

"So what?" she sneered. "I'll replace it. It's only—"

"You don't have any money," I said quickly. "Your access

to funds has been cut off. I arranged it with your grandfather. You're broke. Your so-called friends are on their way to jail. What now, honey? Huh?"

Kennedy put a restraining hand on my elbow. I shut up.

It must have been the news about the money. I figured she'd probably never been broke before. Whatever it was, somewhere inside her, a dam slowly came apart. At first, she seemed to be having trouble getting her breath. Gulping air, without ever exhaling. Followed by a long series of what sounded like hiccups. Then the tears, as she turned away again and began sobbing hysterically, her body wracked by spasms, her shoulders shaking almost uncontrollably as she poured and pounded her collected angst into the mattress. She seemed to cry forever. I became progressively more uncomfortable.

I've never been good around crying women. Most of the greatest, most expensive mistakes of my life have been made in response to crying women. Crying always gives me the uncontrollable urge to do something. Something, anything, no matter how stupid, not just stand around.

I started to move forward, but Kennedy held me back, silently shaking her head. She pointed toward the door.

"Me?" I mouthed silently. She nodded.

I stepped out, closing the door behind me. The frozen leaves crunched beneath my feet as I wandered down a couple of blocks. I stood on the frozen sidewalk in front of Tim Flood's house. Only the hall lights glowed weak and yellow through the crocheted curtains.

Part of me was tempted to ring the bell and turn Caroline over to whoever answered. My job was finished. I'd done what I'd been paid to do. I'd earned my bonus. Who in hell was I to be mucking about in somebody else's life? My own wasn't in such good shape that I could be considered an expert on life management. If my old man hadn't been smart enough to tie up all of his money, I'd probably have gotten myself into even worse trouble than Caroline was in now.

Something wouldn't let me. Probably the memory of the smell. Involuntarily, as I stood in front of the house, my circuits had conjured up the stifling heat and the decaying smell of Tim's solarium. Disgusted with myself, I wandered back down the street.

As I approached the camper from the rear, I could hear the murmurings of conversation from within. Separate voices.

Shivering now, I strolled around some more, once again wondering about the heating bills in this august old neighborhood. Fifty minutes passed as I wandered frozen about the darkened streets.

The camper door opened. Kennedy got out. She closed the door.

"Take us back to my car," she said. "Caroline's going to spend the night with me."

"What then?"

"We'll see."

"You sure?"

"You didn't leave her many other options."

"You better keep both eyes on her. She's—"

"A very mixed-up, very disconnected kid," she finished for me. "I'll make some calls in the morning."

"She'll probably be gone by morning."

"Where's she going to go, Waterman? She's not even wearing a jacket."

I started for the camper. She stopped me.

"You just drive. Right now, she doesn't need any more of your ham-handed moralizing."

Before I could argue, Kennedy climbed back inside with Caroline and locked the door.

26

THE LORD DIVIDES up the good stuff and parcels it out. Charles Hayden's secretary was pretty, but she wasn't quick.

"Mr. Hayden's in conference at the moment. If you'd like to wait—"

I kept right on walking. She'd told me all I needed to know.

"Just a minute, sir. You can't— Sir. Sir."

She was still trying to disconnect herself from her headset when I hit the door. She must have meant conference call.

Hayden had the phone to his ear and was facing away from the door, his feet on the windowsill, gazing comfortably out over the city. He swiveled his chair angrily, his face still registering bemused tolerance when it fell into his lap.

"How's the Toxic Avenger this morning?" I asked.

The secretary was babbling apologies behind me.

"I'm so sorry, Mr. Hayden. I told this gentleman"—her inflection suggested this last word might not be altogether accurate—"that you were—"

"It's all right, Nancy."

He spoke into the receiver. "I'll have to call you back." He hung up.

"Never mind, Nancy," he said to the girl.

She stood dumbfounded. He shooed her off, waving the backs of his hands at her. I could feel her gaze on the back of my neck as she reluctantly sidestepped out of the room. He watched her go.

"What are you doing here? We had a deal. If you think—"

"I lied." Now it was Hayden's turn to be dumbfounded. I helped out. "Quite a splash in the media the other day. Nice suit. Understated, but elegant. Looked good on the tube. I especially liked the part about the months of dogged investigative work paying off for your agency. A nice touch. You could move up a few floors with this one, Charlie."

I pulled the nearest chair over to the side of the desk and sat in close, grinning at him. "Daniel sends his regards."

"What do you want?"

"Nothing. I just wanted to meet a genuine American hero, that's all."

"I don't have any money. Wendy bled me dry. If you want money—"

"I don't want your money." I waited for him to ask me what it was I did want. He was either unwilling or unable to oblige.

"I want some information." I gestured expansively out over his desk. "I'm willing to bet that what I want to know is somewhere here in your tidy little desk. You know what they say about tidy desks, don't you?"

"What do you want?"

"You're starting to repeat yourself, Charlie. Keep that up and you'll have me thinking that you're not glad to see me."

He sat and stared at me. I decided to give him a break.

"How's the investigation progressing?" I asked.

"Slowly."

"Any leads?"

"It's only been a couple of days."

"In an investigation, three days is an eternity. Come on, Hayden. By now, even a government employee must have come up with something."

A wave of color moved up his face. He rose to the bait.

"Take a look at this." He slid a piece of paper across the desk.

It was a bank statement. Everett branch, First Interstate. Howard Short. Present balance, one hundred eighty-one thousand and change.

"The tribe was paying him forty-two thou," he said.

"Frugal fella."

"That's what we thought," Hayden said smugly. "We're checking back on him now."

"What about a list of possible PCB recyclers?"

"Do you have any idea how many users of PCBs there are? It could—"

"Not users. Recyclers, remember. I was there. Too much for users. Has to be a recycler. Let me a see a list of local recyclers."

He started to protest, had a spasm of lucidity, and reached up into his in-basket. He dropped a blue-and-white computer printout onto the desk in front of me and glared at me over laced fingers as I worked my way down the columns of company names and addresses.

The list was statewide, nearly a hundred entries. Ecology was big business. I moved back to the first few listings. The third one down read Rainier Recycling, 400 Second Avenue, Seattle, Washington.

"What's this?" I asked, turning the printout so he could read under my finger.

"Rainier Recycling. They do mostly plastic for—"

"It's downtown on Second Avenue. Yuppies. Suit City. The only thing they're recycling in that neighborhood is cappuccino. What's the deal?"

"That's just the office address."

"Where's the recycling facility?"

"That's in the Inspection Guide."

"Where's the Inspection Guide?"

He exhaled noisily again, turned, liberated a beige hardbound book from a bookcase beneath the window, and plopped it down in front of me.

Grabbing the printout and the Inspection Guide, I stood up.

"Thanks," I said. "Keep up the good work." I started for the door.

"Hey," he whined. "I need those."

"Fill out a requisition form," I said over my shoulder.

I gave Nancy my most dazzling smile as I strode past her desk. Her lovely jawline was spoiled by knots the size of golf balls. I kept smiling.

Two hours and three cups of coffee later I had it narrowed down to four possibles. Four chemical recyclers who had offices within a ten-block radius of Bobby Warren's collection of parking stubs and a recycling facility in Tacoma. Baker Commodities, American Recycling, and Mobius Reclamation in Tacoma and Northwest Handlers in Fife all fit the bill.

Four was better than a hundred, but it was still too many. From what I remembered of the geography of that area, the possibles were widely scattered. I needed to narrow it down. As much as the thought pained me, I needed to talk to Caroline Nobel.

I left the gloom of the coffee shop and squinted my way over to a phone booth. I called Kennedy. Her voice was husky.

"How's the girl?" I asked.

"She's sleeping. We talked most of the night."

"I need to have a few words with her."

"That wouldn't be a good idea."

"Why not? It's important."

"She has enough unresolved issues in her life right now without you adding any more. I'll have to insist—"

"I think I can resolve at least one of them for her."

"Like what?"

I told her. She didn't say anything for quite a while.

"The death of this young man has been quite a trauma for her."

"I figured he was just so much grist for the mill," I said.

"Perhaps you should just take my word for it," she said coldly. "I've already shared more with you than I should have."

"So, how about it?"

"Do you really think you can bring this matter to a successful resolution for her? Give her some sense of closure on the matter? She doesn't need any more trauma."

"I do."

She reluctantly recited the address.

I would have bet it wasn't possible. I would have been wrong. Caroline Nobel looked terrible. Beneath each blue eye hung an ash-colored bag. Several scrapes ran down her right cheek, probably from when she'd jumped through the hedge. Her other cheek was creased with blanket marks. In a voluminous flannel nightgown, she looked young and vulnerable.

She was sitting in a white wingback chair, curled up on her own feet. Kennedy sat protectively on the arm of the chair.

"You know who killed Bobby?" Caroline asked distractedly.

"I'm close. I need your help."

When I didn't get a response, I continued.

"I need to know exactly where you lost the truck you were following."

"I told you. Right at the railroad tracks."

"What was the cross street?"

"I don't know. That was the first time I'd ever been down there."

Dead end. I was busy calculating the risks involved in carrying out a B&E on four separate chemical companies when Caroline said the magic words.

"I could show you," she said in a small voice.

If Saasha Kennedy had shaken her head any more violently, she'd have ended up in a neck brace. Caroline gazed beseechingly up at her.

"Please. I need to. If it wasn't for me Bobby would—"

They went at it, low-key tooth and nail, until Kennedy finally relented. Caroline may have been beaten, but her spirit wasn't broken yet. It was a good sign.

Kennedy found her some clothes and then returned to the living room while the girl got dressed. She was angry.

"You better take care of her, Waterman."

"I will."

"She just shows you the street and then you bring her back here. I mean it. Two hours from right now, I call the police."

"Scout's honor." I held up two fingers.

"Stuff 'em," she replied.

Caroline appeared wearing an oversize pair of jeans and a green cowl-neck sweater. "I'm ready," she said. Kennedy forced a smile. I hustled Caroline out the door.

It was a quiet ride. She never said a word until we passed through Federal Way. Then suddenly, as if we'd been conversing all along, she said. "Bobby was very special to me." I stared straight ahead. Whatever the response was supposed to be was lost on me.

"I know what you think of me. You're probably right, but that doesn't mean I didn't love Bobby. He was special."

"I think you're a hell of a kid," I said.

"You think I'm a pain in the ass."

"That too."

"See."

"Hey, kid. Nobody except maybe Mother Teresa is all good or all bad, and I've got my doubts about her. You've got your finer points. You just need to get a little more mileage out of them."

"What points?"

I thought about it as we wheeled down the hill and into Fife.

"You know, one of the guys that works for me, his name is George Paris, he thought that little trick we pulled on you last night would never work. You know why?"

"Why?"

"Because he said that people didn't give enough of a shit about one another anymore to come running to the rescue at a time like that. He said the average person would just refuse to get involved, that they would just keep on walking. And you know what?"

"What?"

"He was right. Most people don't give a shit," I said. "But you did."

"Maybe I'm just stupid."

"No," I said. "You just care."

"You're telling me that caring is what got me into this mess I'm in."

"No. Being disconnected got you into this mess. That's a word Ms. Kennedy used the other night. It's a good word for you. I've been thinking about it. You're not connected to anything."

"I don't understand."

"Let me put it this way. You've seen some of the people who work for me, right? Who could be more disconnected than them? Society wants no part of them. Half of them live outdoors. Their families, if they've got families, gave up on them years ago. What have they got?"

No answer.

"They've got each other," I said. "It sounds corny, but it's true. Even if it's only whiskey, at least they share with each other. They look out for each other. They know who's in detox, who's in the hospital, who's in jail. They keep track of each other. They're connected."

Mercifully, my lecture was interrupted.

"This is the exit," she said. Same exit I'd taken with Trask.

I moved over in the right-hand lane and eased the camper around the arc to the traffic light. The usual collection of freeway exit gas stations, minimarts, and truck stops lit the intersection as far as the eye could see to the left and right.

"Which way?"

"Straight. What are you connected to?"

"Seattle, I guess. The place. The people. I've lived here all my life. I walk down the street and see people I went to grammar school with. I can drive up to Queen Anne and drive by my parents' house. I've got uncles and aunts and cousins scattered all over the place around here."

"There, up ahead. There's the tracks."

I pulled over onto the right shoulder, the truck's tires smashing the thin layers of ice that had formed in the potholes. A double line of tracks humped the road and bisected the street. No automatic guard barriers.

"So you followed the truck up until right here. Then what?"

"How many times do I have to tell you?" She was tiring.

"Tell me again," I said as gently as I could.

She wiped the hair from her face. "All right. The truck stopped before the tracks like they always do."

"Where were you?"

"Back there. That little turnout behind us."

I looked into the big mirror on her side of the truck. Fifty yards back a similar turnout, its glazed potholes intact, held a newspaper collection bin.

"I was trying not to be, you know, too obvious."

"Then what?"

"I started to pull out to follow the truck when this old bum in a station wagon cut me off. I couldn't believe it. The guy could barely see over the wheel. The thing was smoking so bad I couldn't even see the truck anymore."

I was nearly speechless but managed to squeak something out.

"What kind of wagon?"

"Who knows. Some old American gas hog."

"What happened then?"

"The old fart stops right on the tracks. I think he stalled the damn thing. I thought the train was going to hit him. Then, at the last second, he gets it going and hustles over the tracks right in front of the train."

"Then?"

"That's it. It was a long train. By the time it passed, the truck was long gone." She was on the verge of tears.

"You have no idea which way it went from here?"

"How was I supposed to see through a train?" She channeled her sorrow into anger, but her eyes gave her away. "If the truck left a vapor trail like that damn old car, I would have known where it went too. It's all my fault."

"You know where the car went?"

"Sure. The thing was smoking so bad, it was like he was skywriting. I could see the smoke running all along the top of the train."

She pointed off to the north.

"The car turned right?"

"Who cares about the stupid car? It's the—" She picked up on my tone.

"Was . . . was that your friend in the car?"

"Yes."

"Oh . . . I'm sorry for calling him a bum."

"He was an old fart. Don't worry about it. He wouldn't have minded."

"He took the first right."

We followed in his tracks, turning right up a wide unlit industrial access road. There were no street markers. We were about a mile from where Buddy had been found. Wall-to-wall heavy industry. Big fences, booms, cranes, smoke-stacks, and dispersion towers backlit by the sky. I started out slowly, looking for company signs to identify the buildings we were passing. No luck.

Three quarters of a mile down, we came to a dead end, as the road ran directly into a butte overlooking Commencement Bay.

"What now?" I asked, already knowing the answer.

"No idea," she shrugged. "I went straight back at the tracks. It was a bigger road."

I nosed the truck into a little turnout. In order to get the tailgate out of the street, I had to lean the front bumper of the truck on the chain-link fence. The fence groaned and buckled inward, snapping a couple of the white painted slats that ran through the links. We settled to a stop.

I shut down and pocketed the keys.

"Let's walk around a little. See if maybe we can't get an idea of what some of these businesses are." Caroline was game.

We covered a good half mile on both sides of the street, up and back to the truck, without seeing a single identifying sign. Halfway up the first leg, we were silhouetted by the headlights of an oncoming car, which started up the street toward us, changed its mind, and backed out to the main road.

The momentary flash of headlights served only to heighten the darkness after they were withdrawn. We stood still, waiting for our pupils to dilate.

Huge piles of rough-sawn boards identified one of the yards as a wholesale lumber dealer. The rest, it was hard to tell. Drums of various sorts were scattered about. I needed light.

The frosted pebbles of the road shoulder somehow reflected the meager light and crunched under our feet as we meandered back toward the camper.

"So, what do you care about, Leo?"

"I care about lots of stuff." I was hoping this would suffice. No go.

"Like what?"

"Well, you know," I stammered, "that's why I do what I do. I care about the people I work for and the problems they've got."

"You're a detective." It was a statement.

"A private investigator," I corrected, glancing at her sideways.

"Ms. Kennedy told me. She didn't want me to think you worked for my grandfather, you know, like Frankie."

I made a mental note to thank Kennedy.

"People come to you with problems?"

"Only after they've tried everything else."

"Kind of like Ms. Kennedy."

"You could say that. She sure as hell wouldn't like the idea, but I suppose we do have a lot in common. We're both sort of professional busybodies. We both spend our time dealing with other people's problems."

"You like that?"

"It beats dealing with my own."

"Be serious."

"I am being serious."

We climbed back in the truck. I figured to come back in the morning when I could see better and people would be around so I could ask directions. I threw it in reverse and started back into the road.

My original angle of entry had been too steep. I wasn't going to be able to turn all the way around, so, after backing partway out I crimped the wheel hard and nosed back into the turnout. I mashed the brakes and stared straight ahead.

There it was, right in front of my face. I'd parked on top of it. Two feet off the ground, a two-foot circle of engine sludge and burned oil was etched onto the white slats of the fence. Just like the one the Buick had left on Arnie's fence the day I'd first fired it up.

27

◆◆◆
◆◆◆◆
◆◆◆

I SAT AND stared at the circle.

"What is it, Leo?"

"The Buick station wagon made that mark." I pointed at the fence.

"You're sure?"

"Positive."

"Why would he park here?"

"Because Buddy thought you knew where you were going. He could tell you were following the truck. He figured you'd show up here."

"Here? Why?"

"Because this is where the truck went."

"Here?"

"No. Behind us. He was backed in so he could see."

I shut down the truck and stepped back out into the night. Across the street, a double pair of heavily chained gates appeared to be the sole entrance into an immense quadrangle of interlocking corrugated metal shops and warehouses covering the better part of ten acres. Dim lights glowed in a small central brick building. Probably the office. Acres of cement parking lots stood empty.

Caroline appeared at my side. "Is that it?"

I unlocked the camper and fished the nine-millimeter out from under the seat cushion. I checked the load. Full. No sense in taking the automatic. I'd already proved I couldn't hit anything with it. I turned to Caroline.

"I don't suppose telling you to stay here would do any good."

"What do you think?" she grinned.

"I think you and I started all this, and maybe we ought to finish it."

For Caroline, the gate was easy. We merely pulled on one side until the chain was tight, and she slid in between the halves. For me it was another matter. I had to strip down to my T-shirt before I could wiggle and scrape my way through. The pivoting latch mechanism, directly opposite my chest, caught in my shirt, gouging a trail of bloody scratches across my body as I held my breath and forced my way inside.

I pulled the girl to the dark-shadowed side of the nearest building while I re-dressed and worked on what to do next. Any doubts I'd worked up flew away when I noticed the faded stenciling on the corrugated metal above Caroline's head. The little logo was all I needed. I checked anyway.

"What's that say above your head?"

She stepped back from the wall and squinted at the peeling letters.

"Mobils Reclamation, I think. Something like that."

"Mobius," I said. "Mobius Reclamation."

"A picture that looks like a bent circle."

"It's a Mobius strip," I said.

Two overhead lights at the north end of the lot cast a wavering glow over the parking area. I looked the other way, down the length of the building. As the distance from the lights increased, the shadows became deeper, the building less distinct. A hundred feet away, the south side of the fence surrounding the lot had been totally swallowed up by the gloom. I reached for Caroline's hand. She pulled it back.

"Can you hear it?" she said.

I listened. Somewhere within the complex an engine was running. Then the unmistakable sound of a car door slamming. Faint voices, followed by the rumbling rollers of an overhead door. Then silence again.

"Let's go. Stay right up against the buildings," I whispered, taking her hand and leading her toward the back of the building, away from the lights and the sounds. The jungle of weeds and tall grasses that grew along the edges of the building served to hide a lethal array of cans, bottles, defunct machine parts, and mangled pallets that had, over the years, inexorably gravitated their way toward this single unpaved narrow strip. It was slow going, as we tediously picked our way along the wall, testing our footfalls before committing our entire weight. Couldn't risk breaking an ankle. Twice, my probing front foot stepped off into nothing. Both times we had to risk the flashlight in order to avoid hidden drainage pits.

Forty feet shy of the far end, my concentration welded to the blackness ahead, I stepped on something round, skidded, and fell heavily into the side of the building. The flimsy metal gonged into the night as a wave of motion rattled its way through the decrepit building. We stood still, listening.

Somewhere behind us another engine started. Caroline tensed.

"Don't panic," I whispered. "It doesn't mean they heard us."

"What *us*?"

We stood with our backs to the building, staring back the way we'd come. The unmistakable jittery lights of a motor vehicle suddenly lit up the gate area, bouncing, getting progressively brighter as they drew nearer.

"Now panic," I said through my teeth. I grabbed the girl by the sweater and propelled her around the side of the building. We rounded the corner in a sprint and fell heavily into a four-foot trench.

Fighting for breath, I scrambled up and peeked my head back around the side. A green crew-cab pickup truck, identical to those Daniel and I had encountered at the dump site, hesitated at the gate and then turned right toward us, moving slowly up the wall, zigzagging, using its high beams to sweep the area. I jerked my head back in.

"Quick," I said.

We climbed out and stumbled wildly across the overgrown, furrowed field at the back of the building toward a pile of rusting pipe that rested diagonally in the clearing, its haphazard outline skeletal against the sky. I pulled Caroline down behind the pile just as the driver angled his lights around the corner.

The ditch prevented him from driving around the back. I unconsciously held my breath. The driver got out. I pushed Caroline to the ground and eyeballed out through a narrow chink between two lengths of culvert pipe.

The driver held his right hand down along his leg as he hopped the ditch and started across the field. The lights of the truck lit up the fence to our right. I was confident that he'd have to get right on top of us before he could make us out. Not only was it dark, but the unstructured pile of pipe and twisted metal would make it nearly impossible to pick us out. Caroline started to raise her head. I gently pushed it back down. For once, she stayed put. I waited.

He came on, not taking any chances. Cautiously, squinting and swiveling his eyes over the dim overgrown ground. Two steps and listen. Two steps and squint. Backlit by the truck lights, his wispy hair gave him an almost angelic appearance.

Ten yards short of the pile, he stopped. Decisions, decisions. What side of the pile to come around. The left side, nearest the fence, offered more light, but the pile would be right in his lap, negating the advantage of the gun. The right side, while dark as hell, offered greater distance from possible attack. While he took his time, weighing the alternatives, I pulled the nine-millimeter out from my pocket. Shooting him would just about guarantee that we'd have to fight our way out of here. I stuck the gun back in my belt.

As I'd hoped, he chose the right. On all fours, I went left, keeping the bulk of the pile always between us. As he sidestepped around the far end of the pile, his gun now held forward with both hands, I skittered around the other end and then up the long side of the pile. I was parallel with him now. He stayed cautious, taking it one step at a time, until he spotted Caroline facedown in the grass. I don't know what he'd expected, but she wasn't it. I saw his shoulders relax. He stepped forward quickly. I followed suit.

"You—you there—get up," he said, gesturing with a snub-nosed thirty-eight. Apparently, she didn't budge. He stepped closer. I made my move.

He must have heard the scrape as I dragged the four-foot length of rusted pipe from the pile. It cost him an arm. He had half-pivoted back in my direction, trying to raise his free arm, when I swung the pipe with both hands. The effort lifted my feet completely off the ground. The whistling pipe collapsed his upraised arm with a sickening snap before plowing downward into his forehead. My arms vibrated from the hollow contact.

He went down on his back, one leg splayed out at an odd, impossible angle. I watched as his hand relaxed around the revolver. Blood quickly welled up to fill the deep indentation that ran down his forehead. His yellowed teeth were locked in a last ghastly smile. It was the guy who had fired on us at the dump site. He wouldn't be needing the arm.

Caroline was sitting up, staring at me. I bent and took her arm.

"Let's go," I whispered.

She shook her head violently and didn't move.

"Let's go," I repeated urgently. "The party's over. We need to get out of here. They'll be looking for this guy in a minute."

From behind me, a voice split the air.

"No, pilgrim. That's where you wrong. This here party's just startin'."

28

A STICKY VALVE in the idling truck engine ticked rhythmically into the chilled silence. I started to look over my shoulder. He stopped me.

"Hands on top of your head, motherfucker."

I released Caroline's arm and straightened up, my back still to him. If I'd been alone I might have taken my chances with diving over the pile. As it was, even if I made it, he still had Caroline sitting in his line of fire. I slowly raised my hands. Caroline made small slurping noises.

"Back up toward me," he growled. "Real slow." I took one step backward, relaxing my shoulders, lowering my arms as I moved.

"Up. Up. Keep those arms up. I'll waste you right here."

Imaginary bullet wounds in my back throbbed as I took another step backward, angling out to the right, around the top of the pile, getting Caroline out of the direct line of fire.

I was careful not to step on the guy on the ground. Two more steps and I'd give it a try. I wasn't harboring any illusions. The minute I gave up the nine-millimeter, Caroline and I were dead.

"That's it, pilgrim. Nice and slow." I took another measured backward step, trying to relax my arms. I was going to have to be quick. Either quick or dead.

I never got the chance.

Before I could make my move, Wesley's simian arm snaked around me and jerked my gun from my belt. In one smooth motion, he thumbed off the safety, jabbed the barrel into my navel, and put his face right up in mine.

"Heeeeeee. We got you now, asshole. Heeeeeee."

"Bring that gun over here, Wesley," ordered Frank.

Wesley didn't move. He moved the gun lower, to my groin. His foul breath billowed in front of his face, painting the surrounding air with the smell of rotting meat.

"This one here's mine, right, Frank?" He jabbed me hard with the gun, instantly cramping my abdomen, stealing my breath. I struggled to remain upright.

"Heeeeeeeeeeee." He put his nose right on mine. "I'm gonna cut you. Oh, how I'm gonna cut you."

Caroline started to rise. "Please—"

Wesley took one giant step and kicked her in the face. "Shut up, bitch. She's gonna fix you good. You wait. When she puts the hooks in you—"

"Bring his gun over here," Frank bellowed. Frank obviously wasn't a whole lot more comfortable with the prospect of Wesley waving a gun around than I was.

Caroline moaned, rolling over onto her knees, pawing at her face with both hands.

Ignoring Frank, Wesley skittered over to his fallen comrade. He yanked a piece of frozen grass from the ground and put it on the guy's lips. Nothing.

"Marvin's stone dead, Frank. Heeeeee." He gently ran two bony fingers down the long indentation in the guy's forehead, not stopping just above the eyebrows but continuing on down the full length of the face, striping Marvin with his own blood. He looked back up at me.

"This asshole killed Marvin, Frank. This one's mine."

"The ladies will decide," declared Frank. "Gimme that gun."

Wesley was on automatic pilot. He hopped back over in front of me, bringing the gun up hard between my legs. This time it doubled me over, but not for long. He grabbed me by the hair and jerked my head up level to his. He stuck out his tongue. Not pushed out through his lips, but openmouthed, like he was saying "aah" for a doctor. His mouth was filled with brown, broken teeth. I held my breath. I thought he was going to bite me.

With a long, gray-coated tongue, he licked me once, starting at my chin and moving lovingly all the way up to my hairline, leaving a fetid trail of slime and saliva in his wake. I shuddered.

"Heeeeeeee." He stepped back and waited.

I stood still. I knew that if I moved to wipe it off, he'd kill me.

"That's enough, goddammit, Wesley."

Wesley stepped back, rubbing his thighs together. His eyes were glazed. His breath was coming in short gasps. He raised the gun to my forehead. I closed my eyes, calling to my father, waiting for whatever came next.

What came next was so out of context my brain refused to process it.

"Do I have to tell the ladies?" Frank asked resignedly.

Behind my eyelids, I heard Wesley's breaths lengthen. I slit one eye and peeked out. Wesley had moved back three more steps. The gun was at his side. He was silently wagging his head at Frank. Frank smiled.

"Get the girl."

Wesley stiffened, but kept wagging his head.

"I won't touch the filthy bitch."

Frank sighed.

"You"—Frank waved the gun at me—"pick up the girl."

I bent at the waist and pulled Caroline to her feet. She took her hands from her face. Her nose was bleeding. Bits of grass and debris clung to her hair. She gazed disbelievingly down at her bloody hands.

"Hands on top of your heads," Frank ordered.

I laced my fingers over my scalp. Caroline still stared at her hands.

"Let's go. This way." He gestured with the gun.

Nudging Caroline before me, I started toward the closer end of the building. Frank and Wesley fell in behind. Instinctively, I veered left, toward the darkness.

"Toward the lights," Frank growled. I angled back the other way.

I stepped as slowly as possible toward the small brick building that held down the center of the yard. I wanted the sixty yards to last forever. I shortened my stride. Wesley rewarded me with a kick in the kidney. As I stumbled from the impact, Caroline grabbed one hand onto my belt.

Wesley's electric-motor giggle picked up speed as we neared the building. He loped around in front of us to get the door. A single trapezoid of yellow light fell from the interior of the building onto a small cement porch.

Wesley held the door wide.

I hesitated at the doorway. Frank, using his forearm as a club, drove Caroline into my back and me through the door.

It was stifling in the little building. Ninety degrees, at least. Worn black-and-white linoleum squares clashed horribly with the yellowed pine shiplap on the walls. The single room was nearly empty. The walls were bare. An orange Naugahyde secretarial chair and two gray filing cabinets, their drawers hanging open and empty, were all that was left. We'd walked in on moving day.

The saunalike heat was being produced by a small, black rectangular woodstove in the corner. The little stove was working overtime on the enormous sheaf of paperwork being systematically fed in through the open door by Blanche Hammer. Eunice leaned in the shadows of the west wall, impassive, knitting furiously.

29

BLANCHE HAMMER GLANCED up only long enough to register mild annoyance and then resolutely went back to feeding the last of the documents into the fire. The clicking of Eunice's knitting needles provided staccato percussion to the dull roaring of the flames. After banking the blaze with a final pyre of manila folders, Blanche shut the stove door and turned our way.

"Your timing leaves a great deal to be desired," she said. "Another hour and we would have been gone, and we could have avoided all this unpleasantness. Most unfortunate."

Her tone was that of a tolerant adult scolding a child. She brushed her chubby hands together. Either she was trying to remove loose dust, or she was doing a Pontius Pilate impression. I suspected the latter.

"He killed Marvin, Miss Hammer," blurted Wesley. "Stove his head in with a pipe."

She pursed her lips thoughtfully and shuffled closer.

"Well, Wesley," she said soothingly, "Marvin was a good boy, but I'm afraid Marvin had nearly outlived his usefulness anyway." I was touched by the outpouring of sentiment.

She turned to me, eyeing me closely.

"You were with Tom Romans at the conference, weren't you?" I didn't answer. No matter. She put it together for herself. "You must be the inquisitive Mr. Waterman," she said after a minute.

I must have looked surprised. "Your friend, Mr. Knox, with—er—a little encouragement, was quite informative."

I strained forward. Frank tightened his grip around my throat.

"He was just a harmless old man," I croaked.

"Harmless? Hardly, Mr. Waterman. Mr. Knox was scarcely the type to be acting of his own accord. It was essential that we knew who else was involved. One spies at one's own peril, Mr. Waterman. This is a war we are engaged in. I'm sure you understand."

"Can I have him, Miss Blanche?" Wesley asked impatiently.

"In just a bit," she said distractedly. For the first time, she noticed Caroline standing behind me. She came closer.

"Now what do we have here?" she said, peering around me. "This must be the young lady who's been making such a nuisance of herself down at the transfer station. What's your name, dearie?"

The cultured civility of Blanche's tone gave Caroline false hope. She straightened her spine, wiped her face with one hand, and worked up her most imperious tone.

"My name is Caroline Nobel, and if you have any decency, you will tell these Neanderthals to release Mr. Waterman and me, this instant."

Blanche's face crinkled in amusement. She turned. "Did you hear that, Eunice? Nosey Miss Nobel insists that we release her this instant."

There was no need to raise her voice. Eunice was at her

elbow. She'd stopped knitting and was fixed on Caroline like a pointing retriever. She leaned down and whispered at length into Blanche's ear. Blanche listened patiently. Eunice straightened up, gazing expectantly at Blanche.

"If you must," Blanche said. "But you'll have to be quick about it."

Blanche turned her attention to me. Eunice began rooting around furiously in her knitting bag. Blanche smiled sweetly at Caroline.

"I'm afraid, Miss Nobel, that allowing the two of you to leave is out of the question. It was thoughtful of you, however, to give us this last opportunity to tie up our loose ends. We do like to keep things neat, if we can. What with the boys going their separate ways and the greedy Mr. Short out of the picture, you two were just about the last two worrisome creatures left in the forest, so to speak. Were we to allow you two to leave here tonight, why, that could put an end to our work, and we couldn't have that, could we? There's so much more to be done. I'm sure you understand."

"More PCBs to dump."

"Oh no, Mr. Waterman, I'm afraid your infernal meddling has put a temporary end to that. For the time being, we'll just have to go back to recycling oil, like we've always done. It's a very important service, you know. I can't tell you how many people still pour their used motor oil down the storm drains, never thinking that the drains run directly back into our precious waters."

She put one finger coyly along her cheek. "When things calm down, well, we'll see," she added. "Now—" She looked to Frank and Wesley.

"How can anybody who's supposedly so concerned about our waters justify illegally dumping toxic waste?" I asked quickly, trying to buy time.

"Two steps forward and one step back, Mr. Waterman.

Compromises have to be made. The environment has become big business. It took big business to despoil the land; it will take big business to return the land to its former splendor. You wouldn't believe how much money it takes to thwart the forces of corruption."

Her eyes suddenly got black and hard. Her face tightened up. I flinched. The transformation was too quick. It takes sane people longer than that to go from one emotion to another.

"I'm afraid Papa left his affairs in something of a mess. He didn't leave us nearly enough to fix all the damage he'd done." She looked disgustedly at Eunice. "Not that all of it could be fixed," she added. "The sins of the fathers, you know."

"That's worth ruining several thousand acres of land?"

"I'm afraid you've got it backward, Mr. Waterman. We've saved the land, not despoiled it. Papa did enough despoiling for all of us." She looked heavily at Eunice again. "You see, Mr. Waterman, we were going to tell the EPA about our dumping. Anonymously, of course. We wanted them to find it. It was vital that they find it. How else would it get cleaned up? We couldn't have those poisons leaching their way into the soil in perpetuity, now could we?"

My blank expression seemed to encourage her.

"It's the only way they'll do anything, Mr. Waterman. The government won't save anything, won't reclaim anything, won't protect anything that produces even the slightest ripple of economic inconvenience for business, unless you rub their noses in it." She was on a roll.

"What about the spotted owl?"

"Oh, yes, the dreaded spotted owl," she said sarcastically. "The Endangered Species Act and all that. Makes good reading. Within sixty days of shutting down the logging of old-growth forests, do you know what they did? Interior Secretary Lujan promptly turned around and appointed a special committee with the power to override the act. In Washington, they're calling them the God Squad. They're entitled to decide which species they'll allow to become extinct."

"I don't see how that justifies what you've been doing."

"That's because you, like most of our other well-intentioned citizenry, are a short-term thinker, Mr. Waterman. I can't begin to tell you the good we've done with the money we made on that dumping. Buuut"—she drew it out—"the money from the dumping was only a beneficial side effect. We hit upon that almost by mistake. All we really wanted to do was to save that beautiful property from any more useless development. Lord knows we don't need any more condos or golf courses. We were merely trying to evoke the federal superfund law. The PCBs were just a way to stop the development. We had no idea about the potential profits. Next thing we knew, the money just came rolling in." Her eyes twinkled. "The Lord provides in mysterious ways."

"The federal superfund law?"

"A wonderful piece of legislation." She clapped her hands lightly. "It says that property owners are responsible for the cleanup of any toxic elements found on their property. Contaminated property can't be sold or developed until it gets a clean bill of health from the EPA. That piece of property will be tied up for decades to come." She smiled at the thought.

"It was already tied up in court. You didn't have to—"

"That was us. Who else was going to do it? The government? Don't make me laugh. The tribe? Lately, they're nearly as bad as the government. It's costing us a fortune to keep them in court—those mercenary lawyers have no sense of moral purpose. And do you know what we get for trying to stem the tide of development?" She didn't wait for an answer. She was screaming now. "Legal bills. That's what we get. We lose. We always lose. They own the courts. The developers always win. It was our turn. Our turn."

Before I could say anything, her face turned back into a stone mask.

"Wesley. You and Frank take care of Mr. Waterman. Be quick about it, I want to be out of here within fifteen minutes."

"Fifteen minutes?" whined Wesley. "I need—" She cut him off, cold. "Fifteen minutes is plenty of time for your fun. I'm limiting Eunice to a similar amount of time with Miss Nobel here. Now get to it, young man."

Eunice grunted as she yanked a cluttered collection of ominous-looking crochet hooks and knitting needles from the bag. Several pieces of yarn were caught up in the hooks. She frowned as she worked to free them. Her eyes burned with the same anticipation that made her bony fingers tremble.

It was now or forever hold my peace.

I threw my head back. I heard Frank's nose break under the impact. Half-turning, I clamped his gun arm under mine and swung him back into Wesley. We hit the door in a tangled heap. Caroline, suddenly a snarling tiger, went at Wesley's eyes with her thumbs. He screamed, a high-pitched, inhuman sound, flailing with his arms, trying both to protect his eyes and to get some room to maneuver. Frank and I had him pinned against the door.

Frank, who I suspected had had his nose broken before, staged an immediate recovery. He clamped his free arm around my throat and began to apply ungodly pressure. My own pulse drummed in my ears above the sounds of Wesley's screams."

"Bad move, pilgrim," he grunted.

Mustering one last burst of oxygenated energy, I brought Frank's gun hand down hard over my left knee. The gun clattered to the floor somewhere behind me. No go. The pressure on my throat increased exponentially. I could feel my movements going into slow motion, like I was running underwater. I began to float. Only Wesley's hysterical keening kept me conscious. A muffled shot burped in the tiny doorway. The pressure behind my eyes again increased.

For a second, all sound and movement ceased, as everything waited for the pain that follows the impact. Nothing. Pound by pound, the pressure on my throat began to lessen. Frank began to drop to his knees; his belt buckle caught on the back of my belt as he slid down. Before he could fall, I turned and shouldered him back into Wesley, who was pinned in the doorway, staring disbelievingly upward at the smoking nine-millimeter, now held high above his head. I lunged for the gun, pinning his arm to the wall.

"She touched meee. She touched meee," he slobbered.

My left shoulder caught fire. A searing cramp ran down the length of my body, knotting my hamstring, putting my foot to sleep. Out of the corner of my eye, I could see Eunice using both hands to stir the bright blue knitting needle around in my back. I felt it scrape bone. I opened my mouth to scream but came up dry, empty, and dark.

Wesley, in his fever to escape Caroline, bowled both Frank and me over backward. Our combined weight broke Eunice's grip on the needle. I fell to the floor at her feet, banging the embedded spike on the linoleum as I rolled over. My vision swam and then refocused in time to see Blanche pick up the gun and squint myopically down the sights. I waited for the tearing.

Without Frank to muffle the sound, the second report was horrendous. The sound waves seemed to lodge themselves in the yellowed softwood walls.

The shot took Frank high in the forehead, painting the door behind him with a ghastly collage of hair and tissue. His face didn't register surprise, only a sense of wonder as the impact bowled him over.

Blanche turned the gun on me. Wesley hopped over and

filled the space between the sisters. "I didn't mean to shoot Frank."

He stayed partially behind Blanche while he gazed beseechingly up at Eunice. "It was her fault," he said, pointing at Caroline. "She touched me. You saw her. You'll fix her, won't you?"

"Never mind, Wesley." Blanche kept the gun steadily aimed at my midsection as she spoke. "Accidents will happen. We were going to have to do something about Frank anyway. Get that tape we were using on the boxes from over by the stove."

Wesley hurried over and returned with a full roll of dull silver duct tape.

"Tape Mr. Waterman's hands behind him. He's proven to be quite a distraction. We can't be having any more accidents, now can we?"

As Wesley came around behind me with his tape, Caroline came off the doorjamb like a missile. "You—you—" she screamed. She never made it.

Wesley roundhoused the nine-millimeter up beside her head with a crack, catching her coming forward, midstride, dropping her to the floor. Raising the gun high overhead, he made a move to smash her in the face while she was down. I was paralyzed. Eunice growled like a bear. He stopped.

"Okay, I won't," he said contritely.

Wesley made it a point to scramble the needle in my shoulder around in a wide circle before jerking my hands behind me and taping them together.

I briefly blacked out. From the bottom of a deep fog bank, I barely heard Blanche Hammer's next instruction.

"Drag Miss Nobel out of the way over into the middle of the floor, so your mother has a little elbow room, and then take Mr. Waterman out to the maintenance shed and dispose of him. We've wasted too much time here already. Put him in a barrel when you've finished with him."

My vision blurred back in time to see Wesley take Caroline by the feet and drag her to the center of the room. Eunice picked up her purple knitting bag and followed. Blanche held up her free hand.

"I know how much this means to you two, but I'm afraid we're going to have to hurry. Five minutes is all you get."

Wesley skittered over in front of her. "Nobody heard, Miss Blanche. Five minutes isn't enough time."

"Five minutes," she insisted, wagging a chubby finger at him.

"Not fair," he bellowed. "Not again. You let Frank shoot that old bum before I even got a chance."

"Don't sass me, Wesley. If five minutes is good enough for my sister, it's good enough for you. Now hustle, young man. Time's a wastin'."

Wesley hustled. Grabbing me by the hair, he dragged me out the door and lobbed me off the little porch into the frozen grass.

"Get up," he screamed in my ear. I stayed down. I'd already made up my mind. I was willing to die here. While he was trotting over to kick the door shut, I'd come to the realization that I was prepared to beg. Tears streamed down my face, without the act of crying. In that moment, I had become middle-aged. The imagined invulnerability of youth seemed absurd. I tried to speak, to plead for our lives, but nothing came out. Without intending to, I vomited into the sparkling grass.

"Get up," he screamed. I stayed down, watching white spires of steam rise slowly from the pile of effluent in front of me.

He kicked me in the small of the back, rattling the needle, sending red waves coursing through my head. I fell over on my left side. Wesley knelt beside me. He was breathing heavily. He set the gun down behind him in the grass and fished out a knife. He tilted the fluted blade in front of my eyes, letting the moonlight glint on the surface. "I'll cut you right here then," he breathed.

"I'm gonna feed you your cock and balls," he whispered in my ear. "Heeeeee. They're gonna find you that way. Have you ever tasted your own cock? Heeeeeee. When I was young, I used to—"

He stopped babbling and suddenly went on alert.

I saw it coming for me. When the shadow first emerged, tiptoeing out from the darkness at the back of the little building, I nearly called out to it. I flashed that this was one of those compensatory escape scenarios that a dying man goes through at the moment of his death. I'd seen a movie like that once.

The specter raised both hands above its head. Something about a rod and a staff comforting me ran through my mind. The staff came down with a metallic thud, taking Wesley full across the back of the neck.

He fell onto his side, his face a couple of inches from mine, jumping and shaking uncontrollably, his tongue lolling, his mismatched eyes wide with amazement, and then he was still.

I stared into his lopsided face. "Where's Caroline?" he said, without moving his lips. His body convulsed once more and then repeated the question.

I wondered how he was doing that. Neither his unblinking eyes nor his lips moved when he spoke. He shifted hands with the knife. I saw one hand take the blade from the other. I was stupefied until the blade began sawing at the tape binding my wrists. With a snap, my hands came apart.

Using my tingling arms for support, I got to my knees. I thought I might be dead. Bobby Warren stood above me, holding Wesley's gravity knife in one hand and a length of pipe in the other. "Where's Caroline?"

With my right hand, I gestured toward my shoulder.

"Pull it out," I croaked.

The kid wasn't squeamish. He never hesitated. Bracing one hand around the entrance point, he jerked the needle from my back in one smooth motion. I felt as if my life force had followed the needle out, as if the air filling my body had whooshed out with a long, earsplitting "Ahhhhhhh."

My whole left side was numb. I tucked my left arm in and scrambled over to the gun. I used it to point at the little building. I had to struggle to keep up with the kid. He had the door open and was standing frozen in the entranceway when I slid by him.

Blanche Hammer was contentedly tending the fire with a hooked brass poker. Caroline, her blond hair spread out on the floor toward us, was still unconscious. Her slacks and underwear dangled from one ankle. Eunice knelt by her side, her hands full of shining implements.

"What—?" was all Bobby got out of his mouth before Eunice sprang to her feet and in three amazingly long, mechanical strides closed the distance between them, her needles and hooks thrust before her, her eyes filled with impassive blankness as if she were knitting, her narrow mouth wide open. "Not noooow," she screamed. I shot her in the face.

Her gaunt frame slid to a stop head to head with Caroline. A pool of red began to form, halolike, around her head, sliding along the linoleum, soaking Caroline's hair. I stood and stared. I'd never shot a woman before.

Without Bobby Warren's "Look out!" Blanche would have gotten me with the poker for sure. Hindsight tells me he could have handled her. He was young and strong. She should have been no problem. I guess I just wasn't thinking. Something snapped.

As Bobby stepped forward, holding the piece of pipe in both hands to ward off the blow, I mindlessly turned the gun on Blanche Hammer and kept pulling the trigger until it clicked empty six or seven times.

We stood in the reverberating little office with the smell of burnt powder in the air. "Jesus," was all he said before rushing over to Caroline's side.

I leaned back against the door frame. "Are you real?" I asked.

He was patting her cheeks, checking her throat for a pulse.

"I'd better get a doctor."

"You're supposed to be dead. Burned up."

"I was pissing off the back porch when the place went up. I'd had a lot of beer. One minute I was standing on my back porch with my dick in my hand. The next thing I knew, the back of my shorts was burning."

He shuddered at the memory. "I ran off into the woods. I thought for sure there was going to be an explosion. By the time I got back to the house, man, there was this ghost thing running around in my driveway. I took off. I was scared shitless."

"Call a doctor," I said. "Call the cops." I slid down the wall into a sitting position. "Call everybody."

He started to rush out. I waved the gun at him. He stopped.

"Is she bleeding?" He went back and shyly checked her over.

"Not that I can see," he said finally.

"Then put her clothes back on her."

He did the best he could. Her slacks weren't exactly on straight, but it would have to do. He gently rubbed her cheek.

"Get some help," I said. "If you don't mind, I'll wait here."

He didn't mind.

30

IF IT HADN'T been for the way his fingers kept picking at the arms of the wicker settee, I would have thought Tim Flood had gone to sleep. When I finished, he opened his predatory eyes for the first time since I'd started to talk. Thin gray filaments connected his lips as he spoke.

"Sounds like if I was going to pay the ten-grand bonus to anybody, it ought to be this Warren kid. Sounds to me like he saved everybody's ass."

"No doubt about it," I said.

"Tell me again how he knew where to find you."

"He followed me from the EPA office. He'd spent a couple of days camped out in this old abandoned cabin across the road from the last dump site. He'd been sleeping rough, in some clothes he stole from a neighbor's yard. He lost most everything he had in the fire. Figured it was best if whoever was trying to kill him thought he was dead."

"Not a bad idea," rasped Tim. "Used that trick once myself, back in thirty-five. I was——"

I was in no mood for stories. I kept talking.

"When it turned so cold on Tuesday night, he went into town and got himself a motel room. When he came back Wednesday morning and found the whole area cordoned off, crawling with toxic cleanup teams, he knew that the shit had already hit the fan. He figured he didn't have to worry about anybody making another attempt on his life. The cat was already out of the bag, so he went to see his grandmother. She filled him in on what was going on. They put their heads together and decided that the best thing they could do was to spill everything he knew to the EPA."

"This Charles Hayden jerk?"

"Right."

"Why in hell didn't the punk go to the heat to begin with?"

"It was tribal business. Some folks don't like their laundry done in public. Some folks don't go running to the authorities when they've got a problem. Some people like to handle their own problems."

A glint appeared in Tim's eye. He almost smiled.

"Yeah, I know what you mean."

"He was on his way in when he saw me coming out. He tailed me over to Ms. Kennedy's. When he saw me come out with Caroline, he followed us down to Tacoma."

"And saved your ass."

"And saved my ass."

We lapsed into silence. Only the drumming of Tim's untended fingernails on the wicker. We were alone in the solarium. Frankie was out. The twins waited, sphinxlike, outside the door. Sweat trickled down my neck.

"So, the girl's gonna be all right?"

"The hospital is keeping her overnight, but they say she'll be just fine. She's got a concussion and a shiner you wouldn't believe."

"And this Kennedy broad's found her a job?"

"One of the doctors she works with was looking for

a nanny. They live out on Mercer Island. Need somebody to watch their kids during the day. Kennedy thinks it's the right thing for her. She thinks that maybe if she gets a chance to spend some time in a—with a—" I searched for words.

"A regular family." Tim helped me out, drilling me with his eyes.

"Something like that," I hedged. "Anyway, she thinks it will be good for her. Give her a sense of belonging somewhere to something."

He thought it over for a long time. I adjusted the sling cradling my left arm. The movement made my back throb. The heat was beginning to make my vision swim. The door behind me opened. I turned carefully. Frankie Ortega, immaculately dressed in a solid black suit, slid across the floor and took up his station behind Tim. Tim partially opened his eyes. He made a dismissive gesture with his right hand.

"She gonna come and see me, Leo?"

"I'll see to it, Tim. As soon as she gets settled in."

"Tell her—" I waited. He waved himself off again.

"Tell her to come and see me."

"I'll take care of it."

"I know you will," he sighed. He drifted off, his chin coming to rest on the red cardigan sweater. I looked to Frankie.

Frankie gestured with his hand. We went out together, down the long hall, stopping at the double front doors. He picked up a large blue envelope from a table behind the left-hand door. The twins had somehow materialized behind us. They stood silent, rocking on the balls of their feet.

"It's all here, Leo. A little extra too." He was holding the envelope.

I took it.

"Make sure the girl comes to see him."

"I said I would."

"And you do what you say you're gonna."

"I try."

"Try hard," Frankie said.

31

I WAS THE last to arrive. Even a man of Jed's singular talents had been hard-pressed to pry me loose from the cops. It was nearly nine the next evening before I shuffled up to the Zoo.

The hand-lettered sign on the locked front door read CLOSED FOR REPAIRS. Yessir, that'd fool 'em. Unless a detective like me happened by, nobody would ever suspect that there was some kind of wild, illegal, private party going on inside the Zoo. If you ignored the sound of broken glass, the banshee yelling, and the fact that the front door was actually vibrating in time to the bass speakers on the jukebox, the place was a model of circumspect decorum.

Gingerly, trying not to jiggle my upper body, I banged on the door with my good arm. Nothing. I waited for a break in the howling music. Before I could react, "I Only Have Eyes for You" was suddenly replaced by "Tie Me Kangaroo Down, Sport," which, if the sudden caterwauling was any indication, had been deemed a singalong. Damn. I knocked harder. Still nothing but more yowling in horribly mimicked Australian accents.

From behind the door came a familiar strained mumble.

"We're closed."

"Ralph, it's Leo."

"Leo who?"

"Goddammit, Ralph, open up."

His face was split with a huge grin as he peeked out through the crack.

"Just kiddin', Leo."

He swung the door wide. I stepped into the melee. Norman and Earlene were dancing atop the far end of the bar. Their mutual rhythm was nowhere in the vicinity of the music blasting out of the speakers. Harold and George, their backs resting on the bar, led a group of twenty or so seriously altered souls in fevered singing.

The Zoo may have been closed, but the bar was open. All the liquor had been removed from the glass shelves behind the bar and set out on the bar itself. Waldo was using the curved silver spout on a bottle of V.O. as a makeshift whiskey drip. Hector was slow-dancing in the middle of the floor with Mary. The Speaker was hugging the rail, passed out against the back wall. Might as well join the party.

As I stepped off into the melee, I was stopped by the sound of a familiar voice. "You gotta take better care of yourself, Leo."

I glanced over my left shoulder. Daniel Dixon and Miriam Stone occupied the first two stools along the bar. Daniel was nursing a beer. Miriam had a Coke on which several cherries floated. Daniel's face crinkled.

"First you lose an earlobe. Now they got you trussed up like a steer. You keep this up, there ain't gonna be nothin' left of you but a stump."

"Surprise, surprise," I said. "What are you two doing here?"

"I called your number," he said. "I got—" He pointed out onto the dance floor.

"Hector?"

"Yeah, Hector. He said they was having this party. Said you'd be here. You know I wouldn't miss a party." Miriam gave him a gentle elbow.

"Actually, Mr. Waterman," Miriam said, "we came here to thank you for all of your help."

"Bobby's the one you should be thanking."

She waved me off. "No. If you hadn't kept pushing, I'm sure they would have gotten away with it. As it is, the Tribal Council is taking a serious look at its policies. All because you kept pushing."

"If Bobby hadn't shown up when he did, the only thing I'd be pushing is daisies."

"Your friends sure know how to throw a party," Daniel said.

"It's what they do best."

Someone tugged at the back of my jacket. Ralph.

"We're rich, Leo," he shouted.

I held up a finger. When I turned back to Daniel and Miriam, they were boogieing their way out to the dance floor. I turned back to Ralph.

"Rich, huh? How so Ralph?"

"Buddy left us money."

Before I could inquire further, George spotted me. Dragging Harold away from a spirited rendition of "My Way," he shouldered his way over to me through the undulating crowd. We formed a tight circle.

"You got 'em, Leo. The papers said you got 'em," said Harold.

"*We* got them," I corrected.

"How's the girl?" asked George.

"She'll be fine. She gets out of the hospital in the morning."

"Maybe we should go visit her," Ralph said, a fresh fifth clutched under each arm. "Be a shame if she missed the party."

"Land of a Thousand Dances" came roaring from the jukebox. The crowd went wild, erupting into a primitive shout-and-stomp fest.

"*Na, na na na na—*"

"She's got company. Her boyfriend and Ms. Kennedy are keeping her company. I don't think Caroline's quite up to this yet."

"Neither was he," said George. He pointed to the single stool at the door end of the bar. A young fellow in a blue pinstriped suit slept contentedly, his right ear resting in an ashtray.

"*Na na na na na na na na na.*" The voices rose.

"Who's that?"

"That's the lawyer from Buddy's insurance company," said George. "He tracked us down this morning."

"Ralph poured him a couple," chuckled Harold.

"What's this about money?"

"Buddy had insurance. From the paper," said George.

"Two hundred fifty thousand bucks." Harold's eyes rolled.

"*Gonna do the Pony, like Boney Maroni—*"

"We're buying the rooming house," Ralph said.

"We're gonna be slumlords," said Harold.

"It's a little less than Mrs. Paultz was asking, but she says she wants us to have it," said George. "She was always a little sweet on Buddy."

"We was gonna buy the Zoo," said Ralph, dejectedly.

"We talked it over, decided that might not be a good

idea," Harold noted, more for Ralph's benefit than for mine.

"*Na na na na na, na na na, na na na na na. Na na na na na—*"

" 'Sides that," said Ralph, "we know lots of people got no place to go."

"You know a good lawyer, Leo?" asked George.

"If I didn't know a good lawyer, I wouldn't be here now."

"Cops was a little pissed?" asked Harold.

"Just a little. They got over it."

"This lawyer of yours. He could help us?" asked George.

"No, but he'll know someone who can. I'll call him in the morning. We'll find somebody to handle it for you."

We stood, arm-in-arm, somehow encapsulated in our own little bubble of silence, as the maelstrom swirled about us.

Buddy had been right. I was back.